OLD ANGER

Also by Phillip Thompson

Outside the Law

OLD ANGER

PHILLIP THOMPSON

ISBN-13: 978-1-7343480-7-1

Published by
Brash Books, LLC
12120 State Line #253
Leawood, Kansas 66209
www.brash-books.com

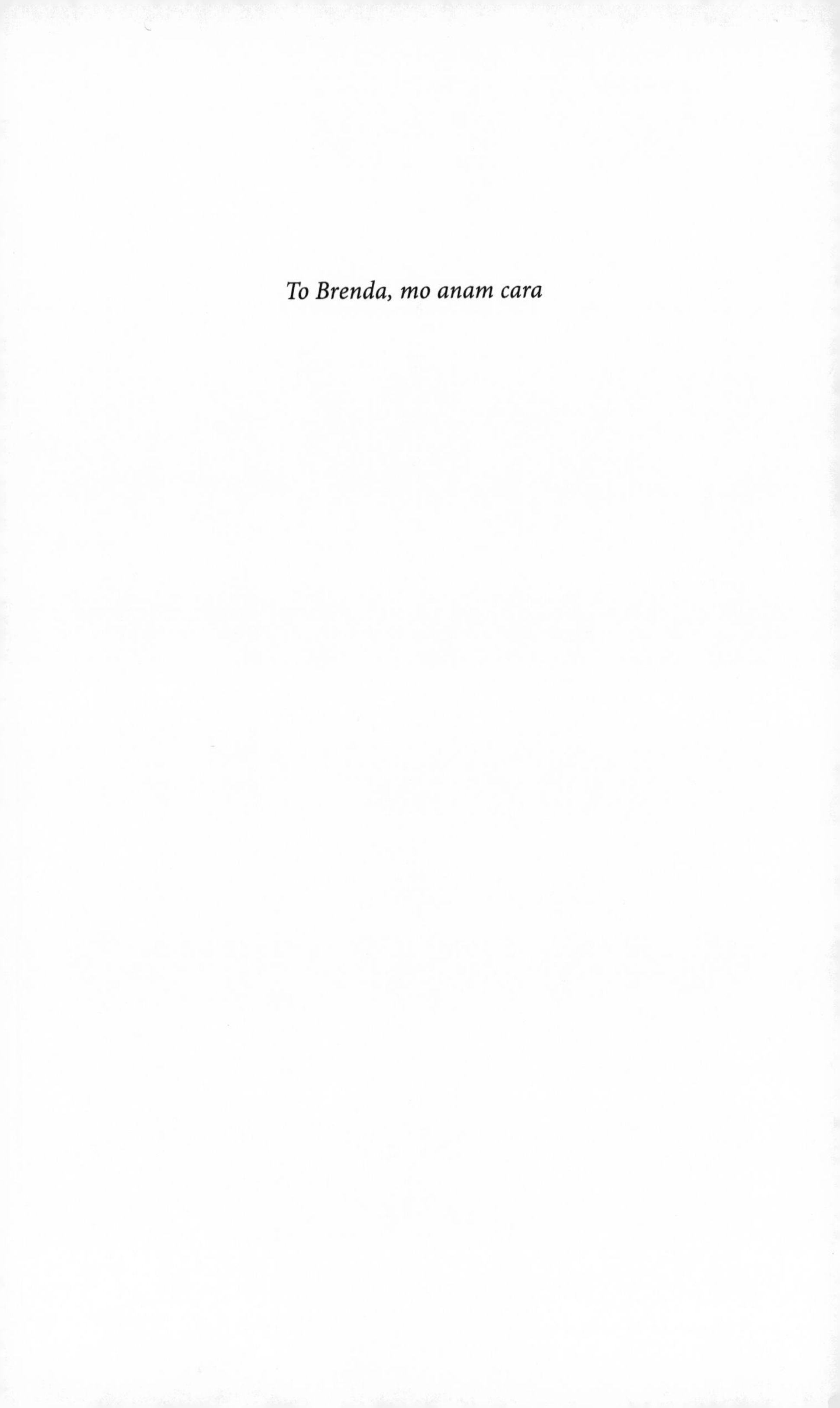

To Brenda, mo anam cara

DAY ONE

CHAPTER ONE

COLT

Sheriff Colt Harper stared at the dead black man dangling from the dragline bucket. The perforated steel basket, as big as a pickup bed, hung over a water-filled gravel pit. Underneath, the corpse dangled like a discarded doll. Colt squinted from the glare of a lemon sun as he scanned the moonscape of craters and dunes before turning to the lanky man standing next to him.

Colt studied Donnie Wample, who looked like he was no more than one generation off a cotton farm. A gristle of a man, his arms were like steel cables that shot out of his short-sleeve shirt and ended in hands that, Colt was sure, made fists like wrecking balls.

Wample turned. "I ain't in no trouble, am I, Shurff?"

"Well, Mr. Wample, you called my office. So, at the moment, I'm gonna say, no, you're not in any trouble."

"Ahite, then. I'm mighty glad to hear that," he said in a Tombigbee sharecropper drawl.

Colt knew that if he bothered to look, which he wouldn't, Mr. Wample had already been in trouble with the law once or twice. "Why don't you walk me through how you found this?"

"Right over here," Wample said, gesturing to his right.

"You touch anything in the vicinity?" he said as they stepped back from the lip of the pit, one of several gouged out of a vast field of gravel just south of the sluggish brown Buttahatchie River, which defined the northern edge of the county before emptying into the Tombigbee.

"Nope."

Colt heard what had to be Freddie Mac Baldwin's ancient government-issued coroner van rattling down the gravel road leading to the foreman's shed. He didn't bother to look back. Wample did, though.

"Who's that?" Wample said.

"That'd be the coroner. He'll join us directly."

"Okay, then," Wample said, then pointed toward the mustard-colored dragline that crouched over the pit like a heron looking for fish. The massive boom angled out over the shimmering water. Wample stood silently by, looking everywhere, anywhere but... at whoever was hanging over the still, green water. Four men stood near the cab of the dragline, two of them smoking and all shifting on their feet, nervous and silent. Across the water sat a dump truck that had been backed up to the edge of the pit. The truck's rusty bed held a pile of wet, shiny gravel the size of a pitcher's mound.

"What happened?" Colt said, still staring at the body.

Wample cleared his throat. "Marvin, my dragline operator, was loading that dump truck when he come up with that." Wample nodded toward the dangling corpse. "Kinda spooked him. He stopped everything and called me on the radio the operators have in the cab. I ran over, saw this here, and then called you."

"Anybody touch anything?"

"No, sir," Wample said. "Nobody wanted to get anywhere near that."

"Which one is Marvin?"

Wample swung his arm. "Blue shirt."

Behind them, the gravel crunched like a ragged metronome, then stopped. Then heavy breathing. Freddie Mac.

"Ain't that something," the coroner said. Freddie Mac Baldwin was panting, his red face beginning to sweat. He wore his usual white short-sleeve shirt. His twisted black tie stopped a good eight inches above his belt and over a belly that belied his claim of losing weight.

He shot Freddie Mac a look. "I just got here myself."

"What you reckon happened?"

Colt shrugged. "Somebody got drunk or high last night and decided to go swimming?"

Freddie Mac turned his bulk to the left, then right. "How'd did he get out here? Walk?"

"Why don't you pull him out and ask?" Colt said.

Wample cleared his throat. "Shurff, no disrespect, but, ah, that's a dead person there. In my dragline."

Colt turned to Wample. "You're right, Mr. Wample. Why don't you head back to your office. I'll stop by on my way out."

"Ahite." Wample was gone faster than smoke in high wind.

To Freddie Mac: "When your photographer gets here, get some shots of the whole perimeter of this pit."

Freddie Mac laughed. "I am the photographer today. All my interns up and left on me, and I ain't hiring a full-time."

"Course not," Colt said. Freddie Mac could be a pain in the ass. He watched the coroner huff and clamber his way down the steep lip of loose dirt, then unlimber the camera swinging from his neck. He snapped here and there. Colt walked over to the men by the dragline, aiming for the one in the blue shirt.

"Marvin?" Colt said to the man.

Marvin tossed his cigarette to the ground and stepped away from the other men. He was shorter than Colt, only about five and half feet, mustache like a shoe brush on a leathery face. Filthy ball cap mashed on his head. "That's me, Sheriff. Marvin Adams."

Colt shook hands with Marvin. "Mr. Adams, tell me what happened."

Marvin told a story similar to Wample's, the only real difference being that the body came up on Marvin's third hoist of the morning. "I's filling up that truck over there, got two buckets in it, then this."

"And you stopped the dragline soon as you saw it?"

"Yes, sir, I did."

Colt nodded. "All right. I'm going to ask that you come down to the station and give a statement to that effect later today. You okay with that?"

Adams shrugged. "Sure, Sheriff."

Colt turned his attention to the other three men, whose appearances were a variation of Adams. "Any of y'all see anything?"

Heads shook no. One man, taller than the other two, wearing glasses, raised his hand. "We all walked over when we saw Wample walking out here," he said.

"All right, well, this is a crime scene now," Colt said, "including that dump truck. So I need you all to clear out of here."

"That's my truck," the spectacled man said. "I need it to work."

"I understand that," Colt said. "And you'll have it back as soon as we can process the scene."

"How long's that going to take?"

Colt looked over at the man. "As long as it takes."

The three men exchanged looks, then shuffled away. Adams leaned against the tracks of his dragline and lit another cigarette.

"Hey, Colt," Freddie Mac called.

Colt turned. The coroner stood near the edge of the pit, looking down. Colt walked over to the spot, saw what looked like drag marks in the gravel. Freddie Mac snapped a couple more pictures.

"What do you think?" Freddie Mac asked.

"Could be anything but looks like some kind of scuffle or something dragged through here."

"That's what I thought, too, and look here." Freddie Mac leaned over and pointed a sausage finger at a red splatter about the size of a quarter. Colt squinted at the blood, noticed several other smaller spots. He straightened up, looked toward the dragline, then back at the blood spots.

"Get a sample," he said.

"Don't tell me how to do my job, Colt."

"Wouldn't think of it. I'm going to have the dragline operator swing that bucket over so we can pull the body down."

"I'll be there in a minute," Freddie Mac said, but Colt was already walking away.

Adams pounced into the cab of the huge machine, cranked it up to an ear-piercing roar, then swung the bucket toward the bank and lowered it with what struck Colt as respect for the dead. Colt watched the body swing toward him, and as it came closer, he could see that the back of the man's shirt had gotten snagged on the bucket and pulled up, giving him the appearance of being hanged. He also could see that the man's head didn't look quite right. Adams maneuvered the bucket some more. Colt signaled to Adams to kill the diesel engine, and the massive machine fell silent. Adams clambered down and stood next to the cab.

"You might as well go get a cup of coffee," Colt said as he approached the body.

Adams took off like a rabbit, clearly wanting nothing to do with a dead body.

Freddie Mac appeared as Colt stared at the body. The man's head didn't look right because of the wide, ragged exit wound on the left side of the forehead and the sunken skull. Freddie Mac snapped a couple of photos.

"Goddammit," Colt said.

"Yeah, I know," Freddie Mac said. "You ready?"

Pulling the corpse of a full-grown man down from the machine took all of Colt's—and Freddie Mac's—strength and had his hip screaming by the time the man's body lay stretched out, faceup, at the water's edge.

"You all right?" Freddie Mac said.

"Fine," Colt said as he wiped sweat off his forehead. His drenched shirt stuck to his back.

"What you make of this, Colt?"

"Somebody who was improvising. Or just not very good at this sort of thing."

"Maybe," Freddie Mac said as he squatted over the corpse. "He mighta been drunk or high, but he got his brains blowed out before he went in here."

Colt leaned over the body. No other distinguishing marks visible. "Turn him over?"

"Yep," Freddie Mac said, moving into position by the corpse's shoulders. They rolled the body over. Colt studied the small hole at the base of the man's skull.

"Another here," Freddie Mac said, pointing at a neat, dime-sized hole in the corpse's back just below the ribs, similar to the wound to the base of the skull. "No exit wound. So that's two gunshot wounds."

Colt reached into the hip pocket of the man's jeans, flipped through the thin, worn, imitation-leather wallet, coming up with only a single bill and a driver's license. He stared down at the body, then at the coroner. "According to this, his name is Lucius Wallace." He handed the wallet to Freddie Mac.

"At least we have an ID," Freddie Mac said.

"Yes," Colt said, squatting down. He recognized the face, or what was left of it, from the driver's license.

"You find a cell phone in his pockets?" Colt said.

"Nope."

"Damn thing's probably at the bottom of this pit," Colt said.

"Good luck with that one," Freddie Mac said. "Help me roll him back over."

Colt pivoted on his haunches, scanned the scuffed-up gravel leading up to the lip of the pit. "Looks like he might have slid down here before he went in."

"That would make sense," Freddie Mac said, staring at the man's face. "Looks like he took a punch to the head, too. See here?"

Colt followed Freddie Mac's pointing finger to a welt just above and between Wallace's eyebrows. "Or he could have gotten that falling headfirst," Colt said.

"I'll know more after I do an autopsy."

Colt stood up straight, tried to stretch out his hip. "I'm gonna call in. I'll leave you to it and catch up to you when you have a report."

"Yep."

Colt walked back to the blood spots. He leaned over and examined the uneven surface of gravel, sand, and loam. He straightened up and spied the metal administrative building squatting next to a ragged line of storage containers a good forty yards away. He started limping toward the building, his hip barking at him as he did so, reminding him that even a year after being shot, his body still needed to heal. He dug a Percocet from his hip pocket and popped it into his mouth as he stepped toward the building he now realized was nothing more than an oversized shed. Wample was leaning against the jamb of the open door and squinting at him, like he was watching a far-off ship come into port.

"Any idea who it is, Shurff?" Wample asked.

"Not at the moment," he said. He pointed toward the interior of the shed. "You mind? I reckon it's cooler inside."

Wample stepped aside.

Colt glanced at Wample's workspace, a rathole cluttered with flimsy papers, several calendars sporting either concrete trucks or women in bikinis, and a five-drawer file cabinet that looked abandoned. Wample's desk was awash in fast-food wrappers, a massive plastic coffee mug, and a computer that should have been scrapped ten years ago.

"You said you're the owner, Mr. Wample?"

"Yep. I'm a one-man operation when it comes to management."

"I noticed you don't have a gate on your property, so it's pretty easy to access. What about security cameras?"

Wample shook his head like a sleepy hound.

"Security guard?"

"Uh-uh. That a problem?"

"Only in trying to figure out what exactly happened. But, you ain't afoul of the law, if that's what you're asking. The coroner's still down there, and I got a car coming out to work this crime scene, so I'd appreciate your cooperation."

"You got it, Shurff," Wample said.

"I thank you. If you think of anything, anything at all, call my office."

Colt left Wample in the shed, climbed into the Crown Vic, cranked the air-conditioning, and wheeled the car around. He stopped at the edge of the highway, watched a pulpwood truck rumble north toward Hamilton. He turned, headed in the other direction, toward town.

Twenty minutes later, he wheeled into the sheriff's office parking lot feeling unsettled, his hip still aching. He made his way through the outer office straight to Becky's desk and stopped when he saw the mop top of blond and Becky's pale arm shoot up, palm out: *Hold on.*

Becky wore a headset and nodded at something a caller was saying. Colt noticed, again, that she reminded him of a fortyish version of Jodie Foster. Becky ended the call, scribbled something on a pad with her trademark green pen, and looked up at Colt. Exhaled loudly. Not happy.

"These people, Colt, I swear," she said.

"Spare me unless it's about this thing out at the gravel pit."

"No, of course not. Some woman complaining about her ex-husband not paying child support."

Colt shook his head. "Not really our problem. You help her out?"

"Yep, I told her to contact the court."

"Good."

The office main door squealed open, and Colt turned from Becky to see Craig Battles coming down the corridor with a full head of steam. Straight at him. "Goddammit," he said under his breath.

Colt started toward Battles, held up a hand. "Stop right there, Craig," he said. "What are you doing here?"

Battles pulled himself to a stop, notebook in one hand, ball-point in the other. As usual, he looked like he'd dressed in the dark: collar points flying in opposite directions, the knot in his tie clinging desperately to his open collar, above which yesterday's shave had begun to wear off. Sleepy face punctuated with squinty dark eyes, curly brown hair combed with his hand.

"Heard about it on the newsroom scanner," Battles said, referring to his place of employment, the only newspaper in town.

"Heard about what?"

Battles cocked his head. "The body at the gravel pit."

"Of course you did," Colt said, hands on hips.

"So, what happened?"

Colt frowned at the reporter. He had to give him something—and not a shove out the door. "We responded to a report of a body found in a gravel pit near the county line, out on Highway 45 North. We're currently conducting an investigation and, as such, you know I can't comment any further."

Battles stared at him. "Foul play? Is this is a homicide or an accident?"

"Not now, Craig," Colt said as he turned and walked back toward Becky's station.

"Sheriff," Battles called after him, "is this a murder or not? Are the people in the county safe?"

Colt stopped. Becky stopped speaking in mid-sentence and stared up at him, her blue eyes showing a hint of alarm. Colt spun, marched back to Battles, and stood an inch away, staring the reporter down. Battles took a step back.

"Like I said," Colt said in a low voice. "Not. Now."

Battles relented, bobbed his head, and ducked away.

When Colt stomped past Becky, she kept her head down, and he was glad she did. He walked into his office and slammed the door behind him. He stood in the cool, dark room, chasing down his profane thoughts, then walked to the window overlooking the ancient cemetery across the road. The gray stones, chipped and tilted, with barely readable inscriptions, smiled back mockingly like crooked old teeth, reminding him that he was still aboveground. But also reminding him that he would one day be as forgotten as the souls under those stones. He shook his head clear.

He stepped out into his doorway. "Becky," he said, "get John on the horn and tell him I need him here."

"You got it, Colt," Becky said, but he was already back in his office answering a ringing phone.

"Harper."

"Colt, it's Freddie Mac. Just wanted to let you know I confirmed our corpse's ID. Fingerprints match the same name: Lucius Wallace. Just figured you'd want to know."

"Fingerprints?" Colt said and sat behind his desk. He spun the chair toward the computer keyboard and started logging into the state police database. "Does our vic have a record?"

"That's your lane, Colt."

Several entries for "Wallace" appeared on-screen, and Colt scrolled down until he found the right one. "Ten years ago, DUI," he said. "First offense. Looks like his only offense."

"There you go, then," the coroner said.

"Thanks, Freddie Mac. Anything else?"

"The two wounds we saw were all he had. One exit wound. So there's probably a bullet to be found. The GSW to the torso probably wasn't fatal."

"And you're doing the autopsy today?" Colt said.

"Soon as I can get to it. You going to notify? You need the address for notification? I got his license right here."

"Sure."

Freddie rattled off Wallace's address, and Colt scribbled it on a page of the notebook he kept in his shirt pocket. "Got it," he said. "Thanks." He hung up the phone and exhaled a long breath, not relishing his next move.

He walked to Becky's desk. "Heard from John?"

"He's working an accident out near the airport.

"Okay, I'm going to notify the next of kin."

Becky looked up at him, kindness and concern in her blue eyes. "Good luck."

"Thanks."

CHAPTER TWO

COLT

Colt stared through the bug-spattered windshield, glints of red and yellow smears casting light like tiny prisms, at the one-story brick residence of Lucius Wallace. His car was parked behind a gold Chevrolet, and behind him the summer sun bled away into a stand of cottonwood trees lined up like skirmishers at the edge of the East Mississippi prairie. The sky had gone orange-purple, turning the green fields outside the hamlet of Crawford to monochrome in his rearview mirror.

He tried to think about what he would say when the dark blue front door opened. Who would open it. And see him—not even him, really, just the badge, then the white face, then the gun. Probably in reverse order. He knew he didn't know exactly what he would say. Of course, he knew what words to use. But those words were never easy or sufficient, and he never got used to them, no matter how many times he'd done it. He also realized he was stalling, allowing himself an unearned luxury.

He climbed out of the car, fixed his eyes on the door, and walked across the yard, parched and going brown from the lack of rain in the late summer. His knuckles had barely finished knocking when the door swung open.

A woman—black, in her forties. Hair short and natural, smooth face, large brown eyes that would have been charming had they not been filled with alarm at seeing a white lawman, armed, at the door.

Colt met the woman's eyes.

"Mrs. Wallace?" he said, guessing.

She nodded. "Yes. I'm Helen Wallace."

"Thank you, ma'am," he said. "I'm Sheriff—"

"I know who you are."

"May I come inside, Mrs. Wallace?"

"What is this about?" Helen's voice betrayed nothing. Not apprehension or fear or resignation.

"Please, ma'am."

He watched the corners of her mouth twitch. Then she looked away, opened the door just wide enough for him to step through. He followed her into the living room. She turned to face him, the long skirt of her white summer dress rustling in the stillness of the house.

"May we sit?" Colt asked.

Helen's face showed she understood the clue. She sank to the sofa, hands in her lap, knees together and head down, as if in prayer. He took a seat in a recliner opposite her, coffee table between them. Maybe she was praying.

"Mrs. Wallace," Colt said, wishing to hell he was anywhere else on the planet than this living room. "I'm sorry to have to inform you that your husband is dead."

He left the words hanging in the air. Experience had taught him that. The weight of those words was enough for anyone to bear—and too much for some. So, he waited.

Helen's shoulders shook as she released a ragged sob, and he saw two spots darken the linen fabric in her lap. She wept silently, shaking her head, for a long moment. Then she looked at him, wiped tears away with the back of a hand.

"What happened?" she said.

"Can I get you something to drink? Some water, maybe?"

Helen shook her head. "I'm fine. What happened?"

Colt took a breath and tried to read the woman. Every case was different. Some wanted to know every grisly detail; others wanted to know nothing, as if the not knowing could invalidate the horrible truth of the moment.

"We're not sure yet," he said at last. "We found Lucius earlier today."

"Found."

He tried not to wince. Failed. "We were called to the scene. The gravel pit out on 45 North. Lucius was found by a dragline operator."

Helen's gaze met his own. "Dragline? I don't understand."

"He'd been in the pit."

"Drowned?"

"We don't know for sure yet. We do know that he'd been shot. I'm very sorry to tell you this," Colt said, hoping to hell Helen knew he meant it.

Helen's eyes brimmed, tears like drops of mercury falling down her cheeks. "Shot," she said in a whisper.

Colt laced his fingers, hands between his knees. He waited until Helen looked up again. Then: "When was the last time you saw Lucius?"

"I would like that drink of water now, Sheriff Harper. Do you mind?"

"Not at all."

She rose, glided into the open kitchen twenty feet away toward the back of the house, where the window over the sink let the evening gloom leak in, clouding over the stainless-steel appliances. Helen drew a glass of water from the tap, pulled a paper towel from a roll suspended under a cabinet, then returned to the sofa.

Colt pulled his eyes from the various framed photographs displayed on end tables and a credenza against the wall, photos of Lucius and Helen, mostly indoor shots of the two of them, Lucius always smiling, Helen not as often. Lucius a good head taller, lean, just going gray, though he kept his hair short.

"When was the last time you saw Lucius?" Colt said.

Helen held the glass in both hands. "Yesterday afternoon. After he came home from work."

"Where does he work?"

"Claiborne Catfish Farm."

"Hank Claiborne's place?"

Helen watched him. "Yes, that's the one. You look surprised."

Colt shook his head. "Not really. It's just that I've known Hank most of my life. We went to school together."

Helen's eyes narrowed. "Oh. I see." Her voice was steady.

Colt noted the tone. "And what time did he leave here?"

"After supper, six or six thirty."

"Any idea where he was going?"

Helen nodded, sniffled. "He and Reverend Mike—that'd be Mike Sanders—were going to a prayer meeting."

"Prayer meeting?" Colt said. "On a Monday night?"

Helen drank, then set the glass on the coffee table. "You got a problem with prayer, Sheriff?"

Colt sat back in his chair and met Helen's eyes, dry now and wary. "No, not at all," he said, smiling to show the woman he really didn't have a problem at all with praying. "It's just that usually prayer meetings are on a Wednesday night."

"Weren't at the church," Helen said. "They met some folks at the community center."

"I think I passed it on the way in," Colt said. "These are just folks in the area?"

"Far as I know."

"What was Lucius driving?"

"His truck," Helen said. "Red Chevrolet."

"Was it common for Lucius to be gone all night at these meetings?" Colt asked.

Helen looked away, off toward something Colt couldn't see. "You'd have to ask Reverend Mike about that."

Damned odd answer for a woman who's just been told her husband was dead. "Yes, ma'am, I'll do that. This may sound like a strange question, but did Lucius have any enemies? Anybody that might want to hurt him?"

Helen shook her head.

"One more thing, and I hate to bring it up, but I have to. I'm going to need you to come into town to identify Lucius."

Helen's eyes went wet again, and her shoulders sagged. A ragged sob tore the still air of the room. Colt thought about reaching over to place his hand on her arm but thought better of it. He stood. Helen nodded and rose, unsteady on her feet.

"When you're ready, Mrs. Wallace. And you need anything—anything at all—call my office." He half turned to go.

Helen sniffed. "Need anything?" she said with a voice like steel. He turned back to face her. She wiped a tear off her cheek. "My husband is dead, Sheriff. How can you possibly give me anything I need?"

"Ma'am, I—"

She cut him off with a wave. "I don't expect nothing from the police. Not a thing."

"Mrs. Wallace," Colt said, sharper than he intended. "You can expect one thing from me. I'm going to find the person who killed your husband. And put him away for a long time."

Helen Wallace met his eyes and scoffed. "We'll see about that, won't we?"

Colt swallowed the rising anger. "I'll see myself out."

In the car, he jammed a hunk of tobacco in his bottom lip and let his mind unwind as he pulled away from the Wallace residence and made his way through the town of Crawford. Or what was left of Crawford. In the blue light of the rising moon, the shattered skeletons of businesses long shuttered loomed like ancient ruins, reminders of a past that might have been only an illusion in the first place. The broken brick of a gas station, pumps ripped out, squatted across the street from a desiccated shell of what had once been a discount store, now an anonymous rubble of concrete and cinder block. The remains of the main street reminded him, vividly, of streets in Somalia he had patrolled as an infantry squad leader decades ago.

It was an image that stayed with him all the way to his own place, until he sat on his back porch with a cold beer in his hand: shattered lives and ruined pasts.

DAY TWO

CHAPTER THREE

COLT

When Colt walked into his office the next morning, Deputy John Carver was standing by the window, clutching a green folder in one hand, coffee mug in the other, reading the contents of the folder.

"Morning, John," Colt said as he made his way to his desk, carrying his own mug.

John turned, grim-faced, and waved the folder at him. "This shit ain't right, Colt."

Colt sipped the Becky-made coffee and winced. "Damn, she makes it strong every time."

Unlike Colt, John wore a full uniform every day and, also unlike Colt, it fit him as perfectly as the dress blues they both once wore in the Marine Corps. Colt noticed, again, that his best friend's height, muscular frame, and chocolate skin reminded him of Muhammad Ali.

"You read my notes?" Colt said.

John walked to the desk, sat in the wooden chair opposite Colt, placed his mug on the corner of the desk. "I did. Like I said. This shit ain't right."

"I know. I heard you."

"Coroner's report?"

"Not yet. I notified the next of kin last night."

John grimaced. "How'd that go?"

"'Bout like you'd expect," Colt said, shaking his head. "But it was, I don't know, odd."

John raised an eyebrow. "Odd how?"

"For one thing, she seemed shocked that her husband was dead. But angry, too."

"Sounds reasonable."

"No," Colt said. "Angry at *him*. And me."

"Go on," John said.

Colt recounted his conversation with Helen Wallace, emphasizing the comment she made about asking Reverend Mike about her husband being out all night.

John thought that over. "That does seem odd," he said. "But she *did* just hear the news."

"Still," Colt said. "Something's not right. I could feel it."

"Could be. What are you thinking?"

"That I need to see Reverend Sanders."

John crossed his arms and stared out the window. "You sure you want to do that? Today?"

Colt sat back in his chair. "Why not? What are *you* thinking?"

John picked up his mug, drained it. "Starting with a black pastor feels wrong, even if we think they were in the same place the night he died."

John's words surprised him. "What do you suggest, then? You know it's the only move we have at the moment."

"It just don't seem right," John said, shifting in his chair. "I think you're better off treading carefully on this one."

Colt stared at John across the desk. His best friend since boot camp despite their differences. Or maybe because of them. John had been steady every day Colt had known him. John had even taken a bullet meant for him. But John had never quite been comfortable with the differences between his native Southside Chicago and rural Mississippi, even if John was now seeing Rhonda Raines, another one of Colt's closest friends.

And because of John's outsider's view, Colt had learned to listen to him.

"Fair enough," he said. "For now." He finished his coffee, set the mug on his desk with a clunk. "Have you talked to Rhonda about this?"

"I mentioned it last night, but that was before I read your report. What does Rhonda have to do with this? Clifford was killed by a drug dealer, not like this."

"Right," Colt said, trying to organize the words rattling through his head. "But she knows this place better than I do. The dynamics of this place. The past. I left for years, but she never did. And she's the only person whose opinion I trust as much as yours."

John shrugged, impatient. "So?"

Colt held up a hand. "So, I'm telling you that eventually we're going to do it my way because I know what I'm doing. You don't believe me, ask Rhonda. Even if you do believe me, ask her."

John huffed out a breath, shook his head. "It ain't that, Colt. I got your back, you know that."

"I do," Colt said. "I surely do. And the black folks here are going to want me to arrest a white guy, hopefully a mean redneck they can point at say, 'See?' And white folks will jump for goddam joy if the killer turns out to be black, you want to know the cold truth."

"I get that," John said. "That kind of shit makes me mad."

"Me, too," Colt said as he got to his feet.

Colt walked around the desk, patted John's shoulder on the way past. "One more thing. Put out a BOLO for a red Chevrolet pickup truck."

"Read that in the report," John said. "Already done."

CHAPTER FOUR

MOLLY

Molly awoke in a rush, her eyes wide. She felt disoriented, then realized she was sitting in an uncomfortable hard-backed plastic chair. A buzz at the edge of her consciousness became voices, then a single voice, off to her right. Her eyes focused and she scanned the room, panic rising in her throat. Around her, men and women of various ages sat in the same kind of chairs in a circle. Most were oblivious to her. A girl across from her, couldn't have been more than eighteen, shredded a tissue in her tiny hands as she scowled at nothing, one leg jittering so bad it looked as if it would separate itself from the girl's body.

Fuck. I'm still in rehab.

She hadn't realized she was dozing. These goddam meetings were enough to drive anybody to drink, especially this circle of addicts and alcoholics. She hoped she'd slept through Teresa's story of woe. Teresa, a housewife from Pennsylvania, told the same story in every meeting—how she drank too much wine, but she wasn't too bad off, and she was proud of the fact that she had detoxed herself on the way to rehab.

Yeah, right. If Teresa had detoxed on the way to rehab, she didn't need to be here in the first place. It took Molly three days of bordering on the DTs, screaming panic attacks, and heavy doses of sedatives for her to detox. And she still felt like shit for two weeks after that.

Today was Day 32, Meeting Number 24, or something like that, and even now Molly still couldn't sit still. She was still prone to moments of abject despair or paralyzing fear—fear of leaving the safety of the facility she'd been buried in for a month. In here, not drinking was easy. But she knew that out there, in the world, it was a terrifyingly different story.

But after listening to the sob stories at the meetings day after day, she was almost willing to try it. The teenager hooked on pills who blamed her parents for not buying her a car for graduation, the drug dealer from San Antonio who'd gotten hooked on the heroin he was selling, the waitress who started drinking at age eleven and just never stopped. God, these people depressed her.

"Molly?"

The sound of her name made her jump in her chair. She whipped her head toward Charlotte, the twenty-something with scores of tiny horizontal scars up her arms. Charlotte was leading today's meeting. "Molly," Charlotte said again. "Would you like to share?"

Molly cleared her throat and looked around the room. She had no idea what to say. Certainly not what was on her mind.

"Actually, I'm a little embarrassed," she said, surprising herself. "I just realized I'm sitting here taking the inventory of every person in this room. And I know I should be focusing on myself. But the truth is, it's a hell of a lot easier to focus on somebody else. What do you call it? Comparing out? That's me." She took a deep breath. "I have tried and tried to figure out how I got here, what I did to deserve becoming an alcoholic. I'm ashamed of that word. And myself. But that's what I am. What I have become. Does the self-loathing ever stop?"

She paused and looked around the room. Every eye on her, even the teenage girl with the shaky leg. "I sure as shit hope so," Molly continued. "Because I can't stand it."

She looked again at the faces around her, tried to see compassion or understanding or hope. She saw confusion and pain. "Thanks for letting me share."

The others clapped politely and murmured, "Thanks for sharing."

She sank back in her chair, drained from the effort of two minutes of baring her soul to strangers. She felt better, but only slightly so. She crossed her arms and let her chin drop to her chest and put her mind in idle.

The meeting came to a close ten minutes later—mercifully, Teresa didn't share—and the group stood to link hands and recite the Lord's Prayer. Molly folded her chair and put it against the wall with the others and nearly bumped into Debbie, one of the counselors.

"Oh, sorry, Debbie," Molly said. "Didn't see you behind me."

Debbie, a short, straw-haired woman with a ready smile and eleven years of sobriety, shook her head. "No problem. Can I talk to you for a second?"

Molly shrugged. "Sure."

Debbie signaled her to follow. "Won't take long," she said.

Molly followed her down a short, dark hall to Debbie's broom closet of an office. Debbie walked behind a desk cluttered with file folders and a laptop. Molly stood opposite her on the other side the of the desk. "What's up?" Molly said.

Debbie slid her hands into the pockets of her jeans. "Two things," she said. "First, I heard you share in the meeting. Don't be so hard on yourself."

Molly rolled her eyes.

Debbie smiled, as she always did. "You're probably thinking, easy for me to say, right?"

"Something like that."

"You think I didn't go through the same thing? That torture of, 'Why me?' It happens to all of us." Debbie paused. "You may be Molly McDonough, ATF special agent, but you're not unique."

"Former special agent," Molly said, angry at Debbie and herself.

"And I'm a former community college professor, big deal," Debbie said. "Second, you want to know why you're an alcoholic, Molly?"

Molly's face flushed, and she looked down at the floor. This was too personal, too real. She managed a nod.

"You're an alcoholic because you drank too much," Debbie said. "It's that simple. Accept it and move on. You have a whole lot of life left. And you get to choose how to live it."

Molly absorbed the words. It made sense but she wasn't ready to accept it. "Okay," she mumbled. "You said two things."

Debbie nodded. "I wanted to tell you that first because we got word from your insurance company. Your benefits are maxed out, so we have to discharge you. Today."

Molly stared wide-eyed at Debbie, the all-too-familiar panic seizing her by the throat. "What?" she said. "That's bullshit, I've got another week here. I can't leave today."

Debbie held up a hand. "It's going to be okay, Molly, really it is. And you are ready. You're more ready than you think. You still need to go to meetings, get a sponsor, and start learning how to live a sober life. But you've learned everything we can teach you here."

Molly's anger flashed again. What Debbie really meant was she'd learned everything her insurance would pay for. She felt Debbie's eyes on her, and she knew the counselor was expecting her to say something. She took a deep breath. "Okay," she said at last. "Can I ask a question?"

"Sure."

"What do I do when I get home?"

Debbie smiled. "Go to a meeting. Get a sponsor. Find someone you trust."

Molly ducked her head, nodded. Easier said than done. Her list of people to trust was painfully short.

CHAPTER FIVE

COLT

Colt parked the Crown Vic in a shaded spot next to Zion Baptist Church, checked his watch. He figured Reverend Michael Sanders, being the shepherd of a flock, would be on duty by ten thirty in the morning. Then he spotted the reverend's new Buick sedan.

Inside the church, he made his way down a narrow hall, past several doors painted white with stick-on signs stating the purpose of the rooms behind the doors. Most were classrooms. He found the pastor's office, stepped into the empty reception area. Against one wall, there were two chairs and a side table stacked with magazines. The opposite wall bore a picture of Jesus above a wooden cross on a hook.

In front of him, a door with a brass plate that read PASTOR was ajar, and a fan of light the color of butter spread out toward him. He stepped across worn green carpet and poked his head through the threshold.

A fierce-looking man the color of ebony sat at a wide oak desk, short-cropped hair just going gray, matching his goatee. Head down, gold wire-rimmed glasses perched at the end of his nose as he studied an array of papers splayed before him. He wore a blindingly white shirt and blue vest, matching tie in a full Windsor knot, which made Colt glad he'd put on a uniform shirt for this visit instead of his usual civilian shirt.

He tapped the door with his index finger. "Reverend Sanders?"

The reverend didn't look up right away. He finished reading whatever had his attention, then raised his head.

"Yes? Oh, I'm sorry, Sheriff, I didn't know that was you." Sanders rose and extended his hand. Colt shook it.

"My secretary is out," Sanders said, straightening his vest. "How may I help you?"

"It concerns Lucius Wallace," Colt said.

"Oh?" Sanders' brow furrowed behind his glasses.

"May I?" Colt said, glancing at an upholstered chair facing the desk.

Sanders flashed a tight smile. "By all means."

"Thank you." Colt sat, as did Sanders. "Reverend, Lucius Wallace is dead. We discovered his body yesterday afternoon."

Sanders' eyebrows shot up. "What?"

"He was found at the gravel pit north of town," Colt said.

Sanders' hand went to his mouth, then rubbed his eyes. "What happened? How?"

"We're still trying to figure all that out," Colt said. "That's why I'm here."

Sanders cocked his head and gave Colt a questioning look. "I don't understand."

Colt watched the pastor carefully. "Time of death, as best we can tell, was sometime late Monday night, after the meeting he attended with you in Crawford." He intentionally left out the word "prayer."

Sanders scowled down at his hands. "I see." He drew a long breath and looked up.

"How did you know Lucius, Reverend?"

Sanders laced his fingers together on the desk. "He's been a member of my congregation for, oh, ten years or so. Very involved with the church. Him and Helen—his wife—both."

"Did you know him outside the church? Socially?" Colt said.

"For me, socially more often than not means church," Sanders said. "But outside of church services and activities, we didn't really socialize. We did pray together from time to time. That's why we were together that night. We were meeting members of the community for a time of prayer."

"Did the two of you do that often?" Colt said. "Meet with folks at the community center?"

Sanders stared at him, brown eyes steady, much the same way Helen Wallace had the day before. He shrugged. "From time to time."

"On Monday nights? My understanding was this was a prayer meeting. I'm not an expert, but don't those usually go on Wednesdays?"

Sanders smiled. "As the spirit moves, Sheriff," he said. "It wasn't a formal worship service like the ones you're referring to. Lucius and I would often call on members of the congregation or the community at large, usually small groups of five to ten people, just to have fellowship, offer emotional support, that kind of thing. He was a very good conversationalist. Good communicator."

Colt nodded his understanding. "Emotional support for anything in particular?"

Sanders cleared his throat. "That, of course, would depend on the people at the meeting. Sometimes I speak for a few minutes."

"What about Monday night? Did you speak then?"

"I did."

"What about?" Colt kept his voice conversational, matching Sanders' tone.

"Book of Matthew," Sanders said. "The meek shall inherit the earth. You're familiar?"

Colt smiled at the pastor. "Quite. I spent a lot of time in Sunday school as a kid."

Sanders beamed. "Good. I hope it serves you in your current position. Anyway, I didn't speak for long; we mostly talked about day-to-day issues: jobs, families, that sort of thing."

"Could you get me a list of names of those at the meeting?" Colt said.

"I'm sure I could come up with some of them."

"Thank you," Colt said. "What time did y'all leave the meeting?"

"Oh, Lucius left about nine thirty, ten o'clock, I would imagine," Sanders said. "Why?"

"I'm just trying to establish a timeline of Mr. Wallace's whereabouts on the night he died." He recalled the conversation with Helen. She'd implied Lucius and the pastor had gone together. "You stayed behind? Were you in separate cars?"

Sanders looked puzzled. "Why, yes. We met at the center."

"Why separate vehicles?"

"Lucius had to get back home," Sanders said, his tone no longer conversational. "I like to linger after the meeting to follow up on some of the conversations."

Colt noticed the change in tone, much like Helen's. "I'd appreciate that list, Reverend. One last question. Do you own a gun?"

Sanders sat up in his chair, looking fierce again and not at all pastoral. "What kind of question is that, Sheriff?"

Colt held up a hand. "I have a lot of details to account for, Reverend. It's not an accusation."

"It sounds like one," Sanders said, watching him with hawk eyes.

"Then I apologize," Colt said. "But do you?"

"As a matter of fact, I do. Perfectly legal, and I have a permit to carry it concealed."

Surprised, Colt said, "Seems odd that a man of your profession would feel the need to carry a gun, if you don't mind me saying."

Sanders crossed his arms. "These are fraught times, Sheriff. You of all people should know that. I carry it for self-protection."

Colt nodded. "Yes, I understand. Do you have the weapon here? May I see it?"

"Do you have a search warrant?"

"I can get one," Colt said.

Sanders leaned forward and laced his fingers together. For a second, Colt thought he was going to pray. "I'm not trying to be difficult, Sheriff, but I know my rights as a citizen. Like you, I believe in the law. Your request, I believe, requires a search warrant, with which I'd comply."

Colt wanted to tell Sanders that at the moment he wasn't being very compliant. Instead, he stood and said, "Thank you, Reverend. I appreciate you taking the time. If you could call my office with that list, I'd be much obliged."

He turned and walked out of Sanders' office without looking back, not wanting to see the fury on the man's face.

On the way to the car, his phone buzzed in his shirt pocket. He glanced at the screen.

"What's up, John?" he said, climbing into the driver's seat.

"Looks like we found Wallace's truck," John said. "At least, a gas station manager reported a red Chevy in his lot, locked up. Been there since last night, he said."

"Where?" Colt said, pulling out of the church parking lot.

"Forty-Five South. Convenience store. Bait 'n' Beer."

"I know it," Colt said. "Meet you there in ten minutes."

"I'm already on the way."

When he pulled into the parking lot of the store, John was already inspecting the vehicle. He parked and joined his deputy. The truck sat in a spot next to a wall, near the air pump. John turned at the sound of his arrival, waited for him to join.

"That's a red Chevy, all right," Colt said. "You talk to anybody inside?"

John shook his head. "Just got here myself. I was about to run the tag."

"Go ahead," Colt said. "I'll go inside."

The manager was waiting just inside the glass door, and he introduced himself as Mike Honeycutt. Colt shook his hand and walked to the counter, where a teenage boy with a shock of straw-colored hair made himself busy behind the cash register.

"Mr. Honeycutt, thank you for calling this in," Colt said.

Honeycutt rubbed his hands together, seemed nervous talking to the Law, like most people did. "Not a problem, Sheriff. That thing's been here overnight. My nighttime associate noticed it was still there when he came off shift this morning, told me about it. Far as I'm concerned, it's trespassing, and I'd just as soon have it moved off my property."

Colt scanned the store, saw that nothing seemed out of place. "You say he noticed it was *still* here when he went off shift. Did he see the vehicle approach?"

Honeycutt shrugged and looked like he'd just been asked a question in math class he didn't have the answer to. "Don't know. You'd have to ask him."

"What's his name? I'd surely like to talk to him."

"Roger Graham," Honeycutt said.

"I'm going to need a phone number, Mr. Honeycutt," Colt said. "And as far as that trespassing thing, that truck is now part of an investigation, so it stays where it is until I decide it can be moved."

Honeycutt drew in a breath. "Investigation? Of what?"

"That's a law enforcement matter I can't comment on right now," Colt said, turning to go. "If you could get me Mr. Graham's phone number, I'd appreciate it."

He walked around the corner to see John working on the driver-side door with a slim jim. "Forensics is on the way, if that's what you're thinking," John said over his shoulder.

"Good," Colt said. "Open it up and let's see what's in there."

John tugged on the metal bar, and the door lock clicked open. Colt pulled latex gloves from a hip pocket, snapped them on, pulled the door open.

An unmarked sheriff's car swooped into the lot behind them, and two men scrambled out, the passenger carrying what looked like an oversized tackle box. The driver, the older of the two, marched to the truck. "Sheriff, I really wish y'all would wait and let us do our job first."

Colt held up his hands in surrender. John slid away, trying to hide the slim jim. "We haven't touched anything inside the vehicle, Steve," Colt said to the older forensics tech. "And John took photos of the truck before we opened the door. Y'all can get in there right now."

Steve sighed and waved the younger tech toward the truck. Colt joined John at his car, watching the techs get to work with photographing and dusting the vehicle.

"You talk to Rhonda?" Colt said as he leaned against the hood of John's car.

John stared down at the asphalt, arms crossed. "No. How'd it go with the pastor?"

Colt recounted the conversation, noting John's growing angst.

"You actually asked him if he owned a pistol?"

Colt pulled a can of snuff from his jeans pocket. "Yes, I did. And I'm glad I did. Because, much to my surprise, he owns one."

"Can't say as I blame him."

Colt put a small chunk of tobacco in his lower lip, spit onto the asphalt. "The hell you say?"

John pushed himself off the hood of the car, arms still crossed. "Colt, do you really not see it? The question is why *wouldn't* he carry a gun? If I didn't have a badge, I'd still carry a gun around here."

Colt stared at his best friend. "I didn't know you felt that way."

John turned his head toward him. "Since day one, Colt. I just keep that shit to myself. Like a lot of black folks around here. Maybe you should be the one talking to Rhonda, not me."

Colt worked the tobacco in his jaw. "You think I don't know what's going on in this county?"

"I think you think you're color-blind, but you don't realize that the rest of the county isn't," John said.

"I think that's bullshit," Colt said, crossing his own arms to wrestle his anger.

John pointed toward the truck; Colt swiveled his head. Steve was taking photos of a cell phone in an evidence bag held by his assistant. Colt walked over. "What you got there, Steve?"

"It was under the seat," Steve said. "Bagging and tagging."

"Let me see it," Colt said. Steve handed over the bag. Colt turned the phone on through the plastic, waited for it to boot up. John joined him at his side. "We're going to need the call records," he said. "Anything else in there?"

"Small black notebook over on the passenger-side floorboard," Steve said. "Bunch of writing in it, couldn't really tell what it says. Already bagged."

"All right, then," Colt said. "We'll sort it out back at the office."

"You headed back?" John said. "I was about to grab some lunch."

"Go ahead," Colt said. "I'll finish this up and talk to Hank Claiborne."

"Wallace's employer, right?" John said. "Good idea."

"Thanks," Colt said, sharper than he intended but not really giving a damn as he walked back to his car. He waited until he was on the highway and out of sight before he mashed the Crown Vic's accelerator to the floor. The big car jumped under him and he let it, keeping one hand light on the wheel, fuming at John's words as he tore across low hills blurring past soybean fields and hardwood trees. He didn't understand John's surliness, or even his own anger at his best friend. But he didn't like the insinuation that John was making, that he didn't know what was going on, race-wise, in his own damn county. Who was he to start pointing fingers and making judgments?

His cell phone chirped from the cup holder between the seats, jolting him from his silent rant. He fished the phone out and answered while staring at the highway.

"What's up, John?" he said.

"Colt?" A female voice. He stared at the screen, read the name.

"Molly? McDonough?" he said. "Is that you?"

"Yes, it is," Molly said.

He smiled. "I have to say, this is a hell of a surprise. Been a long time."

"I know," Molly said, her voice shaky. "Look, Harper, I just need you to listen for a few minutes."

He backed down off the accelerator. "Sure," he said. "Go ahead."

"I've got some, uh, time on my hands," Molly said, "and I was wondering if I could come down there."

He chuckled. "Molly, you don't need permission to come here. Of course you can, but what's up?"

"Not over the phone," she said.

"Okay. When did you plan on coming down?"

"Tomorrow."

"Tomorrow?"

He heard her blow out a breath, tried to get an image of what was going on at her end. "Yes, tomorrow," she said. "Is that a problem?"

"No, no, not at all. I'm in the middle of a case, but, sure. Who knows, maybe you could have some insight on it."

"I wouldn't count on that," she said.

"Call me when you're on the way," he said.

"I will," Molly said. "And thanks." She hung up.

He tossed the phone to the passenger seat. Molly didn't sound like the same federal agent he'd worked with a year earlier. But whatever was going on with her, it'd have to wait until tomorrow.

DAY THREE

CHAPTER SIX

COLT

He could see the man smoking in the moonless desert night, even from yards away. He crouched and broke into a run toward the Iraqi guard, who faced away from him with an AK-47 assault rifle slung over his shoulder.

Colt left his feet and flew, like a glider, up and over the man, silent and airborne against flickering stars and a sky black as pitch. It felt weird being weightless. The knife in his right hand glittered and tugged at him, pulling him into a dive toward the guard's head. He heard air rushing past his ears and felt an anger and hatred rise within him and propel him toward the guard, who must have heard the wind, too, because he turned his head and looked up at Colt. But his face was a skull, bloody and rotten.

Colt screamed and landed on his feet, swung the knife in a wild arc. The guard disappeared, and in his place stood his dead friend Moonpie Jones, in full battle gear, smiling. A gaping hole in his chest gushed blood, and he pointed over his shoulder. "Over there," Moonpie said. "The ones that did this are all over there."

Colt screamed again, spun around, and fell into a bright, deep swimming pool. He loved the water, had his whole life. Swam like a fish before the Marine Corps, so he aced the swim qualification at boot camp. Scuba quals at Camp Pendleton had been even easier. He learned then that he had no innate fear of water.

But now he was underwater, surrounded by the shimmering refracted light through clear, clean water. A pool maybe. He didn't know. Didn't know how he got there or when, and he didn't know why he could barely move or surface. Oddly, he couldn't see down, only up, and he couldn't inspect himself for any clues. He didn't feel trapped as much as captured by the sensation of being suspended, against his will. He looked up, toward the flickering white surface. He couldn't move. He willed himself forward, but he remained motionless. He knew he would run out of air, and thus must break the surface, but couldn't. He felt held down, in the grip of some inchoate evil. He twisted, turned, thrust himself toward the surface. Nothing. Panic. He couldn't hold his breath any longer. He felt himself convulse into a scream, knowing that underwater the scream would kill him. He screamed again, and again …

Screaming. He was screaming again. He lunged toward the foot of the bed, consciousness arriving like a brick to the head, an ungodly moan ricocheting off the walls of his darkened bedroom, a moan he barely recognized as his own voice. The familiar smell of his own sweat confirmed he was awake.

He shook his head, scanned the room, wiped his face. He couldn't recall the dream at all. Just the end, the terrible fear of being held down, panic, and screaming. Always screaming.

The sheets wrapped around him like an anaconda, and he fell back onto the bed, heart pounding, mind tumbling through the dark space like a meteor.

"Goddammit," he said to the ceiling. He swung his legs to the floor, reached for the pill bottle on the nightstand, and shook two painkillers into his palm. Tossed them back, then walked to the kitchen. No sense in trying to sleep now. The just-rising sun peeked through the window over the kitchen. He put on a pot of coffee and got dressed.

Three cups later, he pulled on his gun belt and limped to the car, still haunted by a dead comrade. He tried to shake it off, focus on his first stop of the morning. Hank Claiborne. He recalled a chilly October night thirty years earlier, after a high school football game. Twenty or so kids, mostly athletes and their girlfriends, had found their way down dark country roads to a one-room clapboard shack in the woods for a late-night party. Organized, if that was the right word, by Hank Claiborne. It was his father's property, after all, and the shack was used as a campsite during deer season.

Colt recalled the endless supply of beer from the back of Hank's pickup truck and the heavy, pungent smell of weed suspended by the cool night air that hovered over the crowd. The weed had also been provided by Hank, as he had himself a small patch on his daddy's farm. Bonfire roaring between the cabin and the tree line providing warmth, the orange light casting weird shadows around the grounds.

And he recalled how the party got out of control when, early into the morning, Hank was discovered on the roof of the shack, stoned out of his mind, dancing and peeling shingles off the roof and throwing them toward the fire below. He'd nearly fallen off more than once, until somebody—Colt couldn't remember who—climbed to the roof and hauled Hank down.

He smiled at the memory and almost blew past the sign for Claiborne Catfish Farm. He stomped the brake, fought the wheel, and made the turn. He steered down the main dirt lane that bisected the farm, splitting the pond groups in two: six rectangular ponds, covering the same area as two football fields, three to the north of the road, three to the south. Together, the two groups made up half the farm, with an identical setup across the highway to the east. He appreciated the symmetry of the layout and found some comfort in the near-military precision of the formations.

He pulled up in a cloud of dust to a low metal building. Several cars and a couple of pickups occupied spots near the wall in the afternoon shade. He found a spot, put his mind back on the job. His hip ached as he climbed out of the car, and he dug a Percocet out of a pocket, chewed and swallowed it as he pushed open the door to the farm office.

Inside, an air conditioner whined like a jet engine from a window, with little effect. A woman at a desk fought to keep a sheaf of papers from flying as an oscillating floor fan moved muggy air from one side of the room to the other. She looked up, sweaty and exasperated, and attempted a smile. "Sheriff Harper, how're you doing today?"

He smiled. "Could stand a break from the heat, same as you. Is Hank around?"

The woman blew a wisp of dyed-blond hair from her brow. "In the back," she said, tossing her head in the general direction.

"Thanks very much." He stepped through the door behind her and walked down a short hall into Hank Claiborne's office.

Hank sat behind an ancient double-pedestal oak desk cluttered with folders, papers, and one picture of his two preteen kids, who Colt knew lived somewhere in North Carolina with Hanks' ex-wife, Rita. Photos of Mississippi State football games on the wall to his left, file cabinets on the right.

Wasn't much cooler in Hank's office, either. Hank's blue golf shirt clung to him, dark with sweat. The man who toiled at the desk bore a resemblance to the kid he'd gone to high school with, but clearly with some wear and tear: a belly, red drinker's nose, hair thinning on top. Expensive-looking watch on his wrist.

"Colt?" Hank said, looking up from his papers, his eyebrows raised in surprise. "What brings you all the way out here?"

"Hey, Hank, good to see you, too," Colt said, smiling. "Got a minute?

Hank's face still wore a smile, but it no longer registered surprise. "Sure, uh, is this official business?"

"It is," Colt said.

Hank waved him in. "Sure, come on in." He leaned back in his chair and rubbed his eyes. Colt sat in a metal folding chair opposite.

"Can I offer you something to drink?" Hank said. "Coffee? Water? I figure you're on duty or I'd offer you something stronger."

"No, thanks." Colt shifted on the metal chair, taking the weight off his hip. "I won't take much of your time."

Hank nodded, as if he were waiting for Colt to continue.

"I believe you employ a man by the name of Lucius Wallace," Colt said.

"I do," Hank said. "He's my maintenance chief. Damn good worker."

"How long has he been working for you?"

"About five years," Hank said.

"You seen him the last couple of days?"

Hank gave a low laugh. "No, I haven't. I haven't been out to the ponds or warehouses the last few days. Trying to keep up with inventory, the paperwork I hate but have to do. And I took some days off last month."

Colt smiled again, staying polite. "Yep, I hate paperwork, too. Worst part of the job. Anyway, Lucius Wallace is dead, Hank. We pulled him out of a gravel pit couple of days ago. We're investigating it as a homicide."

Hank sat up straight. "What? A homicide? What the hell happened?"

"We don't really know at this point," Colt said. "Course, I can't get into specifics, but there's enough indicators to lead me to believe it was a homicide."

Hank looked confused. "You sure it was Lucius?"

Colt studied Hank's face, weighing reactions and movement, and not liking himself for doing it to someone he'd known most of his life.

Hank gave a low whistle, wiped sweat from his brow. "Well, goddam. Ain't that something."

"You said he was your maintenance chief," Colt said. "Good worker? Reliable?"

"Absolutely," Hank said. "He's worked here a few years. He can fix any damn thing that's broken or needs fixing. Never missed a day's work that I can recall. Never had a problem with any of his work."

"What about him—I mean, not connected to his work?"

Hank looked puzzled. "No. I really didn't know him all that well outside of work."

"So, nobody you know of that would want to do him harm."

"Absolutely not."

"That's what I figured," Colt said. He heard footsteps behind him, and Hank got to his feet. Colt turned to see a tall bearded man walk through the door toward them. Big as a linebacker, curly brown hair and blue eyes that seemed to inspect everything they saw.

"Hey, Jack," Hank said, crossing the room, "didn't know you were coming by. Come on in, say hello to the sheriff."

Colt stood and faced Jack, who took two steps into the office. Colt noticed he was a good three inches taller than himself. He put out his hand. "Sheriff Colt Harper."

Jack glanced at Colt's hand, then met his eyes. No smile. "Jack Burnett," he said as he shook Colt's hand.

"Colt and I go way back," Hank said, a smile flickering across his face. To Colt, he said, "Jack is my operations manager."

Colt glanced at Hank, then back to Jack. "Operations manager? What all does that entail?"

Jack slid his hands into the pockets of his jeans. "Making sure things run like they're supposed to."

Hank laughed. "Jack started out as my oxygen man."

"And what is that exactly?" Colt said, staring at Jack Burnett.

"You have any idea how hard it is to raise catfish?" Jack said. "The water levels have to be perfect. Feed has to be perfect. Same with oxygen levels. Population of fish per pond has to be carefully monitored. It's all very scientific. That's what I did, check the oxygen levels in these ponds."

"I had no idea," Colt said. "Seems like the kind of job that would take up a lot of time. What else is involved in operations?'

"Transportation, utilities, personnel, security, stuff like that," Jack said.

"Security?" Colt said. "What kind of security do you need at a catfish farm?"

Hank laughed, a little nervously, Colt thought. "You'd be surprised, Colt," Hank said. "It's not like raising soybeans like my dad did back in the day, when me and you was in high school. All it takes is somebody pouring a gallon of gas into one of my ponds and I could be out of business in no time. You should come to the farm and see the operation we have out there."

Colt turned to Hank. "That's not a bad idea. I might do that." Then back to Jack. "So, I was just talking to your boss here about one of y'all's employees. Lucius Wallace. He been at work the last couple of days?"

Jack gave a tiny, tight smile under the chestnut beard. "Matter of fact, he hasn't. I was just coming over here to let Mr. Claiborne know that."

"I already took care of that," Colt said. "We found Lucius' body two days ago at the bottom of a gravel pit," Colt said, watching Burnett's eyes.

"Gravel pit?" Jack said. "What, he drowned?"

"We don't have a report from the coroner yet," Colt said, letting the white lie slide off his lips. "But we're treating it as a homicide."

Jack grunted. Crossed his arms, looked at the floor. "Damn shame."

"You know him very well?" Colt said.

Jack looked up. "Me? No, not at all. I mean, just here at work."

"Was he a good worker, bad worker?"

"Jack, I was just telling Colt here that Lucius was reliable, and we never had no trouble out of him," Hank said. Colt cut his eyes toward the man, wishing Hank would be quiet for the moment.

"That's right," Jack said. "Never had no trouble out of Lucius."

"That's what Hank was telling me," Colt said, hoping Hank and his big mouth took the hint. "Hank, I'll leave y'all to your business. If you hear anything, you'll let me know?"

"Absolutely," Hank said. "Anything else?"

Colt looked at both men in turn. "Not at the moment, no," he said.

"I'll show you out," Hank said.

They walked through the outer office, the clicking of heels echoing off the concrete floor. Colt could feel Jack's eyes on his back. Hank opened the door to a blast of late-morning oven heat, offered his hand, which Colt shook.

"If there's anything I can do, Colt, just let me know," Hank said.

"Thanks, Hank, I will."

He climbed back in his car thinking about Jack Burnett. He looked at his watch and wondered where the day had gone. He called John, who answered on the second ring.

"Hey, Colt, any news?"

He summarized his conversation with Hank and Jack Burnett for John, who listened silently. "So, we're still at square one," Colt said. "You hear from the coroner?"

"About an hour ago," John said. "I put it on your desk."

"Highlights?"

"Generally, what you thought," John said. "Cause of death was the gunshot wound to the head, not drowning."

"Okay," Colt said. "I'm going to come in for a little while and do some digging. Don't wait around for me. And tell Rhonda I said hello when you see her."

"I'll do that," John said and hung up.

CHAPTER SEVEN
JACK

Jack waited until Hank returned to his office, then leaned against the file cabinet and stared at Hank as he resumed his seat. Looking nervous.

"The sheriff?" Jack said. "What the hell is that all about?"

"You heard him," Hank said. "On account of Lucius Wallace being dead."

"You and him buddies or something?"

Hank looked up at Jack, whose frame completely hid the file cabinet behind him. "He's not my buddy. Have a seat."

"I'm good," Jack said. "Y'all seemed pretty friendly when I walked in."

"We went to school together, played football, chased the same girls. That's all."

Jack pulled a snuff can from a back pocket, jammed a chunk of tobacco in his jaw, grabbed an empty plastic water bottle off the top of the cabinet, and spit. "I really don't give a shit about your trip down memory lane, Hank. I don't like having the law around."

"I know you don't," Hank said.

"What's that supposed to mean?"

"You know exactly what it means. But Lucius is dead. It's the sheriff's job to investigate. It won't become a thing. We may have to rearrange our plans, though."

"Yeah," Jack said, "I'd already figured that much out."

"Good," Hank said. "And before you say anything else, let Harper do his job."

"Meaning?" Jack said.

"It means don't screw with him, Jack. Or we'll both regret it."

Jack laughed. Hank could be such a pussy. "You kidding me? Harper ain't nothing but a ten-cent star."

Hank slapped a hand on the desk. "Goddammit, Jack, you're wrong about that. Don't try anything with him."

"You got it, boss," Jack said.

"Thank you," Hank said, a little embarrassed, Jack thought.

"You don't need to worry," Jack said. "I'll keep everything real quiet. The guys I'm working with know only what I'm telling them, anyway."

Hank managed to work a smile onto his face. "Good."

"We're getting there," Jack said.

Hank grunted. "Right. I'll call you later."

Jack waved a hand as he left Hank's office.

CHAPTER EIGHT
COLT

Colt walked through the outer office, poured a cup of stale coffee from the break room, and settled in behind his desk with Freddie Mac's coroner report. He skimmed over the parts he already knew. On the third page, he found the details he was looking for. Lucius Wallace's blood was type A. The blood spatters found on the edge of the pit were type B positive. Colt took a pen and underlined that section.

Someone else had been at the scene. Someone bleeding. He flipped to the back of the report and scanned the scene photos. The spot where the blood lay looked disturbed, like someone or something had been dragged through it. A fight? Maybe Lucius didn't give up easy. Maybe that's why it took two bullets to put him down.

He kept reading. Cause of death: gunshot wound to the head, or that's what he surmised from Freddie Mac's technical language full of medical words that meant the same thing. The gunshot wound to the torso would not have been fatal. No water in the lungs.

He sipped coffee and skimmed past the medical terminology. So, Lucius Wallace was killed—or "most likely" killed, as Freddie Mac wrote—from a nine-millimeter or similar-caliber weapon firing high-velocity rounds. And Freddie Mac noted that even though two bullet fragments recovered from the body were so mangled that ballistics comparisons would "likely not yield satisfactory results, the nature of the exit wound on the body suggests a weapon with a high muzzle velocity." He put the report down.

The door to his office swung open, and John stepped through with a folder in one hand, plastic evidence bag in the other.

"Some people knock," Colt said.

John grinned at him. "I ain't some people."

"I can't argue that. What you got?"

John settled into a chair, opened the folder in his lap. "A couple of things. The notebook in Wallace's truck." He held up the evidence bag, which contained a pocket-sized black notebook. Colt motioned for it, and John leaned over the desk and dropped it. Colt pulled the notebook from the bag and laid it on the desk.

"It's got phone numbers in it, and what looks like dates and some kind of entries that I haven't been able to make much sense of."

Colt picked up the small book, flipped through the first few pages. John was right: it didn't make a lot of sense. He started over, from the front, read slowly.

"Looks like dates, times, and initials," Colt said. "Meetings, maybe? He and the reverend met with church people a lot. It would make sense Lucius keeping some sort of record or schedule."

John shrugged. "Could be. I thought about that, too, but I wanted to hear your take on it."

"You said a couple of things," Colt said, laying the book down.

"I been working on call records from Wallace's phone," John said. "There weren't many. And the phone is a burner, which could be interesting. A couple of the numbers had multiple calls. One got my attention. It was made about an hour before the approximate time of death." He slid a thin sheaf of papers, phone records, across the desk. "So, I called it, just to see."

Colt scanned the list of calls. "And?"

"And," John said slowly, "a Rose Sanders answered. It's her cell."

Colt looked up, met John's eyes. "Rose Sanders? That's Reverend Sanders' wife."

"That thought occurred to me," John said. "But I don't know the man."

"I do," Colt said. "I mean, besides the fact that I just talked to him. He's been in the paper a few times, and she's been mentioned."

"Interesting."

"Yeah, damned interesting," Colt said. He reached for the phone.

John sat up in his chair. "You want me to leave?"

"No, I want you right here."

John sat back. He looked like he wanted to be anywhere but sitting in a chair in Colt's office.

Colt buzzed Becky and asked her to patch him through to the pastor's church. Sanders answered on the second ring.

"Reverend, Sheriff Harper here."

"What can I help you with, Sheriff?" If Sanders was still angry, he didn't let it come across in his voice.

"We're still gathering evidence in the death of Lucius Wallace," Colt said. "We located a cell phone in his truck, and some of the numbers were pretty interesting."

"In what way?" Sanders said.

"Reverend, would Lucius have had any reason to call your wife several times?"

Colt heard Sanders draw in a breath. "What are you talking about, Sheriff Harper? More to the point, what are you implying? Again?"

Colt looked over at John, shook his head. John scowled back at him.

"I'm just trying to put together a complete picture," Colt said. "I'm not trying to imply anything. But if there's something you need to tell me, now would be a good time to do so."

Long silence. Then: "It was a while back," Sanders said. "Lucius and Rose had a, uh, fling. An affair. It was a difficult time in our marriage. But they broke it off after I discovered it. Rose and I have since reconciled, and I have tried, every day actually, to forgive them both and move on from it. I don't see how an affair that ended a year ago is particularly relevant here."

Colt scribbled notes on a page of Freddie Mac's report. "You say it ended a year ago?"

"Yes."

"So, how long did the affair last?"

"Months," Sanders said.

"Reverend, Lucius Wallace called your wife a few minutes after he left the meeting in Crawford. That is to say, about an hour before he was killed."

From the corner of his eye, he saw John shake his head slowly. He could hear Sanders' breathing on the phone.

"Reverend?" he said.

"I... I don't know what to tell you," Sanders said.

"Thank you, Reverend," Colt said and hung up the phone. He laced his hands together and looked at his deputy, whose face was frozen in a scowl.

"I'm getting a search warrant for his pistol," Colt said.

"You realize what this is going to do?" John said.

Colt's eyes wandered to the window. "I know. The black folks in the county aren't going to like this one bit."

"You think?" John said. "Wallace shows up dead and our first suspect is a black preacher?"

Colt nodded. "Yes, but this is a murder investigation. Nothing is obvious, you know that. And before that phone call, I would have agreed with you that this is a crazy line of questioning. But the fact is Sanders has motive, means, and opportunity."

"Only if he's lying about the affair. He said it was over."

"Wouldn't you?" Colt said. "Look at his position. Not just any preacher, he's one of the best-known pastors in this part of the state, active in his community, a leader even. Bad enough his wife is having an affair. Even worse if she won't knock it off. That would make any man rage, but Sanders has a lot more at stake than your everyday churchgoer."

John slumped in his chair. "On that, you're right. But this just don't feel right, Colt. And I personally don't like it."

"Personally? What the hell does that mean?"

John looked across the desk at him. "Sometimes you forget that I am a black man."

Colt opened his mouth, then shut it.

"It's true," John said. "I know you like to think otherwise and all that shit, but this is different. Seeing Wallace in those photos was like looking at a newspaper from sixty fucking years ago, man. How do you think that lands on me? A cop? A black cop?"

Colt felt a shiver of discomfort run the length of his body and felt, for the first time in the years he'd known John, that he really didn't know his best friend at all.

John stood. "Next time, think about that. I agree with you at this point that the most likely course of action is to talk to that reverend some more. Or Rose Sanders. But I'm also saying you need to pay a little more attention to the people around you." He turned and walked out of the office.

Colt sank back in his chair. What in the hell was going on here?

He picked up the phone on his desk and punched in some numbers, waited for an answer.

"Judge Dockery's office." Colt recognized the voice.

"Hi, Mary Ann. Sheriff Harper."

"Hello, Sheriff, how can I help you?"

"I'll be sending a search warrant request a little later today," he said. "Can you make sure the judge sees it as soon as possible?"

"Of course," Mary Ann said. "He's in court today, but I'll let him know."

"Thank you," Colt said. He hung up and spent an hour on Becky's paperwork until his cell rang. Glad to be distracted, he glanced at the screen, checked his watch. "Hey, Molly."

"I'm about an hour out," she said.

"Perfect," he said. "I was about to escape to the shooting range. Want to meet me there?"

"Sure. Where is it?"

"I'll text you," he said. "See you in an hour." He hung up before she could answer and was out the door ten seconds later.

CHAPTER NINE
MOLLY

She felt like an idiot. No matter how many times she tried to tell herself otherwise, that's what it felt like.

She stared ahead through her bug-spattered windshield, at the strip of gray highway, its superheated surface shimmering a ways off. The car sailed south as if it had a mind of its own, an air-conditioned space capsule hurtling along in its own orbit. Her brain barely registered the four-foot snake when it rippled across the road like a black ribbon or the *thump-thump* from her wheels that ran over it.

She checked her watch. She was a good twenty minutes later than she thought she'd be, so she grabbed her phone from the console and punched the number. Harper answered on the third ring with, "Yeah."

"Hey, I'm running behind, but I'll be there soon."

"Ahite," he said, his voice its usual lazy tone, but this time with something of an edge. "Where you at?"

"Aberdeen."

"Okay. You good on how to get there?"

"Yep. Plugged into my GPS."

"See you there." He clicked off.

She tossed the phone to the seat. She still didn't know what she hoped to accomplish by meeting Harper. A connection, maybe? Sympathy? Empathy? A job? This was probably the dumbest idea she'd had since… the last time she decided to come to this state.

All she knew at the moment was that for months after returning to Memphis, all she could think of—all she *wanted*—was to be back here, doing something. Being *in it*. Useful. Having a purpose. She couldn't be a fed anymore, and no bullshit job as a corporate security consultant was going to give her that purpose. She was a disgraced federal agent, plain and simple.

And there had been the nightmares. She knew what caused them. She just didn't know what to do about them besides drink enough to pass out so they wouldn't come. And that's what she did every night until she wound up in a rehabilitation facility in Nashville, broken and scared to death of sleep.

Her GPS alerted her to a right turn, and she put her thoughts away. She wheeled off Highway 45 South onto a side road, then another, until she rolled into the gravel parking lot of the ridiculously named Cool Hand Shooting Range.

She parked, grabbed her ATF gym bag from the back seat, and strode toward the low gray building at one end of the long, covered shooter benches. Three men, spaced apart by a few feet, fired handguns and paid her no mind.

The door to the place swung open, and Colt stepped out into the afternoon glare and grinned at her from behind dark sunglasses.

"What do you know?" he said. "If it ain't Molly McDonough."

She couldn't help but grin. She walked up and stuck her hand out. "Sheriff Harper. You're looking a lot better than you did the last time I saw you."

He shook her hand. Another grin. Harper seemed to have an endless supply of them.

"I could say the same thing about you," he said. "But truth is, I don't remember it all that much."

"Thank God for that."

He gestured toward the firing line. "You ready to kill some paper? Lose a bet?"

"Lose a bet? Harper, you know damn well I can shoot."

"Yeah, yeah," he said, walking toward the shade of the covered benches. She followed him to a spot near the building, mostly away from the other shooters, and slung the gym bag under the bench as Harper pulled a Glock from the low-profile holster on his right hip. She, in turn, yanked her .45 from the concealed holster at the small of her back, released the magazine, racked the slide and locked it, then benched the weapon. Colt did the same—after he deftly caught the round he ejected from the chamber of the nine-millimeter.

He glanced over. "No Sig?"

She shook her head as she bent to her bag to retrieve ear plugs and extra magazines. "Nope. That was my service weapon."

"That new, then?"

"Yep. But don't get your hopes up," she said. "I've put it through its paces."

"We will see, former special agent McDonough. May I?"

She handed him her pistol.

He took it, inspected it, eyes approving. "Always liked Springfield. This the XD model?"

"XDS, and I like it, too. Where's your .45?"

"In my office safe. Cheaper to shoot nine-mil ammo out here, and I like to stay proficient on both weapons." Harper handed the weapon back, picked up his own. "Let's see about this shooting of yours I've heard so much about."

They loaded their weapons and got to the business of shooting, blasting away at the paper targets, first at seven yards, then ten. Two magazines each at each range.

She bore down, determined to make Harper eat his words, but the man could shoot. She could feel her hands shaking with each shot, and she managed to control herself only by an enormous amount of self-will and personal pride. Each time they went downrange to compare groups, she couldn't tell the difference between her shot group and his. She could have covered either with the palm of her hand.

They hardly spoke while firing, each concentrating on the intricacies of marksmanship, a ritual she found soothing and stimulating. Sight alignment, sight picture. Breathe and squeeze, let the pistol do the work. She could shoot for hours—and often did, back when she could.

After they inspected the results of their last string of fire at ten yards, Harper stapled up a new target and cocked his head at her.

"You're damn good, Molly," he said around a grin he apparently couldn't suppress. "But can you still pull?"

She didn't answer; instead she stuck her own target up in the frame, walked back to the firing line. She pulled another holster from her bag, quickly ran it through the belt loops of her jeans, then holstered the .45.

Harper watched her. She couldn't tell if he was bemused or entranced, nor did she give a damn. "You gonna stand in the sun all day?" she said.

He shook his head and walked back to his pistol, loaded and holstered it, then walked back toward the targets.

"This is about right," he said as his boots crunched through the gravel. "Don't have that bench to worry about."

She took her spot.

He took up a spot to her left. "Go ahead, loudmouth," he said.

"Kiss my ass, Harper." She faced the target, feet apart just so, wiped her right hand on her jeans, blew out half a breath.

She homed in on the target, saw where she wanted the bullet to go, and pulled cleanly. The pistol moved as if a part of her own body and she leveled, fired, reacquired, held steady.

Harper grunted. She looked over the top of the pistol and saw the sunlight through the crisp hole, a dime of yellow against the black, just a hair off-center. Not X-ring, but damn close.

Harper faced his own target. His right hand was a blur as he pulled his pistol, fired, steadied, then just as quickly reholstered. Her eyebrows rose.

Jesus, he's fast.

She looked at his target. Impact in the black, top of the bull. Technically, hers was better. But only technically.

Harper stepped toward her. "Damn, Molly, that's the best shooting I've seen in a long time. I see the time away from the ATF hasn't diminished your skills."

She wiped sweat from her forehead with the back of her hand. "Back at ya. For a shot-up sheriff, you're not so bad yourself."

"Least you didn't say 'old.' But you didn't drive all this way just to prove you can shoot. I already knew that."

"Maybe."

"You want to tell me what this is about?" He stared at her long enough to make her feel uncomfortable.

"Not here," she said.

Two hours later, on Colt's back porch, they sat at a table, with disassembled weapons, cleaning gear, and beer bottles between them, the afternoon glare loosening its stubborn grip to the gauzy light of a cloudy evening, the sky muslin colored and low, a vague threat over the flat green expanse of Colt's backyard.

"So," he said as he took a pull off a longneck bottle. "You miss it."

She wiped her hands on a rag, hoped Harper didn't notice them shaking. Her mind ran away from her, and she felt on the edge of panic as she sat a foot away from the first alcohol she had seen in weeks. "Christ, is it that obvious?"

Colt pushed an oily cleaning patch through the barrel of his pistol with a cleaning rod, one eye squeezed shut. The other looked at her. He shrugged. "You weren't too enthusiastic about your new career choice."

She picked up the slide of her pistol. "Sucks. Boring. Know what I mean?"

Colt put his pistol down, picked up the nearby beer, gave her that one-eyed look again.

"We got home from the Saudi, first thing they did was cut us loose on leave," he said. "Damn near all of us, the whole company. We'd been gone eight months, and I guess the head shed figured we needed a break. John went back to Chicago. I came home, here, for about three weeks. And every single night I was here, all I could think about was being back in that goddam desert, which I hated and never wanted to see again. Still don't. But there it was. I couldn't stand being away from those guys. Mostly John. So, I think I know what you mean. What you really mean."

She fiddled with her pistol, more than a little surprised that Harper had just said more words in one sitting than she'd ever heard from him. She turned her head and stared at the tangerine clouds. "It's not just that."

"Oh."

"I, uh, don't sleep well."

"Neither do I."

"Seriously."

He crossed his arms, leaned back in his chair. "Seriously."

"Do the nightmares ever stop?"

He shrugged. "Sometimes. I mean, they come and go. For me, anyway."

"What do you do?"

He waved a hand at the two empty beer bottles. "These help."

She grimaced. "About that."

Harper cocked his head and looked at her with open curiosity. "About what?"

"The alcohol," she said. She drew in a breath, grasping for the guts to speak again.

"Goddammit, Molly, don't show up here after a year and start yapping about my drinking—which you know nothing about."

She recoiled as she realized Harper had misinterpreted her. Forgetting herself, she threw up her hands and blurted, "Not you, you idiot. Me. The alcohol and *me*."

Harper stopped, mouth half-open, and stared. "What are you talking about?"

She picked up a cleaning rag and began twisting it like the young girl from rehab with the mangled Kleenex. "I just got out of rehab, Harper. It's been hell the last year."

Harper looked alarmed, his face more unsure than she'd ever seen it. "Holy shit, Molly," he said. "I mean, damn, I didn't know, you didn't say anything. You want me to get rid of these?" He grabbed up the empties and rose from his chair. "Is that why you called me?"

She waved him back into his seat. "No, don't. I don't want a drink. Well, I don't want one bad enough to take a drink. Jesus, this is hard."

"Tell me," Harper said, and when she looked in his eyes, she could see he meant it. She leaned back in her chair, placed both hands on the table. He sat back down, eyes on hers.

"I don't even know where to begin," she said. "I mean, you know what this life is like. Drinking is almost a requirement in the law enforcement world. I'm sure it was the same in the Marine Corps."

"Sure," Harper said.

"Plus, I've had to kill people," Molly said.

Harper stared at her, silent.

"I know, I know, you have, too," she said.

"That's the cost of doing business for folks like us, Molly," Colt said. "That's what you got to remember. You rather have the alternative outcome?"

She shook her head.

"Then you did your job."

"Do you have any idea how many times I told myself that over the last couple of years?" she said, more sharply than she intended. "Especially after the first one, out in Hawaii. After I killed that guy, I told myself I was responding to my training, doing what I was supposed to do. But it didn't stop the nightmares. Getting shitcanned to Memphis didn't help. At first, I thought it was nothing. Just normal delayed reactions, you know? So, like you said, a couple of cold ones or some good Scotch helps. Until it doesn't. Know what I mean?"

Harper peeled the label off the bottle in his hands as he listened. He cleared his throat, spread the label out on the table between them. "Sure," he said. "I get it. Anybody that's ever been in your shoes gets that, Molly."

"You don't ever worry?" she said.

"About what?"

"That it'll happen to you?"

Harper looked her in her eyes, and she saw him drift off to someplace she couldn't see. "Not really. I mean, it's an occupational hazard. And I grew up around that kind of... craziness, so I know the warning signs."

She let the "craziness" comment slide and tried not to show her irritation. "Your father? He was an alcoholic?"

Harper snorted. "No, he was a drunk. Big difference."

She slapped the cleaning rag onto the table. "You know, you're not exactly making this easy."

Harper leaned back in his chair and looked at her with something close to amusement. "What exactly do you want me to say, Molly? Or do? You show up here after a year, tell me your darkest secret and... what? I mean, I'm sorry that all this happened."

"I don't want your goddam pity, Harper," she said.

"And you're not going to get any," he said. "I spent my whole life, up until a few years ago, dealing with an incorrigible, mean alcoholic who was in jail more than he was out—and he just happened to be my father. So you'll excuse my predisposition to the condition. I just don't know what it is I'm supposed to do here."

"Listen," she said.

"What?"

"That's what I need you to do," she said. "Just listen. When I left rehab, I was told to find somebody I can trust."

Harper put his elbows on the table, his brown eyes burning into her. "And that's me?"

She nodded. "It is. In fact—and you're going to find this hard to believe—you may be the only person in the world I *do* trust right now."

Harper stared down at the table long enough to make her uncomfortable. When he looked up, his eyes met hers again. "Fair enough, Molly. I'll listen. Or try to. And for what it's worth, I trust you, too, but you probably already know that."

She nodded, her voice suddenly gone.

Harper picked up a cleaning rod and twirled it in his fingers. "So, what's next for you?"

"I don't know," she said, realizing for the first time that she really didn't have a clue. "Maybe hang out here a couple of days?"

"Here?"

"In town."

Harper chuckled. "That's what I meant. But if you need a place to stay, I have room."

She held up a hand. "No way, Harper, that's not why I'm here."

"Whoa," he said. "I only meant I have room. You're kind of a mess right now, if you don't mind me saying, so take a couple of days to decompress."

"I'll find a place to stay, don't worry," she said."

"Suit yourself," Harper said. "If you're up to it tomorrow, why don't you come into the office?"

"Why? Something brewing at work?"

"Yes, the murder case I mentioned on the phone. Looks like a hate crime, but my best suspect so far is a black preacher, apparently."

"Apparently?"

Harper started reassembling the pistol, telling her about the homicide of Lucius Wallace, and a connection she didn't fully understand to some guy Harper went to high school with. Sounded interesting, even if she didn't fully grasp the details.

"So, I could use a fresh set of eyes," he said. "You're pretty good at this kind of thing." He grinned at her.

"I'm better than pretty good, and you know it."

"Heard that."

They fell silent, and she felt more exposed—and more seen—than she had felt in more than a year. Hell, years. The relief she felt when Colt spoke washed over her like summer rain. She smiled down at her pistol and started reassembling it.

Later, near midnight, after she'd checked into her hotel room and hauled her belongings inside, she lay in bed, absorbing the black stillness around her. A sudden lightness came over her, an unburdening she didn't expect. It wasn't serenity, but it was a sort of calm she had not known for some time.

CHAPTER TEN

HANK

Hank Claiborne admired the craftsmanship of the bar as he poured himself his second drink of the evening. The small-batch whiskey seemed to taste better when he took the time to savor the moment in an environment he had created.

Actually, he didn't create the bar, he reminded himself as the whiskey hit him with that familiar burn and numbness. He'd only designed the bar, now nestled into a custom-made recess in the foyer where it opened into the wide sunken living room. It had cost him nearly thirty thousand dollars to build the recess into the wall, install wiring and plumbing, and then hire an artisan cabinet-maker to fashion the recycled oak barn wood into shelves, cabinets, and a countertop that reminded him of a wooden sailing ship from the 1800s. Expensive, but he figured why not? It was his house. He could do what he wanted with it. And drink when he wanted.

He swirled the ice in the crystal tumbler, enjoying the aroma of the liquor, as the doorbell rang. He checked his watch—they were more or less on time.

He walked the length of the foyer and pulled the door open to let Jack and a man he assumed to be Reggie Cash into the house. Both men looked like they'd come straight from work—jeans, sweat-stained short-sleeve shirts, work boots.

Jack came in first, eyebrows raised as he took in the drink, the soft hallway light. "Hank," he said, jerking a thumb over his shoulder, "this is Reggie."

Reggie ogled the surroundings and nodded approvingly. He stuck out his hand. Hank smiled thinly and shook Reggie's hand. The man didn't look at all like Hank thought he would. Thin, homely, not at all threatening. He hoped Reggie's bite was worse than his bark. "Nice to meet you, Reggie. You boys care for a drink?"

"Sure," Jack said, now admiring the bar, which, Hank had to admit, pleased him. He plucked two tumblers from the cabinet over the countertop and splashed brown liquor into each.

"Ice?" he said.

"No need," Jack said. Reggie shook his head no.

Hank handed over the drinks, then stepped toward the hall that led to his office. "Y'all follow me."

He led the pair into the room he considered his sanctuary. His office, also custom-built—by the previous owner—offered a panoramic view of the Tombigbee River below the slope of his massive front lawn. One wall was actually a built-in bookshelf, which Hank had filled over the years with books on subjects important to him: sports, fishing, farming, business, but most of all, the War Between the States. A double-pedestal oak desk took up the wall opposite the huge window. He settled into the leather chair behind the desk as Jack and Reggie gazed at the muddy river in the distance. He offered them two chairs, also leather, across from him.

"Reggie," Hank said, "I'm glad you decided to join us. You were the first person Jack mentioned when we decided to do this."

Reggie gulped his drink. "We must secure the existence of our people and a future for white children," he said in a cadence that was more chant than conversation.

Hank held his glass in both hands and smiled. "Yes, we must." He looked at Jack, whose face was blank. "We need to discuss the Lucius Wallace situation."

"What's there to discuss?" Jack said. "He's dead. That don't change a goddam thing as far as I'm concerned."

"Same here," Reggie said.

Hank leaned back in his chair. "I been thinking. We may have an opportunity here."

"How so?" Reggie said.

"The fact that he's dead proves our point, if you think about the big picture," Hank said.

Jack finished off his drink. "I don't follow."

Hank leaned forward. He had only been rolling some thoughts around in his head since Harper had visited him and Jack in his office. Having the law investigate Wallace's death was one thing—and a worry, truth be told—but something else had occurred to him midway through his first drink. "This thing is liable to kick up a shitstorm around here," he said, organizing his ideas verbally. "The law is already onto it, and it's only a matter of time before the paper and TV station get ahold of it. And you know what that will mean. It'll be like the president had gotten assassinated instead of it being one dead nigger. Nobody is paying attention to the big picture. Nobody sees what is really going on around here except for us. Do you think there'd be all this attention over a white man?"

Jack just stared. Reggie drained his drink.

Hank liked his own words. He kept going on. "Hell no. We aren't politically correct. We don't matter anymore. All this attention on one dead mongrel while white men and women—and our children, mind you—have their jobs and culture and their religion stolen from them by the same mongrels."

Jack set his glass on the floor, leaned forward in his chair. "So, what you're saying is we can use this to make the 'public,' as you call it, see this?"

Hank smiled. "Yes, that's exactly what I'm saying."

"How, though?" Reggie said. "I thought we were recruiting people for a march."

"We are, we are," Hank said. "That, by the way, is what we need you to do, Reggie. Keep recruiting. But we can finally make people see—wake these people up to what's going on around them, right under their nose. White people have been preyed on and discriminated against, right in this county, for years. Welfare queens, drugs, racial mixing."

"That's the worst," Reggie said. "Hell, I'd rather see two homos get married than see a white woman defiled. And that shit is out of control."

"Damn right it is," Hank said. "And look how many white men are out of a job because of some goddam equal opportunity hiring quota. I have to bend all kinds of rules to keep my place as white as I can. And you see what happened to one of the few black employees I had on payroll. He ended up dead."

Reggie laughed. "He deserved it. Whatever got him killed, he deserved it."

Jack cleared his throat. "So, Hank, what's your plan?"

"Y'all keep recruiting, of course," Hank said. "That's still our main priority. We need a group of dedicated men who will stand by the cause. We'll still have a rally, just maybe a little later than we'd planned. I'm going to do my own kind of recruiting. There's plenty of people with money that agree with us in this county. I'm going to start looking for way to approach them. People who can remind the politicians and businessmen of this county that we are the ones being left behind. And the church people, can't forget about them."

Reggie and Jack stared back at him, and for a second he thought maybe they didn't get it. But eventually, they began to meet his gaze and nod their approval.

"What about Harper, your sheriff buddy?" Jack said.

Hank raised a hand. "You let me worry about Harper, Jack. I just need you two to keep doing what you're doing. Speaking of which."

"It's going," Jack said. "Me and Reggie are still buying ammo."

"Right," Reggie said. "And I picked up a bunch of burner phones we can distribute when the time comes. I'm still working on weapons from a contact over in Alabama. That's going to be the hard part. That's going to take a little more time. And money."

Hank had already anticipated that part. But he had money. "How much? You've already spent a few thousand. Not complaining, just wondering."

Reggie shrugged. "Depending on how many rifles we get, probably ten thousand."

Hank glanced at Jack, who remained passive. Reggie noticed the look and put up his hands. "Getting the weapons is one thing," he said. "High-capacity magazines is another. Getting harder to get those. And then there's transport."

Hank smiled. "It's okay, Reggie. If it's ten grand, it's ten grand. Money well spent, wouldn't you agree?"

Reggie's head bobbed. "Yes, I would."

"All right, then," Hank said. "Y'all keep up the good work." He pushed himself out of his chair. "Y'all want another drink?"

Jack picked up his glass; Reggie's face lit up.

"Yes, sir," Reggie said.

DAY FOUR

CHAPTER ELEVEN

COLT

Colt pushed his way through the door to the main office, coffee cup in hand, thinking about the previous evening's conversation with Molly, and stopped short, hit by a sonic wall of ringing phones and the conversations of several deputies and citizens, most black. The dozen or so people clogged the lobby and blocked his view of Becky.

"What's all this?" he said to no one in particular. His words caused the crowd to turn as one to stare at him, each citizen realizing the Sheriff Himself was here. He threaded his way through hostile glares, the crowd hushing as he scanned the brown faces looking back at him. He stopped at Becky's desk, where she sat like a hostage, headset gripping her skull, brow furrowed, her face scowled in consternation.

"What's going on, Becky?" Colt said, eyes on her and not the men and women clamoring around him.

Becky huffed out a breath, shook her head. "I guess people read the newspaper," she said in a low, calm voice. "This is the reaction. They're here about the murder case. Oh, and Craig Battles has called twice."

"Craig Battles is the least of my worries," Colt said.

Becky looked down at the phone panel in front of her; several lights twinkled, yellow and white. "If you ask me, he's the cause of this. John's in your office."

"Thank God," Colt said.

He turned and nearly stepped on a woman who blocked his path to his office. Short, with a fierce visage behind cat-eyed glasses, the woman looked at him like a schoolteacher at a wayward pupil.

"Sheriff Harper, I'd like to know what you plan to do about this murder," she said.

Colt raised his chin and spoke loud enough so that the entire room could hear. "Ma'am, I opened an investigation on this homicide as soon as we identified Mr. Wallace," he said. "Believe me, we are moving as fast as we can. Now, if you all will kindly excuse me, I'm going to go into my office."

The woman was having none of it. She stood, hands on hips, defying him to take a step further. Behind her, the crowd agitated. A male voice called out, "You don't seem to be moving very fast."

Colt searched the crowd but couldn't identify the speaker, as his words started a chorus of angry outbursts. He held up his hands.

"Folks, please," he said. "I don't know who killed Mr. Wallace. And I haven't read the newspaper, so I don't know what you may or may not have read. I understand y'all's concern. But I can assure you I will find the person who did this."

The crowd quieted, but several men still glared at him and muttered to one another, including one who yelled, "Bullshit!" from the back of the crowd. He sidestepped the woman and made it to his office door without further incident, stepped inside, clicked the door shut behind him.

John sat with one hip perched on the windowsill, arms crossed, staring at the world. He turned when Colt walked in, gave him an "I told you so" look that pissed him off.

"Don't you say a fucking word," Colt said.

"Wasn't planning on it," John said. "At least not today."

Colt sat behind his desk. "Becky is going to need a hand with those folks. Last thing we need is a scene."

"Already got a scene."

Colt stared at his deputy. John stared back. "Goddammit, John, you know what I mean."

John walked to the chair in front of the desk, sat. "Sorry," he said. "I'll take care of it. Also, Sanders sent over a list of people who were at the meeting in Crawford the night Wallace was killed. Said you asked him for it."

"I did," Colt said, relieved for a change of subject before his anger got free. "We need to start running down that list."

The intercom on Colt's desk buzzed, and he punched the speaker button. "What is it, Becky?"

"Can I come in?"

"Please."

Becky appeared after a moment. The look on her face was a warning to Colt. "What's on your mind, Becky?" he said.

"Woman just showed up," she said. "That agent from last year. Molly McDonough. She said you told her to stop by."

Becky's words sounded like an accusation. The noisy clutch of citizens in the lobby had distracted Colt, and he'd forgotten to tell Becky about Molly. "Yep, I did tell her that. She's in town for a couple of days. Could you send her in?"

Becky hesitated a beat. Then: "Sure, Colt." She spun on her heels and strode out of the office.

John looked at him, his face a question. Then he turned as Molly came through the door.

"Well, I'll be damned," John said as he jumped to his feet. "Special Agent McDonough."

"It's just Molly now, John," she said. "It's good to see you again." She offered her hand, and John shook it.

"What brings you here?" John said.

Molly glanced at Colt, whose face remained impassive, then turned back to John. "I have a lot of time on my hands these days, so I just wanted to get away from the big city and see how things have gone since last year."

"I see," John said, though Colt could tell he clearly did not see.

"John," Colt said, "I was thinking that Molly, if she's amenable, could serve as a temporary deputy."

Colt could see the surprise register on both John's and Molly's faces. Nobody spoke for what seemed like a long time.

"Molly, one of our deputies—Townsend—is set to retire in about a month, and he's in the process of getting his affairs in order. Which means I'm down a badge that I could surely use with this murder we just had. What do you think?" Colt said.

She looked toward the window for a long moment, then back at Colt. "Sure," she said. "A little unexpected, but I think I can make that work."

"John?" Colt said.

John still looked stunned. "Uh, sure," he said slowly. "Welcome aboard, Molly. I'd be happy to work with you again. But try not to kill Colt before we're done."

Molly laughed, a real laugh, and Colt realized it was the first time he'd ever heard it. He reached down and pushed Becky's number on his phone.

"That'll be enough out of you," he said to John.

A tap on the door made them all turn just as Becky stepped into the office. She glanced at Molly, raised an eyebrow, then looked at Colt. "You wanted to see me?"

"Becky, Molly is our newest temporary deputy, effective immediately. Can you make sure she gets whatever she needs? And can you send Moore in for a second?"

The eyebrow again. "Sure, Colt." She stepped back into the hall.

He shot a look at John, who looked surprised. "What was that all about?" Colt said.

John shook his head. Molly put her hands on her hips. "I know what that was all about. Jeez, guys."

John chuckled and looked at his feet.

Colt wondered what the joke was, then decided to let it go, just as Deputy Randy Moore appeared in the doorway. Colt waved him in and introduced him to Molly.

"Molly's our newest deputy, Randy," he said. "Can you find her a desk out in the bullpen and get her set up on a computer?

Moore, sporting a fresh Marine Corps Reserve haircut, flashed a quick grin before looking as serious as a twenty-something cop can and said, "Sure thing, I'll get on that right now."

"Thanks, Randy," Colt said, but Moore was already marching out of the office. Colt looked over at John, who couldn't help a smile at the new kid.

"John, I gave Molly a quick rundown on this case last night, but I'll leave it to you to get her up to speed on the details. Molly, first thing you should focus on is a list of people who were at a community meeting with a local preacher the night the victim was killed."

"Were any of those people out in the lobby at the meeting?" Molly asked.

Colt looked at John, who shrugged. "Good question," Colt said. "Start there."

Molly looked at John, then back at him. "Guess I get on that right now?"

Colt grinned. "Go. Both of you. Help Becky clear that crowd out there. I'm going to be out of the office for about an hour."

John took the cue. "Come on, Molly, let's get you that desk."

After they'd left, Colt picked up the phone, got an outside line, punched in the numbers.

"County Clerk's Office."

"Hey, Rhonda, it's me," he said.

"Hello, Colt, what can I help you with?" Rhonda said in her business—not friend—voice.

"Free for lunch?"

"It's a little early for lunch, isn't it?"

"Maybe," Colt said, "but I need to run some things by you, and, frankly, I need your advice on something."

"Something having to do with this latest crime?"

Colt winced at Rhonda's sharp tone. "Yes, that. Do you have the time?"

He waited, picturing Rhonda mulling over the prospect of being seen at lunch with the sheriff. The white sheriff. The one she had a history with.

"Okay," she said at last.

"I'll be there in about ten minutes."

"No, meet me at that new little place in Fairlane Shopping Center," she said.

"I'm on my way," he said and hung up.

He drove to the Fairlane Shopping Center, a faded cluster of 1950s architecture clinging to the old highway in the east part of town, to Joe's Family Restaurant. He got a table and had just picked up a menu when Rhonda walked through the glass door. His heart caught a little, as it always did, whenever she came into a room. Tall and graceful, with soulful eyes, she beamed when her eyes found him.

She sailed over to the table and sat, still smiling but also hiding something with her eyes. He found it astounding she could smile at all, considering the fear and loss she'd endured the last few years.

"Have you been here before?" Rhonda asked.

"No, but Freddie Mac swears by the fried chicken here," he said.

Rhonda chuckled. "Well, if anybody knows fried chicken, that man certainly does. Has he lost any weight?"

"Hell no," Colt said. "He's still big as a house. He's back on his blood pressure meds so his face ain't as red as it could be, but still red enough to make me wonder about him. And he still goes to work in his white shirt, black tie."

"He likes being official."

"That he does."

A waitress whose name tag read LORETTA took their orders. She had a face vaguely familiar to Colt. She smiled at him as if they knew each other, so he smiled back. Loretta weaved her way to the kitchen through the tangle of legs, chairs, and tables of the early lunch crowd.

"Old friend?" Rhonda said.

"I have no idea," Colt said as he unrolled his utensils from the paper napkin at his right hand.

"Hmm," Rhonda said. "I guess that little extra twitch in her hips was natural."

"I didn't notice."

"Right," Rhonda said.

Loretta returned a few minutes later and set a plate in front of Rhonda, then put Colt's on the table, between his hands.

"Y'all need anything else, just let me know, all right?" Loretta said.

"Sure will," Colt said, as she turned to head back to the kitchen.

Colt looked down at a lunch he knew he'd scarcely be able to finish. Fried chicken, okra, mac and cheese, completely covered the plate. Not to mention a plate of biscuits between him and Rhonda.

"So, what's on your mind, Colt?" Rhonda said.

He twirled a fork in his hand. "I need your perspective on something. But let's eat first."

They ate in silence as they plowed through their lunches. When he'd picked the chicken bones clean, he wiped his hands and drained the glass of iced tea. Rhonda pushed her plate away just as Loretta swooped in to whisk the plates away as both of them declined pecan pie for dessert.

"So, out with it, Colt," Rhonda said. She fixed him with a stare that never failed to make him feel like an errant schoolboy, even after all the years. "What's got at you?"

He brushed away crumbs from the table, laced his fingers together. "John's what's got at me."

Rhonda cocked an eyebrow. "John?"

"Come on, Rhonda, I know he's told you about Lucius Wallace."

Rhonda leaned toward him, her voice low. "Of course he has. And Reverend Sanders."

"I thought so."

"So, what exactly is John doing that you don't like?"

Colt frowned. "Don't say it like it that, Rhonda. He's really pissed off about me questioning the preacher, and I can't understand why. This is a murder case, plain and simple, and the logical—and most obvious—starting point is Sanders. But he's not happy about it. Furious, even."

"I see," Rhonda said. She looked down at her hands, then back up at him. "Colt, did it ever occur to you that this case affects him as a black man—not just as a deputy sheriff?"

Colt sat back in his chair in disbelief at Rhonda's words. "That's almost exactly what he said."

"Maybe he has a point."

Colt shook his head. "Then it's one that I don't get. The implication is that I'm somehow targeting a black man out of, what, convenience? Because I'm white? Rhonda, you know better than anybody in this county that's not true. And I'm not talking about Clifford. Or last year."

He saw her stiffen at the mention of the horror of the previous year's encounter with a murderous drug mob enforcer named Hack. He had chased bodies for weeks until he finally caught up with the most heartless and ruthless killer he'd ever encountered, a psychopath who'd gone for one victim too many when he abducted Rhonda and forced Colt into a confrontation.

Colt and Rhonda stared at each other as memories came back to haunt him—Hack's ice-blue but merciless blue eyes mocking him from a doorway, Rhonda in his grip, terrified, her own eyes pleading, *Help me.*

Rhonda had trusted him, as she had her whole life, and he'd put a bullet in Hack's forehead. And then passed out from a loss of blood caused by three gunshot wounds, one of which nagged at him today.

"I'm sorry," he said, forcing the memories from his mind. "I didn't mean to bring that up."

Rhonda swiped at a tear that had appeared in the corner of an eye. "It's okay." She cleared her throat. "But that was different. You know that."

"Is it, though?" Colt said. "My job is to enforce the law and ensure justice is served, regardless of the color of the person committing the crime."

"Nobody's denying that, Colt, but the fact is—and you may not like hearing it—but you're white," Rhonda said, fidgeting with a pink packet of artificial sweetener. "And you're the law. And you just pointed the finger at a man who means a lot to this community. My community. The black one. My community believes in justice, too, but we all know how justice goes. I don't know of a single black person who doesn't believe a white man killed Lucius. Not a single one. But the first person you question is a black man. It just reinforces the notion that justice is always white around here."

"That's bullshit," Colt said.

"Don't use that language with me, Colt," Rhonda said.

He held up his hands in surrender. "Sorry. I just find it hard to believe."

Rhonda sat up and scoffed. "Really? You don't remember anything from the past?"

His mind flashed back to a long-ago night when he steered his father's car to the curb behind the Fred's Discount Store. And seeing Rhonda the instant she stepped out into the cool fall air, still wearing her red smock with her name embroidered over the left breast. She flashed a tentative smile as she crossed the lot—it jolted him like a bolt of lightning.

Their first and only date. That night ended in violence when three boys—white boys—jumped them coming out of the movie theater. They were foul-mouthed and drunk and made the mistake of thinking that they could pummel Colt Harper into submission. They never saw him reach into the back seat of his father's car for the ax handle and never stood a snowball's chance against the rage they had unleashed. Colt had only stopped when he became conscious of Rhonda's terrified screams.

Now he looked across the table at the woman who, even through the years, had remained the same person even as he had changed. Maybe Rhonda was right. Maybe he had forgotten things. But not that.

"I remember," he said.

"I know you do," Rhonda said. "Do you know that every time you come to my house, I know there could be a price that I pay for that? Not because you're the law, and not because of our movie date, but because you're white. You're white first and then you're the badge."

Colt wanted to reach across the table and put his hand on hers, but he knew he couldn't. Maybe not ever.

"So, what do I do?" he said.

A wisp of a smile came to Rhonda's lips, and Colt felt relief. And something else. "Reverend Sanders' congregation is holding a community meeting tonight at the civic center downtown to talk about this," she said. "I arranged to get them the room on such short notice. Why don't you come down, take some questions, talk to people face-to-face?"

His mind flashed to the angry crowd in his office earlier. "I don't know about that."

"It's a chance for you to speak to people straight, on your terms and theirs."

He knew Rhonda was right, and that this was a chance to set things straight for his own sake. "Okay, it's a deal."

Rhonda's eyes twinkled. "Good. I'll let them know."

"Thanks, Rhonda," he said. He stood. "I guess I should let you get back to work."

As they walked to the door, Colt said, "Oh, one other thing. Molly McDonough is in town."

Rhonda stopped and turned, her eyes mischievous. "Really? On business or..."

"Sort of," he said. "I just made her a deputy."

"Oh, you're going to have to tell me all about that," Rhonda said as she unlocked her car door.

"Later, Rhonda," he said as he climbed into the Crown Vic.

CHAPTER TWELVE
JACK

Jack Burnett had a lot on his mind. Ever since yesterday when that asshole sheriff had shown up at Hank's farm asking questions—and Hank had acted like he and the sheriff were best buds. And then that evening meeting at Hank's house.

He steered his pickup down the main farm roads past the placid green ponds, cranked up the radio when he heard Tammy Wynette's voice. Even an oldie like Tammy didn't take the edge off his growing anger.

He slowed to a stop at the highway's edge, then bounded onto the asphalt, headed east. Ten minutes later, he turned onto a dirt road, this one leading to a line of pines across a soybean field. He drove into the shade of the trees for a quarter mile, then turned right onto an even narrower path and bounced along hard-packed clay ruts until he spied another pickup parked in a clearing just large enough to accommodate a battered-looking single-wide trailer.

He came to a stop, noticed the door to the camp house ajar, then noticed Reggie Cash emerge from behind the trailer, headed to his truck. Jack climbed out of his vehicle and stomped toward Reggie, his steps muted by the thick carpet of pine needles beneath him.

Reggie looked up at the sound of Jack's door slamming shut and grinned. "You coulda just called, man."

"Stay off the fucking phones, how many times I got to say that?" Jack said.

Reggie leaned over the hood of his pickup, and Jack followed suit.

"Listen," Jack said. "We might have a problem. And by that, I mean the goddam sheriff."

Jack looked over at Reggie. The man looked like a two-by-four: skinny, straight, and flat. Hatchet-faced with a permanent snarl under a thatch of brown hair. "What you mean? I thought Hank said that wasn't a problem," Reggie said.

"He's been down to the farm, asking questions about Lucius Wallace," Jack said. "And seems he and Hank know each other from way back. That's probably what caused that meeting at his place."

"So what exactly is the problem?" Reggie said.

Jack glared at Reggie's near-black eyes. Reminded him of a shark. "The sheriff investigating that situation is one thing. But him and Hank are too goddam close. He might start thinking he can show up anytime he wants, and Hank's liable to talk too much. You heard him—and he'd only had a couple of drinks in him last night."

Reggie shrugged. "Might be a good thing. I mean, Hank knowing the sheriff. He'd be less likely to suspect anything."

"Did you not hear what I just said?"

"Yeah, I did," Reggie said. "Sounds like we might have a Hank problem."

Reggie was starting to piss him off, like he often did. Sometimes Jack thought he did it just to amuse himself. "We ain't got a Hank problem. I can handle Hank."

"Then what the hell are you so worked up about?"

Jack pushed himself off the hood and began pacing. "We need some kind of distraction to throw the cops off. Point them in a different direction. And I ain't talking about going around and talking to bankers and deacons."

"What kind of distraction?"

"Talk back at the farm is that Harper's been questioning some black preacher and it's got all the niggers riled up, even more so than they already are. Maybe we play off that," Jack said.

"Like maybe they're so mad they, what, riot?" Reggie said.

Jack shoved his hands in his pockets. "Think you can pull that off?"

Reggie grunted, then started pacing the length of his truck and back and started clicking his teeth together like he did when he was thinking. "You mean, like a robbery or something? Where somebody gets shot and that causes a protest? And then we can make our move?"

Jack grinned. He knew Reggie could think of shit like this. It was his specialty. One of them, anyway. "Something like that."

"I can do that," Reggie said. "Give me a couple of days."

"What do you need from me?"

"Not a goddam thing," Reggie said. "There's this stupid kid works at the shop with me. Lamarr. Typical gang-banger thug, right? He's always looking for a big score. I been kinda stringing him along."

"Stringing him along? How?"

"Playing off his whole 'I'm a thug' vibe," Reggie said. "Feeding him little pieces to make him think I get him, and that I might have some connections."

Jack looked at Reggie like he'd grown another eye. "Why in God's name would you want to do that?"

"For this reason right here," Reggie said, his rat eyes shining. "I'll work Lamarr into something that will definitely distract the sheriff."

"Like what?"

"Don't worry about it," Reggie said. "You said you wanted a robbery. You'll know when it happens."

Jack wanted to say, *Don't fuck it up*, but instead he said, "I have to get back to work. And don't use the goddam phones. Never know who is listening these days."

"Whatever you say, boss," Reggie said.

Jack ignored the sarcasm and walked out to his truck, feeling his anger subside. A little.

CHAPTER THIRTEEN

MOLLY

Molly made her way through downtown traffic, then pulled her car to the curb under a towering oak tree and checked her watch: twelve forty-five. She still had fifteen minutes. In rehab, several counselors had told her to get to meetings, and to get there early so she could get to know people, get phone numbers of people to call when she felt like drinking. And get a sponsor. Work the steps.

All of which filled her with dread at the moment, and she felt she was drowning in a sea of anxiety. She closed her eyes, took three deep breaths, then stared ahead at the brick Baptist church that loomed a block away, white columns gleaming in the morning sun.

Even from this distance, drunks and addicts were easy to spot, especially in broad daylight and near a church. She'd learned that much as an ATF agent on stakeouts. The men were leathery and skinny, with drawn faces and milky, ratlike eyes. Twitchy from the detox and the nerve-jangling newness of being dried out and the panicky emotional rawness it caused. They had the faces of the craven, the hunted, the defeated yet defiant. Even the three men who smoked easily on the sidewalk near the entrance to the church, the ones who obviously had some semblance of recovery. They, too, had shadows behind their eyes, shadows caused by the demons of shame, sin, remorse, and the twin terrors of jail and the DTs.

Addiction was harder on women, she'd learned and seen in rehab. They looked like a cross between electroshock-treatment patients and horror movie wraiths, stringy and old before they'd had a chance to be young, bellies distended, jumpy like alley cats, shabby in disaster-relief clothing. She hoped to God that she had not begun to look like that. No women loitered outside to smoke with the men.

She checked her hair in the rearview mirror, climbed out of the car, locked the door.

"Here we go," she whispered to herself.

She crossed a street with the light and turned right, toward the small white door on the side of the church building, behind the group of smoking men.

"Molly?"

The voice came from behind, and it froze her, both from surprise and from her recognition of Rhonda's soft voice.

Dammit, she thought, panic climbing up her spine. What the hell do I do now?

She turned. Rhonda stood a few feet away, smiling but with surprise in her eyes, which was how Molly always remembered her. A sad smile and brown eyes that always radiated compassion.

"It *is* you," Rhonda said as she rushed up and threw her arms around Molly before she could react. "Colt told me you were in town. And, my goodness, girl, you're shaking."

Molly smiled and wiggled just enough to escape the embrace. "Hey, Rhonda, this is a surprise. Yeah, I'm in town for a couple of days."

Rhonda cocked an eyebrow, faint smile lingering at the edges of ruby-red lipstick. "To see Colt?"

Molly nodded as she scrambled for a believable explanation. "I had some time, so I thought, why not, you know?"

Rhonda beamed, her caramel skin glowing in a bright green-and-yellow summer dress, and Molly marveled at how a woman who had been through as much as she could still smile at anything. Losing a son and being kidnapped by a psychopathic killer would extinguish the joy in most people.

"I'm glad to hear that," Rhonda said. "But what are you doing *here*?" She took a look toward the white door—only men remained outside—then back at Molly.

Molly felt trapped and angry and ashamed. "Ah, hell, Rhonda," she said in a quavering voice. "I'm going to an AA meeting. I just got out of rehab and I didn't have anywhere—"

Rhonda thrust up a hand, silencing her. "You don't have to explain, dear," she said. "I'm here for a meeting, too. A support group I found after Clifford got killed. When I thought I would go insane. So, you go on. Take care of you today. We can talk later."

Molly didn't know what to say. She tucked an errant strand of hair behind her ear.

Rhonda's smile returned and she held out her arms. "Come here, girl, you need a hug. A real one."

Molly sobbed and fell into Rhonda's arms, confused, angry, and grateful all at the same time. She rested her head on Rhonda's shoulder, then calmed herself and stepped away.

"Thanks, Rhonda," she said.

Rhonda patted her shoulder. "You're welcome. Go on, now, you don't want to be late."

Molly wiped the corners of her eyes, managed a smile.

"Good girl," Rhonda said. "Let's talk again soon."

"Sure," Molly said. "Bye." She went through the door into a multipurpose room with about twenty folding chairs—half of which were taken by mostly men, but also three women—arranged in a half circle facing a table, at which sat a sixty-something man, white hair and glasses, reading from a binder.

"Okay, next, anyone new to this meeting?" the man read aloud.

Molly slid into an empty chair on the right of the table, took a breath, and raised her hand. Here goes nothing.

"Yes?" said the man leading the meeting.

"Hi, I'm Molly, and I'm an alcoholic."

"Welcome, Molly," the group said as one.

CHAPTER FOURTEEN

COLT

Colt sat at his desk working his way through Becky's paperwork, trying to ignore the throbbing in his hip. After he'd been released from the hospital last fall, he'd taken several weeks off to further his recuperation. The time off had been good for him. He'd done a lot of fishing on the Tombigbee and had even put in a garden for the first time in years. But it hadn't fully healed him physically. The nagging hip reminded him of that nearly every day.

A loud knock on his door forced his eyes up.

"Colt," John said as he strode through the door. "I got a couple out in the waiting room. They are concerned."

"Come in," he said to John.

"Oh, sorry," John said. "Anyway. They're a nice older couple. They asked if they might have a word."

He sat up straight. "Concerned about what?"

John crossed his arms. Looked at him.

"Okay," Colt said. "What are their names?"

"Mr. and Mrs. Lowell T. Jernigan."

"Show them in."

The Jernigans were just as John described, gray-haired, serene, and polite. After introductions and handshakes, they took the two chairs John offered before he retreated to his usual roosting spot, the sill of the window overlooking the old city graveyard.

"So, Mr. Jernigan, what can I do for you?" Colt said. "John said y'all have concerns and wanted a word with me?"

Mrs. Jernigan smiled.

Lowell T. Jernigan nodded. "That's right, Sheriff. Deputy Carver was gracious enough to ask on our behalf."

Colt nodded.

"First, Lucy and I," Jernigan said as he tilted his head toward his wife, "just wanted to personally thank you for the job you're doing. We both voted for you, and it weren't no easy thing you did last summer when you... got shot. I'm sorry."

He held up a hand. "Quite all right. I appreciate the kind words."

Lucy Jernigan leaned forward. "Broke my heart to know you was hurt that bad. I knew your momma, back when she was young and worked at the theater downtown. Sweet girl."

He glanced at John, who watched with interest.

"Thank you, Miz Jernigan, I appreciate that," he said. "I'll be sure and let Momma know you spoke kindly of her."

Lucy smiled again and sat back in her chair.

"Now, Mr. and Mrs. Jernigan, how can I help you today?" Colt said. He picked up a pen, pulled a legal pad out of the desk drawer. Lowell watched his hands with a kind of professional intensity Colt had not seen in years.

"We have been members of Reverend Sanders' church for near on forty years," Lowell said. "And, frankly, our concern is that you would even consider him capable of doing something like killing somebody."

Colt stopped writing. Looked Lowell T. in the eyes. "Mr. Jernigan, there may be a misunderstanding of what has actually taken place. I have yet to make any considerations in this case. Deputy Carver over there and I are at the very beginning of investigating a homicide. Interviewing Reverend Sanders is just one part of that process."

Jernigan looked down at his hands like he'd been called on in class and didn't know the answer. "That's not what I hear," he said. "If that is true, my wife and I would like to hear your side of it."

Colt sat up in his chair. "Mr. Jernigan, I believe I just gave you my side of it."

Lowell started to speak, but Lucy placed a hand, light as a feather, on her husband's arm. "Sheriff Harper, we consider Reverend Sanders to be almost a part of our family. He baptized our three youngest kids, and he married the oldest two. Lowell and I have known him nearly all of our lives. At least since Lowell got back from the war."

Colt looked over at Jernigan, who saw the question in his face. "A Shau Valley," Lowell said.

"I didn't know you were in Vietnam," Colt said.

Lowell Jernigan sat up in his chair, the old pride still present. "Yep. Hundred and first. I was a machine gunner, then got promoted to corporal. Squad leader."

"Hamburger Hill?" Colt asked.

Lowell locked eyes with him, one combat veteran to another. Then Lowell's eyes took on a far-off look that was far too familiar to Colt. "Yes," Lowell said.

Colt smiled to reassure the man. "Mr. and Mrs. Jernigan, I understand your concern."

Jernigan's head bobbed slowly. "I know you do, Sheriff. That's part of the reason why we're here."

"Part of the reason?"

Jernigan placed both hands on his knees, and Colt could see plenty of fight left in the ancient soldier sitting across this desk. Whatever Lowell Jernigan was today in retirement, the man was still a warrior. "Like I said, Lucy and I think you're doing a fine job. But, as a voter and a homeowner, I have to say this: last year's violence was a bloodbath in this county. And now this. A black man murdered—and a man of God accused of that murder. It's more than shocking for both and me and Lucy to know that such people could do the things they did in our community."

"Wait," Colt said, cutting the older man off. "Nobody has accused Reverend Sanders of anything."

Lowell clearly didn't like being cut off. He glowered at Colt. "I got to ask you, Sheriff. Is the county safe? Are me and Lucy safe? What are you doing about it?"

Colt sat back in his chair and met Lowell T. Jernigan's steady gaze. The man deserved an answer. A real one, not the flippant political one he was sometimes tempted to give just to move a pesky citizen along.

"Mr. Jernigan, Mrs. Jernigan, last year was a very unusual circumstance, and, yes, it was extremely violent," he said, measuring his words, "because I was dealing with some very violent people. But I think what happened then was an exception, rather than the rule. That group is out of business for good. You have my word on that." He paused, aware of his own words. "Now, this current case, I'll be dead honest, we don't really know what's going on with that. Meaning, we don't know who did it or why, for that matter. But I can tell you, we have an investigation going and we're going to get to the bottom of it. And to answer your question, yes, sir, the county and you are safe."

He could see the Jernigans weighing his every word, just as he would were the situation reversed. Lucy's head had moved in a slow, barely perceptible nod as he spoke. Now she stared at him, lips pursed, coming to her own judgment. Lowell had not changed his steely-eyed expression one whit. Still steely-eyed.

"Thank you, Sheriff," Lowell finally said. "And thank you for hearing us out."

"My pleasure," Colt said, and he meant it. "You need anything else from me, you let me know right away."

The Jernigans rose as one, the way old married couples do. John pushed himself off the sill.

"Thank you both for coming down," Colt said.

The Jernigans nodded. Then John led them out.

John stepped back in when the couple had left. "That was very reassuring, Sheriff Harper," he said, not a trace of snark in his voice.

Colt stared out the window at the cemetery and its chipped, tilted headstones and uneven ground. "Thanks, John. I think they may feel more reassured than I do."

John sighed at his long-suffering boss. "Then you're doing your job," he said.

Becky appeared in the office doorway. Colt waved her in, and she stepped into the room.

"Craig Battles is here," she said.

"Let me guess," Colt said. "He heard about this morning's gathering on a scanner."

Becky shrugged. "Who knows? But he wants a statement."

"Tell him I'm busy."

"Already did. He said he'd wait. Seems pretty aggravated."

Colt threw his hands up. "I'll give him five minutes."

John chuckled. "The bane of Colt Harper's existence," John said.

"Clear out for a second," Colt said. He began turning the various reports and files on his desk facedown. "This won't take long."

John walked out behind Becky, who returned less than a minute later with Craig Battles trailing behind her. Colt stood at his desk, hands on hips.

Battles stopped next to a chair, and Colt measured him up. Even though the man was a few years younger, he looked much older than Colt. Brown hair thinning on top, but still a long, unruly mess on the sides. Wrinkled blue button-down shirt with a burgundy tie hanging loosely from the open top button. Beginnings of a beer belly poking over his belt and jeans.

"Afternoon, Craig," Colt said after a long moment. "Have a seat."

Battles did and produced a reporter's notebook and a pen that he clicked half a dozen times, enough to make Colt wonder if it was intentional. "What can I do for you?"

Battles cleared his throat. "So it looks like we have another murder after all."

Colt sat in the big leather chair behind his desk, taking his time to let Battles' tone pass by before he got angry. "Who told you it was a murder?"

Battles clicked his pen. "Nobody. But a dead body in a gravel pit."

"Could be a bunch of things, Craig. We discovered the body of a black male between, I'd say, thirty-five and forty-five years old three days ago. We are currently investigating the circumstances surrounding the man's death. But you already know that. I do read the paper."

"Identified him yet?"

"It's an ongoing investigation, you know how that works," Colt said, keeping his voice level despite his rapidly diminishing patience with the reporter. "We don't release the names of victims until after notification of next of kin." He knew he was willfully withholding information and would have felt at least a twinge of guilt if anyone else had asked the question. But since it was Craig Battles, his official policy was to not give a damn.

Battles wrote that down. "Anything else?"

"Such as?"

Battles flipped a page in his notebook. "For one thing, this county has seen a serious increase in violent crime since you took the job. There are people saying the county was safer before you became sheriff."

Colt stayed casual in his chair. Not reacting. "What people?"

"You know, citizens. People I talk to when I'm working."

Colt wasn't going to rise to the bait. He could sit here all day long and play word games with Craig Battles, same as he had done since he'd taken office. But Battles wanted something else. "Craig, put your notebook down for a second."

"Why?" Battles asked with just enough surliness to make Colt want to slap him.

"Let's just talk, you and me," Colt said. "I want to try to get some shit straight between us. You seem to have a special ax to grind with me, and I don't know what it is. I don't think you've written one single positive thing about me or my department since I got elected."

"Look, Sheriff, I know you don't think I'm worth the price of the dirt in the ditch you want to see me in," Battles said. The notebook lay in his lap, and his pen was still.

That surprised Colt. What the hell was Battles talking about? "Okay, that sounds like a therapy topic I really don't want to get into. But I got to be honest with you, Craig, I don't have an opinion of you one way or another, besides the fact that you're a huge pain in my ass on the job. I know we're about the same age, but we didn't go to school with each other. I don't even know you, really. So there has to be more to it than that."

Battles sat with his arms crossed and gave away nothing. "Do you shoot pool?"

"What? Yeah, from time to time. What difference does that make?"

"My dad used to shoot a lot of pool. He liked to drink, too, every now and then. Nothing like your father."

And just like that, Colt felt the old anger stir within him. He pushed it down. "Winston—my father—was a drunk," he said.

"Your father was an asshole," Battles said. "A petty criminal with a mean streak."

"You'll get no argument from me on that."

"My dad was shooting pool one night over at the El Camino. You remember that place?"

"Sure." Colt remembered it all too well. One of Winston's favorite places to go get drunk, fight, cheat on his mother, and generally spend a night being a dick. He'd spent several nights as a kid sitting in the passenger seat of his father's Impala waiting for Winston to come reeling out the side door, drunk, dangerous, and stupid.

"Your father walked in one night, drunk, of course, started a fight. Broke my dad's jaw."

"My God, Craig, how long ago was this?" Colt said. "I don't remember anything about this. Not that I would, anyway."

"I was about ten."

"And that's what this is about? A fight between our fathers decades ago?"

"No," Battles said. "You probably don't remember, because nothing happened. My father wanted to charge your father with aggravated assault and the cops couldn't have cared less. Just another bar brawl with Winston Harper, town drunk. He wasn't worth the time and paper."

"I see."

"No, you don't," Battles said, a little louder than was necessary in the office. "My father got laid off because he couldn't work, and it took him two years to get another job. Two years. My whole family had to suffer through that. We ended up out of a house, had to move into the projects over on the south side of town. You have any idea what that feels like? Meanwhile, your father kept right on doing what he always did—stealing, bullying people, and getting drunk all over town."

He tried to keep his patience, but Battles was surely testing him with this ancient grudge. And even though he knew exactly what it felt like to be out of a home, scrambling for food and money and living with the shame of being poor and broke, he wasn't about to get into that conversation with Battles. Not here. Not fucking anywhere. "Look, Craig, that was truly a long time ago. And I'm sorry the police let you down. But that's not my sheriff's office. My office has some fine law officers. Not perfect, but solid. You can't hold that against them. You can't hold my father against me."

"Maybe not," Battles said. "But I can do my job and keep people like you accountable."

"People like me."

"I think you're a man of dangerous conceits, Harper. Like a lot of the elected officials around here. And your badge has limits."

Colt stared at the wall over Battles' head and felt a familiar darkness creeping into the edge of his consciousness. And he could feel it metastasizing into a rage he had not felt since he had last seen his father and had left him sitting in a room with a loaded .45.

"You may not believe this," Colt said, "but I agree with you on that. At least the accountability part. I've never thought otherwise."

"Really? You'd be surprised at the number of people who would disagree with you."

"I'm never surprised at that."

"Maybe you should be," Battles said, a little too quickly. "There's plenty of folks who think you're not much different than your father. That you're just as arrogant and mean-spirited. A bully with a badge."

"That's enough, Craig," he said as calmly as he could. He leaned forward, elbows on his desk. "You know, we're both living in the shadows of our fathers. Probably always will. I've accepted that there's nothing I can do to change people's perceptions, so I don't even try. What I do try to do is my job. If that makes some people mad, that's too bad. If they don't like the methods or the outcomes, well then, they can vote me out of office. That's been my attitude since I took the oath of office, an oath that I take very seriously. You don't like me, I get that. Frankly, I don't lose any sleep over that. But I'm my own person, same as you."

Battles fidgeted, clicked his pen several times. Cleared his throat. "Fair enough, Sheriff," he said, without the bravado he'd had a few minutes ago. "Fair enough."

"Anything else?" Colt said.

"Back on the record?"

"Okay."

Battles scratched his stubbled chin like a man with nothing but time on his hands. "The woman who was with you when you got shot last year. ATF gal. What was her name?"

Now Colt looked the reporter in the eye. Craig Battles might be a halfway decent writer, but guile was not his strong suit. He smiled at Battles. Who grinned back, so that they sat there three feet apart, grinning at each other like simpletons in front of a mirror.

"You wrote the story, Craig," Colt said.

Battles bobbed his head. "Right. Molly McDonough."

"What about her?" Colt said.

"Why is she here?"

"What do you mean?" Colt said, knowing Battles knew damn well he was making a lame-ass attempt to stall.

"Come on, Sheriff." Battles tapped his pen on his notebook.

Colt wanted to tell Battles to get out of his office and be done with him, but after the acrimony of the last few minutes, he knew that wouldn't work.

Colt took a breath, let half out, like he did on the rifle range all those years ago. "You probably already know I'm a little understaffed," he said, figuring lying to Craig Battles wasn't the worst thing he'd done, or would do, in his time in office. "I needed a deputy. She was available. I hired her."

"I thought she was ATF."

"Not anymore."

"Is that standard Lowndes County government policy? To hire a deputy on a whim?"

"I have the latitude to make personnel decisions based on the urgency of the circumstance, and it wasn't a goddam whim," Colt said. "I could deputize you right here on the spot if I deemed it necessary. Not that I would."

Battles almost smiled. "That explains why I've seen her around here."

That surprised him. "You stalking her, Craig?"

Battles grunted, shook his head. "Due diligence. It's called reporting."

"You say so. Now, get out of my office. I have an investigation to run."

Battles stood. "I do appreciate your candor," he said. "Thank you for at least being honest about that." He turned and left with a swiftness surprising for a man his size.

He sat with his eyes closed for a long minute, thinking about Battles' accusations and fighting a mighty urge to destroy every stick of furniture within view. "Son of a bitch," he said, but he didn't know if he meant Craig Battles or his father. John's footsteps broke his train of thought, and he watched as his deputy walked in, pulled a chair to the desk, and sat, hunched on his elbows over the desk.

Colt sat back in his chair, studying his best friend's face. "What's on your mind, John?"

"This thing with McDonough," John said. "You think this is a good idea?"

"I do. Why?"

"I was just talking to Rhonda, and she was on her way to her support group when she ran into Molly outside the church where the meetings are. She told me that Molly was on her way to an AA meeting. Did you know that?"

"Know what?"

"That she has, you know, a drinking problem?"

Colt leaned back. "Yes, as of yesterday. She told me all about it. She got out of rehab a couple of weeks ago."

"A couple of *weeks*?" John said. "You think this is a good call? I mean, what if something goes wrong?"

"What if it doesn't?" Colt said. "Besides, she can still shoot."

"Still," John said.

Colt felt himself getting annoyed. "Still, nothing. Look, Townsend is retiring soon, we're going to be short an officer. Molly's here and qualified. If I say she can do the job, then it's on me."

"Okay, Colt, sorry," John said.

"Anything else?"

"No."

Colt rose. "Good. I'm going to talk to Rose Sanders."

⚜ ⚜ ⚜

The drive to the Sanders residence took ten minutes, long enough for him to second-guess his decision to do this alone.

Rose Sanders invited him in immediately, led him into a wide, richly furnished living room, offered him a recliner. She sat opposite him on an expensive sofa. Apparently, the Reverend Sanders had been blessed financially by the Lord.

"Thanks for seeing me on short notice, Mrs. Sanders," Colt said.

"Call me Rose."

"Rose. I have some delicate questions to ask, but this is only because of the investigation I'm conducting concerning the death of Lucius Wallace."

The flickering of her eyes told him the answer to the next question and more.

"Did Lucius call you last Monday night about ten p.m.?" he said.

Rose sighed and looked away. Nodded.

"Why was that?" Colt said.

Rose turned her head, met his eyes. "I thought he would stop by later, like he usually does."

"Usually?" Colt said, surprised.

Rose pursed her lips together.

Colt put his elbows on his knees. “Rose, I know y’all had an affair some time back. Your husband told me. But he said it was over and that you and your husband had reconciled.”

A tear leaked from Rose’s eye, and she flicked it away with a red-painted nail. “It was over, for a little while. But then he started calling again. And I started seeing him again.”

“And I take it your husband didn’t know?”

“He thought something was going on, I think. But we really don’t talk much after the ‘reconciliation,’ as you call it.”

“That was his word, not mine,” Colt said. “When did Lucius start calling again?”

A shrug. “Few months ago.”

“What makes you think he suspected the affair had started up again?”

Rose looked at him. “You ever been married, Sheriff?”

He nodded.

“You ever know something about your wife without ever asking her about it, or saying anything?” she said.

He thought about his own failed marriage and the looks and the things not said. “Yes, I did.”

“When Mike found out about me and Lucius—this was about a year ago—we really hit a rough patch,” Rose said. “We prayed a lot. Together and alone. We even found a marriage counselor over in Tuscaloosa that we could trust to keep things quiet, on account of Mike’s job. It was hard and ugly. Lots of name-calling, bitter arguments. It took months for us to make our way back to each other, but even when we did, it wasn’t the same. I knew it, and I think Mike knew it, even though he probably wouldn’t admit it.”

Colt watched her catch her breath. “Go on,” he said.

“We got back to a point where we got along,” she said. “Like I said, it wasn’t the same, but we were a couple again. In a new normal. We smiled. We talked.” She let out a ragged breath and looked away. “But then Lucius called, and I don’t know why but I didn't discourage him. And not long after that, I noticed Mike becoming distant. He'd look at me when he didn't think I noticed. He'd watch me on my phone sometimes. So, yes, he could have been suspicious of me. Trust is a hard thing to build, Sheriff Harper, and it's even hard to build again."

"I understand," Colt said. He watched another tear, another flick. He let her collect herself, decided to change the subject. "What time did he call the other night?"

"Sometime around ten. The exact time would be in my phone."

"It was ten twenty-three, to be exact," Colt said, raising a hand when Rose shifted to get to her feet. "How did Lucius sound?"

Rose clasped her hands together. "Sound? He sounded normal. He said he was going to stop and get a Coke on the way over. He drinks about four a day."

"He wasn't concerned your husband would be coming home?"

"You mean if," she said. "Mike never comes home early, especially after church or one of his meetings."

He noticed the bitter tone. Waited a second. "About that meeting," he said.

Rose shifted again, her body language instantly defensive, though she tried to look cool. "Yes?" she said.

"I asked your husband about it," Colt said. "And he said he and Lucius did this kind of thing often—meet with members of the congregation."

"That's true."

"I don't doubt it," Colt said. "But what I'm wondering is why. Why the meetings and why with Lucius? Especially after he already knew about the affair."

Rose's eyes betrayed her. She looked away. Her hands fidgeted in her lap. Colt let her stew for a minute. Then, her voice a whisper: "I told him to stop."

"Stop what, Rose? Those meetings?"

Rose's bottom lip trembled. She nodded.

"But why?"

Rose held up a hand, her composure regained. "You'll have to talk to him, Sheriff. That's his business, not mine."

Colt sat back in his chair, watching her. She wasn't going to say anything more, no matter how long he waited. He pushed himself to his feet.

"Thanks again, Rose," he said. "I'll see myself out."

He sat in his car while the air-conditioning ran, blasting out hot air until it cooled off. His mind felt like a shuffling deck of cards, each a piece of information that had some relation with the others, but not in any way that made sense. Rose was as evasive as her husband. And their marriage was over; they just didn't know it. But the state of the Sanders marriage wasn't the thing nagging at him.

CHAPTER FIFTEEN

COLT

Colt walked into the sheriff's office and saw John and Molly hunkered over John's desk.

John looked up from the stack of papers he and Molly were focused on. "Hey, Colt, glad you're back."

Becky appeared at his elbow. "Colt, Judge Dockery signed off on that warrant you requested."

John's head snapped up. "What search warrant?"

"Thanks, Becky," Colt said. Then to John and Molly: "Y'all come on in my office."

He waved the two of them toward seats as he walked in and sat behind his desk. John and Molly trailed behind him.

"Y'all were reading the coroner's report?" Colt said.

Both nodded.

"So, keeping that in mind, and that Reverend Sanders owns a handgun, I requested a warrant to get that weapon after he refused to provide it in my interview with him."

"Jesus, Colt, this again?" John said.

"Hold on, John," Colt said. "I spoke with Rose Sanders today."

"And?" John said, a little louder than was necessary.

Colt pulled notebook out and slapped it on his desk. "Her story corroborates everything we already know, plus a couple of new points." He recounted the conversation with Rose Sanders and her revelation of the real state of her marriage—and her evasive answer about the meeting.

"John, what does your gut tell you?" Colt said.

John cleared his throat. "That Sanders is still in play."

Colt looked at Molly, who stayed silent. "Right," Colt said. "So, that's why I have a warrant, which I plan to execute right now. And, John, you're coming with me."

John crossed his arms and stared at him with eyes like stone, but he didn't say anything.

CHAPTER SIXTEEN

COLT

Colt put the car in park in the shade of an oak tree that cast a wide shadow over the asphalt parking lot of Zion Baptist Church. He left the engine running, air-conditioning going full blast. Looked over at his passenger.

"You okay with this, John?"

John cleared his throat and looked back at him. "Much as I hate to say it, yes, I am."

"I'm glad to hear that."

"How you want to do this?"

Colt killed the engine. "As straight up as I can. I want to hear his side of things on the affair his wife had with Wallace, and I'll take the weapon into custody." He reached into the back seat for a plastic evidence bag. John climbed out of the car and waited for him to walk around.

Inside the church, Colt retraced his steps to the pastor's office, tapped on the open door. Sanders looked up, friendly enough until his eyes registered his visitors. He stood.

"Reverend," Colt said.

"What now, Sheriff?" Sanders eyes darted from one badge to the other.

"This is my senior deputy, John Carver," Colt said.

Sanders gave John a solemn nod. John returned the gesture.

Colt glanced over at John, whose face was blank. Whatever their differences on this case outside the room, John was a stone-cold professional at the moment. Face like a statue. "I have a search warrant for these premises, which I plan to execute in the course of this visit."

From the corner of his eye, he saw John shift his weight from one foot to another. Sanders' breathing was audible in the enclosed office space.

"Reverend?" Colt said.

"I... wait, am I a suspect, Sheriff? Do I need a lawyer?"

Goddam right you're a suspect. Colt waited a beat. "You're of course free to consult an attorney at your discretion," Colt said. "But at this point, this is a conversation to clear up some details about your original statement to me. I don't expect this to take long."

Sanders thought that over. A little too long, in Colt's opinion. "Go ahead," Sanders said.

"Thank you, Reverend Mike," Colt said. He gave John another a quick glance, mostly for his own reassurance. Still a statue.

"Did you know that Lucius and Rose stayed in touch with each other?" Colt said.

Colt watched the fierceness drain out of the man, leaving a much older person, sadder, a face that looked like all of the other people of the world, the ones without the light of God shining on them. Just a man.

"No, of course not," Sanders said.

"Really? Rose thought you suspected it."

Sanders' head snapped up at that.

"I talked to her," Colt said. "She was a lot more forthcoming than you. So, you'd have no idea why Lucius would call her after leaving y'all's meeting and just about an hour before he got killed?"

"None whatsoever," Sanders said. He looked up. "Except for the obvious."

Colt cleared his throat, pulled his notebook out of his shirt pocket. He flipped it open, flipped a few pages, stopped at one. "What time did you say the meeting ended?"

Sanders shifted his feet, rubbed his chin. "About nine thirty or so, if I recall."

"You said between nine-thirty and ten, actually," Colt said. He noticed John look at him. So, John noticed the change in the tone of his voice. "Can you be more specific?"

Sanders crossed his arms over his vested belly, cuff links twinkling for an instant before disappearing into folds of expensive suit material. "Not really, no," he said. "But it had to be about that time, because I stayed after the meeting for a few minutes to chat and Lucius left before me. I do remember the clock on the dashboard of my car said ten oh seven when I got in."

Colt glanced at the numbers under his finger. "Lucius called Rose at ten twenty-three."

Sanders looked at him, stone-faced. "You have made it abundantly clear that he called her, Sheriff. And, as I have told you, I knew about the affair, and I made my peace with it. And Rose and Lucius. I had no idea that they had resumed their ... sneaking about."

"How is it you were able to come to peace with Lucius over this?" Colt asked. "I mean, you and him going to prayer meetings and such together. It seems awfully magnanimous of you, in my opinion. I'm not trying to sound flippant. I'm just having a real hard time understanding that."

Sanders' head sagged. "I'm a man of God, Sheriff," he said. "I don't have the luxury of anger or jealousy or revenge, like some men. My job—my calling—is to heal and forgive. Even those who have done me grievous harm."

"You consider the affair grievous harm?" Colt said. John cleared his throat. Colt ignored him.

"Wouldn't you?" Sanders said.

Colt's mind involuntarily flashed to Irene and their failed marriage. Infidelity. Rage. "I would consider it harm, certainly. Did you ever confront Lucius when you found out?"

"I didn't have to," Sanders said. "He came to me. I'd already found out from Rose after I caught her in a lie and she told me the whole story. And, of course, she told Lucius, too. He came to my house, literally hat in hand, to apologize. He was a mess. Scared, regretful. In a terrible state. I have to admit, I wasn't in a much better state. But I asked him in and we prayed together in my study. It wasn't easy, Sheriff. Forgiveness seldom is. It's a process and an imperative for those who truly desire to follow the Lord. But try to forgive I did, and we prayed there together for a long time."

Colt found himself nodding, agreeing with the man's words about forgiveness and knowing that forgiving the truly misbegotten fuckers of the world was a hell of a lot harder than this preacher was making it out to be.

"And then what?" Colt said.

Sanders cocked his head. "What do you mean?"

"So that was the end of it? Forgive and forget?"

"Forgive, yes, forget, no, of course not," Sanders said.

Colt stepped to the desk, searched Sanders' tired face. "Never any thoughts of revenge?"

The question ignited Sanders. He slapped both hands on the desk. "Revenge? Are you suggesting that I killed Lucius Wallace?"

John took a small side step toward Colt.

"I'm asking if you ever thought about revenge," Colt said.

Sanders curled his fingers into fists. "I swear to you and to the good Lord above, I never once thought about harming Lucius Wallace. How dare you even ask the question."

Colt looked over John, whose eyes were warning him. Colt closed his notebook and pocketed it, then pulled a folded piece of paper from his pants. His hip was starting to ache, again, from all this standing. "You said the clock on your dashboard read ten oh seven. What time did you get home?"

Sanders shrugged. "Probably about one o'clock."

Colt turned his head to look at John, whose face wore the same question as his.

"Did you say one o'clock in the morning?" Colt asked.

Sanders' eyes narrowed. "Yes."

"So where were you between ten oh seven and one o'clock?"

"I went for a drive."

"A drive? To where? And why?"

Sanders sighed, looked away from the both of them. "Just around, nowhere in particular. Just to be alone with myself. And with God."

"Any particular reason for this late-night drive on this night? Do you do this a lot?"

Sanders rubbed his chin again. "I don't know what a lot is. But sometimes, yes. Helps clear my head."

"Clear your head?"

"Of the troubles of the people under my care."

Colt and John exchanged a look. Colt saw something in John's face that had not been there when the interview began, and it made the next step easier. Not more pleasant, but at least easier. He unfolded the paper and set it on the desk between Sanders and himself.

"Reverend, this is the search warrant. Specifically, for a handgun. I'd ask you to hand it over. It'll make this go a lot faster."

Sanders looked stricken but moved his head up and down. He bent over and opened a drawer on the lower right-hand side of his desk and came up with a snub-nosed .38. Colt and John instinctively put their hands on their own weapons while Sanders lowered the revolver to the green blotter on the desk.

"Please take a step back, Reverend," Colt said. Sanders obeyed.

Colt pulled a pair of latex gloves from his back pocket, snapped them on. He picked up the weapon and popped the cylinder out, then dumped six hollow-point shells into his hand. "Ammunition, too, please."

Sanders ducked into the drawer again, produced a box of bullets. Slapped them onto the desk.

Colt could smell the gun oil, but he raised the small pistol to the light, inspected the barrel and cylinder. Clean. He snapped the cylinder shut and put the weapon on the desk, laid the bullets next to it. The box of ammo contained a dozen or so ninety-grain bullets. Colt recognized the brand and make. High-velocity for a lighter-grain bullet, and it packed a punch. Surprising amount of heat for a preacher.

He pulled an evidence bag from his back pocket, slid the box of ammo, the loose bullets, and the pistol into the bag, sealed it. He looked over at John, whose frown told him his thoughts.

"Reverend Michael Sanders, I'm placing you under arrest on suspicion of murder," Colt said. "You have the right to remain silent. Anything you say can and will be used against you in a court of law. You have the right to an attorney. If you cannot afford an attorney, one will be provided for you."

Sanders glared at them both, fists clenched at his sides. "I think I'd like to call my lawyer," he said, his voice shaking.

John stepped forward with his handcuffs. "Reverend, I need you to turn around and place your hands behind your back."

Sanders trembled with rage, but he complied with John's orders. John clapped the cuffs on him and led him out of the office and down the hall, Colt close behind.

In the parking lot, Colt noticed, with no small amount of fury, Craig Battles standing by the Crown Vic. John stopped, his hand grasping Sanders' elbow.

"Dammit," Colt said. "John, please see the reverend to the car." He stepped away from them and intercepted Battles. "Craig, what are you doing here?"

"I was in the area, saw your car," the reporter said, which was bullshit as far as Colt was concerned. "Are you arresting Reverend Sanders?" Battles said as he watched John put his hand on Sanders' head and ease him into the back seat of the car.

"Yes," Colt said. "And since this is an open investigation, I'm not saying anything more than that."

He left Battles standing with notebook in hand and climbed into the car. There was going to be a shitstorm at the meeting tonight if anybody heard about this. He looked at his watch. Battles was probably already past his afternoon deadline. Maybe he'd get lucky.

CHAPTER SEVENTEEN

COLT

The crowd was much larger than Colt had expected, and people were still coming through the double doors at the back of the civic center.

He stood at the opposite end of the room, on a slightly raised stage, Rhonda on one side, Molly and John on the other. He'd decided at the last minute to bring Molly along. An impulse. Looking at the sea of faces in the rows of seats and lining the walls, he couldn't put a finger on why he'd chosen to bring her. He rationalized that she'd had his back once, so having her here might not be a bad idea. But now she looked as nervous as a cat, shifting her weight, eyeballing the place, pushing her hair over the ragged scar just above her left ear. A couple of times he'd noticed her hands shaking, and he wondered if he'd made a mistake by bringing her. He leaned toward her.

"You okay?"

"Nothing a goddam drink wouldn't cure," she said through gritted teeth.

He looked over her head at John, who kept his eyes focused on the people taking seats.

"You need to leave?" he said to Molly.

"Hell no," she said. "I'll get through it." She swiped an errant strand of hair from her forehead.

He glanced over at Rhonda, who couldn't be cooler. Smiles, small waves for folks she knew—which was damn near everybody.

"You set all this up today?" Colt asked her, making sure he was a safe distance from the microphone perched on a stand in front of them.

"I did," Rhonda said, smiling, waving. "Hello, Molly, good to see you again."

Molly smiled, nodded, still nervous as hell. She took up a position to Colt's right, slightly behind, a move that reminded him—again—of the day he took Hack down. Molly, bleeding from a head wound, pushing him forward, even though he'd been shot three times. Toward the psychopath holding Rhonda by the throat. He forced the images from his mind and tried to look calm. His right hand drifted to its usual position on the butt of his .45. Then he realized the folks here might get the wrong idea, so he eased both hands behind his back, like he was taking a photo with city hall dignitaries.

Rhonda stepped up to the microphone, and he was relieved because his mind was running away from him. She waited a moment for the people—had to be more than a hundred—to settle down.

"Good evening, everybody," she began. "Thank you all for coming on such short notice. I know we're all busy, and I appreciate each of you taking the time."

Colt couldn't help but smile a little. Rhonda was a natural at this shit. She could probably be the mayor if she wanted to.

"This was just going to be a community meeting amongst ourselves," she continued, "but, given the subject, Sheriff Harper has been gracious enough to take time out of his own busy schedule to speak to you all about what's going on with the, uh, investigation."

She turned to him. "Sheriff?"

Rhonda moved away a couple of steps, and he stepped over to the microphone. A smattering of applause. And even that sounded forced. He cleared his throat and gazed at the group. Half the faces he saw were hostile, the other half disinterested. This was going to be one tough-ass crowd.

"Thanks, Rhonda," he said. Then, to the crowd: "After talking with Rhonda today, and knowing there are probably a lot of questions about what's going on in the investigation into the death of Mr. Wallace, I took her advice and decided to talk with y'all tonight. I hope y'all will understand that I can't go into details about the investigation itself, but I can say this, and I mean it: whoever killed Lucius Wallace will be found, arrested, and sent to jail."

A middle-aged man built like a baseball bat sprang to his feet. "Then why'd you arrest Reverend Mike?"

Colt did his damnedest not to flinch at the mention of Sanders' name, especially since he'd only made the arrest a couple of hours earlier. And that meant he'd not been lucky at all. Craig Battles must have put something on the web version of the newspaper—and now the whole county knew.

"Sir," he said, then scanned the rows of seats. "I'm investigating a murder, and I'm following the evidence. To discuss the details of that investigation at this point wouldn't be professional, or even necessarily accurate on my part."

"You ain't got no evidence," the man said, crossing his skinny brown arms.

Colt let that one slide.

"You looking to polish that badge is all," the man went on. "You don't care about what's happening to black folks around here."

That one pissed him off. Must have been obvious because he sensed Molly step up beside him as if to warn him not to say anything stupid. And she was cool now. Not the least bit jumpy, just super-cool, red hair and ice-blue eyes looking right at him.

But he never got the chance to speak because Rhonda was on her feet.

"That'll be enough of that talk," Rhonda said to the suddenly silent crowd, her voice steady but loud enough to be heard in the back row. Colt couldn't see her face, but he knew the look in her eyes—it was reflected on the faces staring back at him and her. "You all know as well as I do what Sheriff Harper has done for the people of this county, *all* the people of this county. He's put his life on the line for me, and so have Deputy McDonough and Deputy Carver here. You all know he was the one who made sure that the man—the *white* man—who killed my son went to prison. I won't stand here and let you slander a man who's doing his job. I just won't have it."

She put her hands on her hips and glared at the crowd. Colt felt naked, such was his discomfort. Everybody here knew his history with Rhonda, except Molly. And it was hard to tell if they were buying what Rhonda had to say.

"Thank you, Rhonda," he said into the microphone, the sound of his voice booming like a thunderclap over the heads of the gathering. "Like I said, this is a murder investigation, and it's a process. My office is working as fast and as thoroughly as possible. I'd just ask that you all be patient and not jump to any conclusions."

A heavyset man in the front row stuck a hand in the air. Colt didn't know what to do but point at him.

With his hand still in the air, the man said, "What about them crackers in the woods planning to kill us?"

The question was so random and unexpected that Colt wasn't sure he heard it right. But it caused an immediate, menacing stir in the crowd, like a water moccasin uncoiling on a riverbank. The man's hand went down as a whispered murmur whistled among the seats.

Rhonda was on her feet again, coming at him, brow furrowed. He stepped aside, baffled.

"Y'all," she said, "we're here to let the sheriff give us an update on his case, not to waste his time on stories."

Colt shook her off. "Sir, can you explain that to me?"

The heavyset man folded his arms across his chest and narrowed his eyes. "Like you don't know."

"No, sir, I'm afraid I don't," Colt said, feeling like he was easing out onto some mighty thin ice.

"Then you don't know what's going on in your own county, Sheriff," the man said. "But we do. Same shit been going on for years. One white sheriff after another."

Colt felt his face flush from anger, and he fought it down. "Sir, I'd be happy to talk to you after this meeting, if you don't mind."

The big man waved him off, dismissing him.

From the back of the room, a youngish man yelled, "What about you, Deputy? What do you think about this?"

Colt swiveled his head, first to Molly, then to John, who stood at a loose parade rest. He stepped over to the microphone. "Excuse me?" John said. "I'm not sure I understand the question."

"Question's pretty simple," the man at the back of the room snapped back. "Whose side you on?"

Colt, two feet from John, watched with something akin to horror as his best friend's face contorted with uncertainty as to how to answer. Come on, John, there's no sides here. Just answer the man.

"Sir, we are conducting a homicide investigation," John said slowly. "I'm on the side of the law."

Colt inwardly relaxed but still felt unease at John's struggle. What was so hard about that answer, anyway?

Someone in the crowd, Colt couldn't tell who, yelled, "You still working for a white man, though."

Colt and John exchanged a look. This shit was about to get out of hand. It certainly wasn't going the way he thought it would. Colt nudged John away from the microphone.

"Look, everybody, let's just catch our breath for a second," he said in what he hoped was a calming voice. "This isn't about sides. This is about finding out who killed Lucius Wallace. And that's what I'm trying to do. Same with my deputies. We'll investigate every lead and consider every piece of evidence. If you have something that you think needs to be brought to my attention, then by all means please get in touch with my office." He turned to Rhonda, hoping she'd get the hint.

She did. She smiled and moved to the microphone. "All right, you heard the sheriff. If there are no other questions, then, thank you for coming, Sheriff Harper."

Colt hoped his mouth wasn't hanging open. "Certainly, Rhonda," he said. Then, lamely: "Y'all have a good evening."

Several people jumped to their feet, making for the doors in a clamor of shuffling feet, chairs scraping the concrete floor, and the buzz of conversation. Colt watched the commotion and wondered what had just happened.

"Wait," Colt called as his last questioner moved toward the back of the room—quickly for a man of his size. But he was already out of earshot in the noise. Colt turned to Rhonda.

"What the hell was that?" he said.

Rhonda turned the microphone off. She looked at Molly, then at him. "Foolishness," she said. "Rumors."

"Of what?" Colt said.

"Same rumors that have been around since we were kids," Rhonda said. "Vigilantes. Night riders. Klan."

Colt closed his eyes, counted to three. "The Klan? I know for a fact there's no Klan in this county.

"That don't stop the rumors," she said.

Colt glanced at Molly, who gave him a look that said, *What do you expect me to say?* John stood behind Rhonda staring off into nothing but looking like he was ready to bite a steel bar in half.

"That man," Colt said. "I want his name. He was specific—white men in the woods. I want to know what he was talking about."

"Harold Bell," Rhonda said. "He's one of the biggest rumor-mongers in town, and, frankly, nobody really thinks he's right in the head. But he's not the first one I've heard spread that rumor. Few months ago, some folks started whispering that there was a group of white men looking to do the kinds of things the Klan did years ago."

He didn't have time for this, but he'd be goddammed if he was going to let it go.

"You believe it?" Colt said.

"I wouldn't be surprised," Rhonda said. "Been that way my whole life."

Colt noticed she said "my" and not "our."

"Rhonda," Molly said. "Anything specific? More than a rumor of white men?"

"Oh no, nothing more than that," Rhonda said.

"But that's enough," Molly said. She looked at Colt. "That's why they're here tonight. They're worried. Scared."

"Yes," Rhonda said to Molly. "Like I said, been that way my whole life. And the past usually points to the present." She turned to Colt. "Thank you for doing this. You needed to see it from our perspective. Molly's right. People are scared."

Colt ran a hand through his hair, scanned the now half-empty room. "I can see that now."

"I have to get back to these folks," Rhonda said. "Molly, I'm so happy to see you."

"You, too," Molly said.

Rhonda gave Colt a quick hug. "John, you staying here?" he said.

John didn't look at him—he just nodded. Colt stepped off the stage toward the back doors, Molly trailing behind. When she had exited the room, Molly said, "I've never seen anything quite like that. And Rhonda knows something about those rumors."

Colt shook his head. "You heard her."

"I did," Molly said. "She's right about all of it, and I think she's just afraid to tell you."

"Rhonda's not afraid," Colt said, annoyed at Molly's insistence. "And if she knew more, she'd tell me. So drop it."

Molly shrugged. "If you say so."

They left the building and crossed the downtown street in sparse traffic. Replaying the meeting in his mind, Colt nearly forgot Molly was beside him as he stepped to the curb on the far side, still fixated on the odd question he'd heard.

"Hey, you still with us?" Molly said.

"What?" He looked but didn't see her. She'd stopped ten feet behind him. He waved her forward. "Sorry, thinking."

Molly caught up to him. "About?"

He resumed walking, Molly in step with him.

"I need to check out the notebook John found in Wallace's truck."

"Already did," Molly said. "John let me see it when I was checking out the names Sanders provided—the people from his meeting. None of those names matched any of the initials, or whatever they are, from Wallace's notebook."

They turned a corner onto a side street. Night had fully come, and they passed through yellow discs of light from streetlamps lining the street.

"You get through all those names already?" Colt said.

"No," Molly said. "But so far, the ones I have talked to check out. Right down the line. In fact, maybe too much so."

"What do you mean?"

They stopped at Colt's vehicle, and Molly leaned against the Crown Vic.

"Everybody has, literally, the same story," she said. "And I don't mean generally. They say almost the exact same thing, in the same order."

"Give me an example."

"The meeting started at eight thirty, right on time," she said. "Reverend Mike and Lucius got there at about the same time, and Reverend Mike opened with a word of prayer."

"That's it?"

"That's not a report," Molly said. "That's nearly a verbatim account given to me by four different people. And there's more."

"Go on."

Molly nodded. "Nearly every person I spoke to also said this: 'Reverend Mike spoke to us about the book of Matthew. The subject was "the meek shall inherit the earth." That was all we talked about. That we, as Christians, will inherit the earth. Lucius closed the meeting with a prayer.'"

Colt thought on that, silently agreeing with Molly's observations that it was odd. "And they all said that?"

"Almost like they were reading off a script," Molly said.

"Something's up," he said. "Sanders' wife was real cagey about that meeting when I asked her about it. She clammed up."

"I agree something's up," Molly said. "Why did you need to check out the notebook?"

Colt opened the car door. "You just said part of it. None of those initials match the people at the prayer meeting. So the initials have to belong to somebody else. I'll bet you fifty bucks they belong to white men."

Molly pushed herself away from the car. "White men? Oh, 'crackers in the woods.'"

Colt climbed into the driver's seat, cranked up. "Right. Question is, does that connect to these prayer meetings?"

Molly shook her head. "Not following."

"Maybe Lucius had a target list. Maybe those prayer meetings were planning meetings."

"That's a huge guess, Harper. We don't even know who those initials belong to."

"I know," Colt said. "I'm going back to the office. Go get some rest."

"After I go to a meeting," Molly said, flashing a nervous smile that made her look guilty as he drove away.

He threw his keys onto his desk and walked to the window of his office. He leaned against the window jamb to take the weight off his hip, gazed over the long field of gravestones. Pinpoints of light twinkled in the shanties lining Cemetery Road. At the far end of the cemetery, low buildings, now dark and awash in the faint blue moonlight, stood like sentinels. Those businesses were sort of the lucky ones, still standing next to collapsed hulks of shops destroyed by a tornado some years back.

The dark streets below him didn't lead to a ghost town, but it was a town of ghosts. Everywhere he dared look, every face he encountered, conjured up a haunt, an incessant reminder of this place—and his place in it.

He'd grown up fascinated by stories of his grandfather's grandfather, Cabe Harper, a fierce man who'd fought alongside General Forrest in the war, as far north as Nashville and back before being shot out of his saddle and captured at Tupelo, killing three Yankees with his pistol in the process. At least that was the family lore. Cabe had taken up "overseeing" after the war, a sort of foreman on a farm, his grandmother had explained during long storytelling nights on her front porch. It was decades before he'd learned what an overseer really did and of Cabe Harper's notorious reputation for his frequent and ruthless application of the whip—on black sharecroppers only a few years out of slavery.

And then there was his own father. Winston, besides creating a lifetime of wreckage and generally being an asshole, had killed a man—a fellow Marine for fuck's sake—just for being black and for outranking Winston. And got away with it for decades, until his own son gave him only two options: jail or a bullet. Winston chose the latter, and Colt had never lost a night's sleep over that decision. Winston was just one of the ghosts he'd created, and that was just his family. There were others: Kuwait, Somalia, and in his own county.

The ghosts were black and white. That would never change.

CHAPTER EIGHTEEN

JOHN

John stood on the stage with his arms crossed as he watched Rhonda say good-bye to the last person through the exit. The slow burn that had started when Colt arrested Sanders had just ticked up a couple of notches, thanks to tonight's questioners. Rhonda walked back to him, climbed the stage. He tried to put on a neutral face.

"Out with it," Rhonda said, her face serious as she looked up at him.

He shook his head. "That was bullshit."

"John."

"I know, I know, language," he said. "But, dammit, Rhonda, that guy all but called me an Uncle Tom."

Rhonda crossed her arms and cocked an eyebrow. "Nobody called you that. Yes, it was a heated conversation. What do you expect? These folks are angry and scared."

"I know that," he said, more sharply than he intended. "Sorry. I just don't like having my loyalty—or my identity—questioned."

Rhonda put a hand on his arm, stroked him gently. "I understand that."

The caress softened his mood. A little. "I don't understand the people here. I thought I did, but this is really pushing it. They're questioning *me*? I'm not the white sheriff here. I *see* the racism around us every day."

"Let's sit down for a second," Rhonda said. She stepped down to the first row of chairs and took a seat. John followed her, sat. He waited for her to continue.

"John, of course you see it. Because you're not the white sheriff. Or white, period. But it's different with Colt. He's going to get blindsided. If he hasn't already."

"What do you mean? Colt can handle himself. He's a damn good lawman."

Rhonda nodded. "He's everything you could want from a sheriff. Or a friend. His blind spot is people, always has been. And in this case, it's the thing causing all the problems."

"How so?"

"He expects people to be as forthright as he is," Rhonda said. "It's like he has this need for people to be exactly who they say they are. But his life has been filled with people who were anything but."

"I'm sure living with Winston had something to do with that."

"His father had everything to do with it," Rhonda said. "But others, too. Irene."

"I never knew her all that well," John said. "By the time I got here, I think their marriage was already in trouble."

"It was trouble from the start," Rhonda said. "She carried herself like she was a movie-star actress. Had the looks. She acted like she was special—above all of the rest of us. But then you realized she's just haughty. She saw something in Colt she could use."

"That sounds a little jealous," John said.

Rhonda cocked the eyebrow again. "No, just observation. I've known Colt a long time."

"Longer than me," John admitted. "What you say makes sense, but what I don't get is how he hasn't really been able to see the blatant racism right in front of him. Hell, I saw it the first damn day I crossed the state line."

"It's Mississippi," Rhonda said.

"It's racism," John said.

"I know I can't tell you anything really new about that," Rhonda said. "And I know growing up in Chicago was not an easy life for you. But that's militant, overt racism, maybe because it's a big city, I don't know. Here it's different. It's generational and it's not out in public like it used to be. No more colored bathrooms. But private schools that are really nothing more than a way for white people with money to keep their kids away from schools with black kids. Social segregation. It's part of the fabric of all our lives. White and black."

"You're right," John said. "You can't see it, so you can't fight against it."

Rhonda nodded. "That's part of it, and believe me, Colt knows that. In our social fabric, the racism here is like a stain on the couch."

John laughed. "What?"

"Seriously," Rhonda said. "It's one of those stains that just won't come out. No matter how much you clean it or how many different cleaners you use, it's always there. And always will be. So, even though everybody knows it's there, nobody talks about it because it's embarrassing and ugly."

"So you just pretend it isn't there?"

"I didn't say that," Rhonda said.

"But what about Colt?"

"Colt is the person expecting company, so he's still scrubbing that stain trying to make it go away before anybody sees it," Rhonda said.

John thought about that. Colt was exactly as Rhonda described. Which caused the blind spot she talked about.

"Watch him, John," Rhonda said, making him think she was reading his mind. "Don't let him be his own worst enemy. He needs you. He'll never say that, but he does. He needs Molly, too."

"Molly? Are you kidding?"

"That woman is good for him," Rhonda said.

"How you figure?"

"She's not you, for one thing."

"Or you." He was starting to see what Rhonda was getting at.

"Exactly. He hears her and listens to her. I see it. He respects her."

"That's true," John said. He leaned over, kissed Rhonda's forehead. "Don't worry, I'll have his back. But what am I supposed to do?"

"Be yourself," Rhonda said. "That's the best thing you can do—for yourself and for Colt."

"I know who I am, Rhonda," he said. "I'm just starting to wonder if Colt is who I've always thought he was."

CHAPTER NINETEEN

MOLLY

Molly steered her car to the curb by the church, killed the engine, then yanked her badge from her belt. She felt around under the driver's seat until she found the strongbox. She locked up the badge and her pistol and shoved the box back under the seat. Took a deep breath and climbed out.

The meeting was just getting started as she threaded her way through the group of about twenty, mostly men, and found an empty spot. She settled in on the metal folding chair just as the meeting leader asked if anyone in the room had a topic for discussion.

She noticed her hands shaking in her lap, then surprised herself as she watched her right hand go in the air.

"Yes," said the man seated at a table at the front of the room. He looked to be in his fifties, balding with a kind face.

She cleared her throat. "I'm Molly, and I'm an alcoholic."

"Hey, Molly," the group answered in unison.

She scanned the room, now terrified at her own disobedient hand. "I, uh... I really want a fucking drink right now," she said. "I've been in town for just a couple of days. Out of rehab last week. And it's a lot harder than I thought it would be."

The men and women stared back at her like one gigantic organism. Some nodded, understanding. She knew she had to keep going, because needing a drink wasn't necessarily a topic.

"I just came from a work thing," she said, remembering to share in a general way, as she was taught in rehab. "I thought I was good. Just a meeting, you know? But as soon as I walked in the room, I was shaking. Wasn't even any alcohol there. Just a bunch of people. I don't know what happened, and I don't know how it happened. But I wanted to get the hell out of there as fast as I could, and all I could think about was the fact that a few shots of vodka would smooth me right out. Is it always this hard? When does this stop? I mean, I guess that's my topic. What do you do when every instinct you have goes haywire and the only thing you can think about is a drink?"

She had their attention, that was for damn sure. The room had fallen silent as she spoke, and now every person looked at her with a wild mixture of compassion, pity, and amusement.

"Thanks for letting me share," she said. She exhaled, relieved and spent.

"Thanks for sharing," came the chorus.

The room remained silent for a few moments—nobody ever wanted to go first in these damn meetings. Finally, off to the side of the room, an ancient man in tan slacks and a golf shirt shifted in his seat.

"I'm Ron, and I'm an alcoholic," he said from under a thick shock of snow-white hair.

The room responded and Ron acknowledged the crowd with a nod. He looked like a sage, or an oracle, perched and about to dispense knowledge.

"I panicked all the time for the first three years I was sober," he said. "And every time, I called my sponsor. That's the first thing. Second thing is, and my sponsor taught me this, is always have an escape plan. Ain't nothing worse than having your back against the wall with nowhere to get to. I'd let him know when I was going somewhere, when I was leaving, hell, everything. And those first three years, I needed that. I couldn't do this alone.

None of us can, really. That's why we don't venture out by ourselves. Thanks for letting me share."

Escape plan. Of course. She swore at herself in her head. Why were the simplest things hard? She listened to the remainder of the group share stories, several of which were very similar to hers, with a lot more realism than the stories she'd heard in rehab. Some didn't end with a meeting, but with a drunken binge. She'd come close herself.

When the meeting drew to an end an hour later, she'd made two decisions: never get caught unprepared and find a sponsor. She scanned the women's faces in the room. None made eye contact.

She was halfway to her car when she heard her name being called out on the dark sidewalk. She stopped and turned. One of the women from the meeting was hurrying to catch up with her.

"Hi, I'm Michelle," she said, wrestling a purse onto her shoulder with one hand while offering the other. "Molly, right?"

"Right," she said. Up close, she could see Michelle was older than she appeared, a common trait for AA women, she'd noticed. Taller than her, blond with washed-out blue eyes, Michelle smiled with an ease of someone not hounded by the constant craving of an addiction.

"Look, you said you're new in town," Michelle said. "Take my number. And call me if you need to talk."

Molly surprised herself again with the sense of relief she felt, rather than the throat-tightening apprehension she expected. She pulled her phone from her pocket. "Sure. Thanks."

Michelle rattled her off her number, and Molly put it in her phone.

"Thank you for being honest and sharing," Michelle said. "We've all been there, trust me."

"Thanks. It was good to hear other people say that."

Michelle smiled again. “Okay, you have my number, so, you know, call. But before you take a drink. Nobody wants to talk to a drunk.” She gave a small wave, turned, and disappeared up the sidewalk.

Molly stared at her phone for a moment. It was a start, at least.

DAY FIVE

CHAPTER TWENTY

COLT

"Holy hell," John said as he stepped into the office. "You sleep here last night?"

Colt swiveled his chair away from his computer screen, and an electric shock of pain shot from his hip, causing him to flinch. "And good morning to you," he said with a grimace. "No, I didn't. You're in early."

"So are you," John said. "What's up?" He pulled a chair to the desk and sat, sipped steaming coffee from his battered mug with USMC on one side.

Colt wondered absently in his tired brain how many mornings he and John had shared this early morning ritual, in the barracks, in the field, at a crime scene, in an office, over a cup of coffee. At least a thousand, he thought.

"Okay, so I was here late last night," Colt said, wondering now just how bad he might look. He'd spent an hour the night before trying to make sense of Wallace's notebook, but failing that, he'd gone home and stewed on his back porch for another hour with a cigar and half a bottle of bourbon. "I can't shake that meeting last night. The comments about 'crackers in the woods.'"

John sipped, looked at him over the top of his mug. "Rhonda and I talked about it after you and Molly left."

Colt sat up. "What'd she say?"

John plunked the mug back down on the desk. "About that nut that brought that up?"

"She said 'nut'?"

"No, that was me."

"What if it's not a nut?" Colt said.

"What do you mean?"

Colt recounted what Molly had told him about the rehearsed stories of the people at Reverend Sanders' meeting.

John shook his head. "I still don't see how that connects to 'crackers in the woods,' or Lucius Wallace, for that matter."

"I think Wallace's notebook contains the initials of white men he—and the good reverend—suspected as being part of that group. And that's what the two were meeting with the local folks about. That's why all the accounts from the attendees are so similar. They're not covering for Sanders. They're covering for the meeting."

John leaned back in his chair, looked up the ceiling, then back down at Colt. Thinking. "I don't know, Colt, that sounds like a hell of a stretch. That's like chasing boogeymen."

"Ghosts," Colt said, looking toward the window.

"What?"

"Nothing," Colt said. "You're right, it's a stretch. But there was something to that comment last night, John. I can't ignore it."

"I'm not saying ignore it. I know you won't. I'm saying it's a stretch."

Colt leaned back and closed his eyes. He needed more coffee. And more clarity than he had on this case.

John stood. "What about Molly?"

"What about her?"

John looked down at him. "She okay?"

Colt looked up at John. "She's fine. Why?"

"Just checking." Colt watched John disappear into the main office, then checked the notebook on his desk for Roger Graham's number. He dialed it up on the desk phone and got an answer on the third ring. Graham said he was about to clock out at work and, but sure, he could stay long enough to answer some questions.

Colt hung up, then called Molly.

"Hey, Harper, I'm on my way," she said.

"I'm on my way out," he said. "To talk to a witness. When you were a fed, did you ever handle hate crimes? White-supremacy groups?"

"Not on a case," Molly said. "Used the federal databases to cross-check a lot of suspects and perps, though, so I know my way around that kind of thing. Why?"

"I'm thinking some research might be useful."

"I was hoping you'd say that," Molly said. "I've been thinking about that, too. I still have some contacts that might get me access. It's a long shot, since we don't have a lot to go on. We'd probably do just as well checking over at the Southern Poverty Law Center website."

"Do it anyway," Colt said. "I thought you were a whiz at this kind of shit."

A pause. "I'm the best goddam researcher you know, Harper."

"That's what I figured," he said and hung up.

Half an hour later, Colt swung the Crown Vic into the cracked asphalt parking lot of the Bait 'n' Beer. He could see the man he figured to be Roger Graham at the cash register of an otherwise empty store.

Inside, his guess was confirmed.

"Yes, sir, that's me," Graham said with a grin. He was mid-twenties, rail thin, with what he likely considered a mustache decorating his pale upper lip.

Colt shook Graham's extended hand, then pulled a notebook out of a breast pocket. "Thanks for staying past your shift,

Mr. Graham. I won't take up too much of your time. I just want to ask you a few questions about your shift a few nights ago."

Graham's head bobbed. "Yep, Honeycutt told me you'd call."

"So, tell me about the pickup truck," Colt said.

Graham slid his hands into his pockets, ducked his head as if deep in thought. "Well, like I told Honeycutt when I first told him about it, I saw the truck—it was a Chevy—roll in sometime after nine thirty."

"You sure about the time?" Colt said.

"Oh, yes, sir," Graham said. "I have a habit of looking at the clock every time a customer comes in. I'd had a guy come in about that time. Buying rubbers and beef jerky, of all things. Guess he was planning on working up an appetite, know what I mean?"

Colt managed a smile as Graham cackled at his own joke. "So, the truck came in after that?"

Graham recovered. "Yep, few minutes after. Pulled in off to the side." He pointed to his left. "No lights over there. Cameras neither."

"And then what?"

"I didn't pay it much attention," Graham said. "Folks pull in here all the time. Then a fella came in from the same direction, bought a drink, and left."

"What did this fella look like?" Colt said.

Graham squeezed his eyes shut, thinking. "Forties, maybe. Black guy, dressed casual. Jeans. Button-up shirt."

"What kind of drink?" Colt said.

"Soft drink," Graham said. "Coke, I think."

Colt looked from the counter in the direction of the truck. From where Graham stood, he couldn't actually see the truck parked out there.

"Did he walk back to his truck?"

"Far as I know," Graham said. "I mean, I didn't pay him no mind."

Colt looked up from his notes. "And you didn't notice it when the truck didn't leave?"

Graham scratched his chin. "Not really. People come and go, you know? And I couldn't exactly see the truck from here. I just assumed that he left."

"So, when exactly did you notice the truck was still there?"

"That would be about three fifteen or so," Graham said. "It was slow, and I was really bored, so I took the trash around back to the dumpster." Graham pointed in the general direction of the truck. "When I turned the corner, I saw the truck sitting there. I thought that was odd, because there wasn't anybody in it. When it was still there in the morning, I told Honeycutt."

"You were still working the next morning?"

"You bet. Pulled a double," he said, the pride obvious. "Other kid up and quit, and I need the cash. Child support payments."

"And you didn't see anybody else drive up? Over there by the truck?"

"Nope," Graham said.

Colt flipped the notebook closed. "Thank you, Mr. Graham." He fished a card from his pocket, handed it across the counter. "You think of anything else, give me a call."

Graham beamed the smile Colt had come to associate with citizens who felt like celebrities when assisting an investigation. "Sure thing, Sheriff."

He sat in the car and let the air-conditioning run. Something didn't fit. It nagged at him.

"Crackers in the woods," he said.

Rhonda's words that sounded like a warning.

John's anger.

What was he missing?

He looked up Helen Wallace's number on his phone and dialed it.

"Mrs. Wallace, it's Sheriff Harper again," he said when she answered. "Sorry to bother you, but I was hoping you could help me out with something."

"You want *me* to help *you*?" Helen Wallace said.

He ignored the sarcasm. "Mrs. Wallace, did Lucius have any friends outside of church, maybe somebody he went fishing or shot pool with?"

"No, not really," she said. "Most of the people he knew were from church."

"What about at work?"

"Lucius didn't socialize with those guys much," Helen said. "I mean, Archie Parrott was a friend of his. They used to work together, before Lucius worked at the farm. They stayed in touch."

"Do you have his number?"

"I don't, I'm sorry," Helen said.

"Not a problem. One more question. Did Lucius have any white friends?"

He heard her scoff on the other end. "You must be joking."

CHAPTER TWENTY-ONE

COLT

Archie Parrott sat across the table, shoveling fries into his mouth like a raccoon over a garbage can, as if he hadn't eaten in days, which seemed unlikely, given the paunch stretching his light-blue O'Brien's Maintenance uniform shirt.

"Mr. Parrott, I appreciate you taking off the time from work to meet me," Colt said. He'd picked an old burger joint on Old 45 North, a couple of miles out of town. "I'm sorry it's under these circumstances."

Archie swallowed and reached for the soda in a cup as big as an oil can. "Me, too. Lucius was a good man. Sorry for eating like this. Don't get much time for lunch, even on a Saturday. But when you said you wanted to talk about Lucius, I got over here soon as I could."

"I'll try to be brief so you can get back to work," Colt said. "How did you know Lucius?"

"Used to work together, doing maintenance work out at the hospital, about ten years ago," Archie said, slurping his soda. "At the time, weren't that many brothers working there, and I guess you could say he took me under his wing. When he left to go to work for Claiborne, he told me he'd stay in touch, and he did."

"Seems like a decent man," Colt said. He reached over the table, stole one of Archie's fries. "Tell me about him."

Archie wagged his head. "He was. Damn shame what happened to him. Christian man, always willing to help a brother out, you know?"

Colt nodded. "So, he got along with people?"

Archie stopped chewing. "Meaning what?"

Colt hunched forward. "Just that. He didn't have any enemies? Nobody looking to cause him harm."

Archie's eyes narrowed and he stopped slurping his drink. "Nobody that I know of."

It was the way he said it that set off the alarm in Colt's head. "Come on, Archie. Who didn't get along with Lucius?"

Archie pushed the remains of his lunch to the side, leaned over the table. His eyes scanned the room as if he were about to impart a state secret. "Look, Sheriff, I really don't know that much about it, ahite? All I know is a few weeks ago, Lucius got into it with somebody out at that farm."

Colt studied Archie's face, saw he was telling the truth. "Who?"

Archie raised his hands like he was surrendering. "I only heard about it through the grapevine. I never talked to Lucius about it. I mean, I never got a chance to. But from what I heard, it was his boss."

Colt looked at Archie's eyes. "Hank Claiborne?"

"Dunno," Archie said. "I just heard it was his boss."

Colt thought back on his conversation with Hank, wondered why this didn't come up when he questioned Hank. Because Hank didn't want him to know about it, that's why.

"What were they arguing about?"

Archie leaned back in his chair with a pained expression on his face that could have been mistaken for heartburn from the fast food he'd just devoured. "I really don't want to get involved in all that, Sheriff."

Colt sat up. "Don't want to get involved? I thought Lucius was a friend of yours."

"He was."

"And you don't want to get involved? If Lucius had an argument with somebody he worked with a few days before he was killed, that could have a huge bearing on the case, Archie."

Whatever spirit of cooperation Archie had walked in with seemed to vanish like vapor. "I need to get back to work," he said. "I can't help you with any of that."

But Archie wasn't going to get off that easy. "What do you know about white vigilantes and Lucius trying organize black folks to stop them?"

That one shook Archie. "Whoa, whoa, whoa, Sheriff Harper," he said, his voice lowered to a near whisper. "Where you hear that?"

"Same grapevine you use, I guess."

Archie poked his head up, looked around like a prairie dog, ducked back down. "Dammit, man, you got the wrong man. I'm going to tell you this, but that's it, and then I'm out of here. Lucius thought he was going to get fired. He had a huge argument with his boss—and I don't know no names—and it turned into something racist. I swear to God that's all I know. I heard it from a guy who goes to those meetings you talking about."

"What about you?" Colt said. "You go to the meetings, too?"

"No, I don't," Archie said. He spit out each word.

"Why not?"

"Because I don't want to end up dead like Lucius," Archie said. He stood, and Colt noticed his legs trembling. "I have to go." He turned and made it to the glass door across the room in about three steps.

CHAPTER TWENTY-TWO

COLT

Colt walked past Molly's desk on his way to his office. She looked up, flagged him down. "Hey, while you were gone, I found something pretty interesting."

"What's that?" Colt said.

Molly stood. "Wait, I'll get my notes."

"I'll be at my desk," Colt said.

He'd just chewed a pain pill and settled into his chair when Molly blew in, lugging her laptop. She pulled a chair to the desk, sat, and flipped the computer open. She clacked a few keys.

"Okay," Molly said, blowing her hair from her eyes. "We couldn't make any sense out of Wallace's notebook, right? We didn't really have anything to compare it against until we got the list of employees from Hank Claiborne's farm."

Colt held up a hand. "Wait. When did you get that?"

"Came in this morning," Molly said. "Becky gave it to me. Anyway, I checked what we thought were initials against the list of employees. And, yes, they were initials. At least in one case."

"Okay, I'm interested," Colt said.

"The initials TD," Molly said. "That correlates with Tommy Dowd, one of Claiborne's employees."

"Wait," Colt said. "Tommy Dowd?"

Molly looked at him, her eyes a question.

"I arrested Tommy Dowd for possession a while back. I think John busted him, too. He works out at the farm?" Colt said.

"If my cross-reference is right, yes," Molly said. "Also, several of the entries, including these two, had the letters 'WNC' written beside them."

"Meaning?" Colt said.

Molly shrugged. "Don't know. Still working on that."

"Good work," Colt said as he swung his chair toward his computer as John walked in.

"Hey, John," Colt said. "You remember Tommy Dowd?"

John grunted. "Sure do. Little weasel I arrested twice. Drunk and disorderly and disturbing the peace. What about him?"

"He works for Hank Claiborne now," Colt said. "And his initials are in Wallace's book. At least that's Molly's theory."

"I'll bet I'm right," Molly said.

"He won't ever be employee of the month," John said.

Colt grinned, called up one of the databases the various sheriff's offices in the region used, typed in Dowd's name. A file appeared immediately. "Address listed is Columbian Arms apartments."

"Of course," John said. "Fuck that."

Molly turned to him. "What's up with that?"

Colt turned to look at John, who looked like he could snap a tire iron in half. Then at Molly. "Last time we were there, it didn't go all that well for us. John especially."

"That's putting it mildly," John said, his jaw tight. He glanced over at Molly. "We were investigating the murder of Rhonda's son, and we went to question Bennie Stilwell at those apartments. Bennie, asshole that he is, decided to greet us at the door with a pistol. I was the first one through and he took a shot at me." He pointed to his ragged left ear.

"Oh," Molly said.

"Scared the shit out of us," Colt said. "I shot Bennie in the legs and arrested him. He's currently sitting in a cell at Parchman for murder."

"And," John said, "every time I think about that little asshole, I hope he gets shanked."

"Anyway," Colt said. "Looks like we need to go back out there." He looked at the screen again. "There's something about that address, though. I thought it seemed familiar, but it's not because of Bennie. Wait." He hit a few more keys, then slapped the arm of his chair. "That's what it is."

"What?" Molly said.

"Same apartment number as Tina McGraw," Colt said. "I arrested her a while back, too. She's got a longer rap sheet than Tommy. Disturbing the peace, public drunkenness, a DUI, a ton of speeding tickets. Possession twice. One of the charges is brandishing a weapon."

"Just great," John said.

Colt turned to look at him. "You don't have to go."

"The hell I don't."

"I'll go," Molly said.

Both men looked at her. Then Colt looked at John, who suddenly seemed uncomfortable being part of the conversation.

"No, goddammit, I'll go," John said. "No offense, Molly, but I couldn't sit here and feel good about myself if I don't go out there with Colt."

"Suit yourself," Molly said. She closed her laptop.

CHAPTER TWENTY-THREE

COLT

Colt killed the engine and stared at the door of Tina McGraw's apartment. Drummed his fingers on the steering wheel.

John started to say something, stopped.

"What?" Colt said.

"Just a reminder, this is inside city limits," John said.

"That didn't stop us the last time we went there."

"And look how well that turned out," John said.

"Good point."

Colt noticed John's nervousness. "This is just a conversation, John. That's all."

"Yeah, that's it. I can handle it, Colt."

"I know you can handle it. Just try not to get shot this time," Colt said.

John opened his door. "My man has jokes," he said.

They climbed out of the cruiser. "But if this bitch pulls a gun on me, I'm putting her ass down," John said.

John banged on the door of the first-floor apartment harder than was necessary, but Colt kept his mouth shut. The door snapped halfway open, held by a woman who strongly resembled a mop with blue eye shadow. Faded jeans and a spaghetti-strap top that left little to the imagination, not that there was much to imagine in the first place.

She eyed him back, taking in the tan uniform, the badge, his height, and—most assuredly—his blackness.

"Tina McGraw?" John said.

Narrowed eyes. "What do you want?"

Colt stepped forward. "Ma'am, I'm Sheriff Harper. This is Deputy John Carver. We're looking for a man named Tommy Dowd. You know who I'm talking about?"

She sniffed. "Nope."

"You sure about that, ma'am?"

"I said no."

"Okay, then. Why don't we head back to the sheriff's office, so you can tell me that officially. That way, I won't have to bother you again since you'll be on the record and all?"

She looked at him like he'd just slapped her.

"Wait," she said. "Did you say Tommy Dowd? Yeah, I know him. I mean, I see him from time to time."

"Mm-hmm," Colt said. "And do you happen to know where he might be?"

She shook her head and moved into the space of the open door another couple of inches. "Like I said, I see him from time to time. Ain't got no idea where he is."

Colt stared her down, knew she was lying. "Is he here, Ms. McGraw?"

"Uh-uh."

"So you wouldn't mind me and Deputy Carver looking around your place?"

"You got a warrant?" she said, colorless lips in a snarl.

Colt smiled back at her. "No, I don't. But since you're a known drug user in these parts, I reasonably suspect that you may be in possession of narcotics. Which, as I'm sure someone as legally astute as you are would know, means I can search your premises if I have a reasonable suspicion a crime is being committed."

"That's bullshit."

"Is it, now?" Colt said.

From somewhere in the back of the darkened apartment the sudden sound of glass shattering made Tina jump. Before Colt could take a step inside, Tina's eyes went wild and she started screeching, "You can't come in here! Get the hell outta here!" Then, over her shoulder, "Get the hell out, Tommy!"

Colt shoved her aside and drew his pistol in one motion and sprinted down the central hallway toward where he thought the sound had come from. "John, get control of her!" he yelled. He ran into a bedroom that looked like a cyclone had hit it. The smell of weed, sweat, and sour food nearly knocked him over. Behind him, he could hear John reading Ms. McGraw her rights as he handcuffed her.

The bedroom window was smashed. Glass shards scattered on the dirty green carpet. He looked out the window, thought he saw a head of red hair duck behind a dumpster at an adjacent office plaza.

"Son of a bitch," he muttered as he ran back through the apartment, shoved Tina out of the way. "Stay here," he said to John.

"Colt—" John said.

But Colt didn't hear him as he jumped in the driver's seat again and fired up the cruiser. Just as he dropped the car into gear, he heard a gunshot from behind the apartment building, in the vicinity of the dumpster he'd glimpsed. He called Becky on his cell, told her to send backup and that he was in pursuit of a white male, thirty, red hair, vicinity of the apartments. "And, Becky, make it fast. Shots fired behind the building." Then he tore out of the complex, slung the car through a right-hand turn, then floored it.

He slid the car into the office plaza and jumped out, weapon drawn. Heard sirens and allowed himself to be impressed with that kind of response time.

Dowd had to be close, and now Colt knew he was armed. Couldn't have gotten that far.

"You hear that, Tommy?" he yelled, hoping Dowd was in fact within earshot. "You ain't running away now. You're just going to get caught."

He started toward the dumpster, pistol level, eyes scanning the parking lot. Behind him, he heard a cop car skid to a stop.

Behind the dumpster, two bloody hands popped up. "I'm shot," Dowd screamed.

Colt kept the pistol aimed at the container. "If you have a weapon, toss it out where I can see it."

A groan. Dowd's hands dropped out of sight, then a pistol flew out from behind the dumpster and clattered across the cracked concrete, spun to a stop.

"All right, Tommy," Colt said. "You come on out now, real slow."

Dowd's shaggy mane of red hair emerged from the side of the dumpster; then the rest of him followed, hands raised. He limped, his right foot pumping blood out of his shoe to splash onto the concrete, leaving a bright red trail. He grimaced with every step.

"Walk toward me," Colt said.

"Goddam, man, I'm shot," Tommy squealed.

"So I see. Walk."

When Dowd got a few feet away from the dumpster, Colt told him to stop. "Knees," he said. "Hands behind your head."

He heard two cops come up behind him. A glance revealed blue—city cops. They had their weapons drawn as well. "That was fast," he said as he moved toward Dowd.

"Don't thank us," one cop called after him. "You're likely going to have to explain to our chief what you're doing in town. This ain't your jurisdiction."

Colt walked behind Dowd. "Who shot you?"

Another groan and grimace. "I did," he said in a low voice. "That stupid gun went off while I was running."

Colt shook his head, patted Dowd down and cuffed him, dragged him, howling, to his feet. To the city cops he said, "Call an ambulance. I'm arresting this suspect in connection with a murder. In the county. And I'm taking that pistol over there with me. As for jurisdiction, take it up with your boss. I'm the goddam sheriff."

He marched a whimpering Dowd to his car, stuffed him in the back seat. "Ambulance is on the way," he said.

He walked back to the city cops.

"Look," he said. "I know I probably should have coordinated with the city police. But this all happened so quick, I didn't really have time. But I do appreciate the backup." He walked away and lifted Tommy's snub-nosed .38 pistol by the trigger guard with a pen. He left the city cops standing by their own squad car, shaking their heads.

CHAPTER TWENTY-FOUR

COLT

Colt finished off a double cheeseburger and fries from a drive-through on the way to the hospital. Every bite felt like he was swallowing a grenade.

"Next time, don't let me get this shit," he said.

John chuckled. "Next time, don't threaten to shoot me if you don't get to eat."

"Fair enough," Colt said through a mouthful.

John wheeled the car into the parking lot and killed the engine. Colt gathered up wrappers and ketchup packages, shoved it all in the paper sack it came in, and dropped it on the floorboard. They climbed out into the afternoon swelter, and Colt straightened, favoring his aching hip and hoping John didn't notice.

"After you," John said as they strode through the automatic doors of the emergency room and into a blast of cold from the air-conditioning.

They walked down a quiet, cool corridor past reception. They reached the elevators and John punched the button. Colt looked at him. "What are you thinking?"

John shook his head, looked away. "That we should stay the hell away from that apartment complex."

The elevator doors opened, and they stepped in. "Hey, at least you didn't get shot this time," Colt said.

"That's not what I meant and you know it," John said.

Colt pushed the button and the doors closed. "I know what you meant."

They stepped off the elevator on the fourth floor and walked in silence down the hall until Colt pushed his way through the heavy door to Tommy Dowd's room. Colt stopped short at the sight of Gideon Hayes standing by Dowd's bedside. The brown suit and shaggy hair made his scrawny frame more apt for a cornfield than the concerned attorney he presumed to be at the moment.

"Hello, Gideon," Colt said as John stepped around him. "Lowndes County's busiest public defender. You must be the fastest lawyer in town."

"Hello to you, Sheriff." Gideon frowned at both of them, then cut his eyes back to his client.

Colt smiled at Gideon, then the wounded Tommy Dowd. The overhead fluorescent lighting gave Dowd's wax-paper complexion a blue-tinged cast. He looked like a mannequin. Clearly, he'd been availing himself of the hospital's painkillers. A TV mounted on the wall added an absurd low-volume soundtrack as cartoons flickered on the screen, like a sort of digital fireplace. Dowd rolled a glassy, bovine eye at him and gave him and John a dead stare.

Gideon stood quietly over his client, hands behind his back.

"You must have broken land speed records to get here," Colt said to Hayes.

Gideon flashed a mustard-colored smile. "I try to do my job to the best of my abilities, Sheriff."

"Sheriff? Little formal, aren't we?"

Gideon shrugged, hands still behind his back. "You've made it abundantly clear that you despise me calling you by your given name."

"You're right," Colt said. "I do like you calling me Sheriff. And since you're here, *Counselor*, I have some questions for your client. And you know Deputy Carver."

"Has Mr. Dowd been apprised of his rights?" Gideon asked, not even acknowledging John, who glared at Hayes hard enough to break glass.

"Of course he has, Gideon," Colt said. "Same time I arrested him after he shot himself. Now, if you don't mind, I'm going to ask him some questions if he ain't too high to speak."

"Mr. Dowd may answer your questions, Sheriff," Gideon said, frowning at Colt and trying to nudge John out of the way. "But I'm going to stop you anytime I feel you're crossing the line and trying to get him to discuss matters that are outside the incident that brought him here."

Gideon clenched his jaws. Dowd seemed completely zoned out. Colt stepped to the bed rail and moved the magic morphine button out of his reach, which instantly brought the suspect around.

"Hey, man," Dowd said with a thick tongue.

"Tommy," Colt said as he leaned over the bed like a gargoyle. "I'm going to get straight to the point. Why'd you run?"

"You're kidding, right?" Tommy's mouth worked its way into a smile.

John stuck his hands in his pockets and leaned against the wall opposite the foot of the bed, under the TV. He kept his eyes on Gideon, who fidgeted like a sparrow on a twig.

"Come on, Tommy," Colt said. "You got nothing to hide, right? Other than a couple of possession charges. It's not like you're involved in a murder or anything."

Gideon snapped to his full gangly height. "Sheriff—"

"Shut up, Gideon," Colt said.

"I ain't killed nobody," Tommy said.

"I know that," Colt said. "Even though you managed to shoot yourself. How's that foot, by the way?"

Dowd pouted, looked over at Gideon, who just nodded. "Hurts like hell."

"I bet," Colt said. "Wait 'til the painkillers wear off. But looks like you got that under control. Look, Tommy, me and Deputy Carver over there just stopped by to ask you a few questions, before you decided to go off half-cocked." He smiled at his own joke, as did John. Gideon did not.

Tommy didn't catch the joke. He just looked up at Colt and said, "Questions about what?"

"Well, for one thing, why you ran."

Gideon stepped toward the bed. Tommy's eyes roamed the room. "Why you think? I thought you were going to arrest me. I had weed on me and a bunch of pills."

Colt looked up at Gideon. Shrugged. "I really wasn't planning to arrest him," he said.

"Then why were there at all, Sheriff?" Gideon said.

Colt frowned at Gideon, then turned his attention back to Dowd.

"Tommy, you work for Hank Claiborne, don't you?" Colt said. "What is it you do out there?"

Dowd's eyes drooped from the morphine, but he was still coherent. "Mostly in packaging," he said. "Packing up fish to send out on the trucks."

"Did you know Lucius Wallace?" Colt said.

"Who?"

"Lucius Wallace. He was the maintenance chief. He was killed this week."

Dowd's eyes grew wide. "Killed? How?"

"Don't matter right now," Colt said. "Did you know him?"

Dowd wet his lips with an equally dry tongue. "Yeah, I knew him. I mean, I know who he is. Was. Whatever."

"Y'all didn't work together?"

"Nuh-uh."

"Okay," Colt said. "So, why would your initials be in a notebook we found in Lucius' truck?"

Dowd suddenly seemed wide awake. "What notebook? I don't know what you're talking about."

Colt and John exchanged glances. They both knew Colt was onto something. "I think you know damn well what I'm talking about."

Dowd's head lolled side to side. "No, I really don't. Look, like I said, I don't know the man. Only thing I know about him, really, is that him and Mr. Claiborne got into some kind of argument a while back and after that he stayed away from just about everybody else."

Colt stood up straight. "What was the problem between him and Hank?"

"Ah, it was some stupid shit," Dowd said. "Mr. Claiborne had put up a Confederate flag on the farm. I didn't think nothing about it. I mean, hell, he had an American flag up, too. But I guess Lucius didn't like it, on account of his being black." Dowd rolled his eyes toward John. "No offense."

John crossed his arms over his chest. "Answer the sheriff's questions, Tommy."

Colt watched John for a second, then turned back to Tommy. "So, what happened?"

"I wasn't there when it happened," Dowd said. "But from what I heard, Lucius confronted Mr. Claiborne one morning when he was running the flag up the pole. Said it was offensive or some shit, that it was a sign of slavery or hating blacks, stuff like that. Him and Mr. Claiborne started yelling at each other, until finally Mr. Claiborne took the flag down."

John stepped toward the bed. "He took it down?"

Dowd nodded. "For about a week. Then he put it back up. And nobody said shit about it that time."

John looked over at Colt. Colt understood: *crackers in the woods…*

"Do you know if anybody else saw this argument?" Colt said.

"I ain't got no idea," Dowd said. "Probably that Jack Burnett guy. He's always around Mr. Claiborne, like he's an attack dog or something."

"Attack dog?" Colt said.

"He's some kind of military badass. Or was. Nobody ever wants to piss him off."

Colt thought back to Jack Burnett and understood why someone like Dowd would be afraid to piss him off. "Okay, Tommy, thanks." He moved the morphine button back to Dowd's pillow. "One more thing: what does WNC stand for?"

Dowd wrinkled his brow. "WNC? I don't know."

Colt put his hands on the bed rail, leaned over. "Tommy, don't start lying to me. I can't stand people who lie to me. Right now, you're not in that much trouble. Resisting arrest, discharging a firearm. But I'm sure Deputy Carver is going to find narcotics in that rathole you share with Tina when he searches your place."

Gideon cleared his throat. "Not without a warrant," he said.

John straightened up, pulled a folded document out of his hip pocket, waggled the pages at Gideon, who frowned, opened his mouth, then shut it.

"So, even though you haven't killed anybody, you're involved in this somehow, Tommy. So what does WNC mean?"

Dowd turned sullen and got interested in the cartoons on the TV.

John stepped past Gideon and dangled the search warrant over Dowd's face. He held it there as Tommy's eyes went wide.

"Stop intimidating my client," Gideon said.

"Gideon, the best thing your client can do at this point is cooperate with us in the hope for leniency," Colt said.

John, still boring holes into Tommy's skull with his cop stare, nodded. "The sheriff is right, Tommy."

Dowd's eyes sent a plea, or a surrender, to Gideon, who, for once, relented.

"I didn't kill nobody," Tommy said in a faraway voice.

Gideon held up his hand. "Sheriff, may I remind you my client is under sedation. I've had no advance notice of this alleged crime. If you intend to charge Mr. Dowd with a crime, I'll need time to consult with him."

"Oh, we intend," Colt said, shaking his head. Good old Gideon. "Me and John can step out in the hall and let you consult all you want, but the outcome is going to be the same."

"If you have information relevant to the matter at hand, Sheriff, that is, Mr. Dowd's alleged discharge of a firearm, I should know about that before we go further."

Dowd let out a whine like a squeezed puppy. "I don't know, man. I really don't. Ask some of the other guys that work there, the ones that were really pissed off at Lucius."

"Like Jack Burnett?" Colt said.

"He was one," Dowd said. "He said he was going to call a meeting about it. Never did, though. Not that I knew of, anyway."

Colt glanced at John, nodded toward the door. "All right, Tommy, that's enough for now."

Tommy's head jerked toward Gideon, then toward Colt. "Wait. What about me?"

"What about you?" Colt said. "You ain't going anywhere, and you got a lawyer. What more do you want?"

He and John walked into the hall.

"What are you thinking?" John said.

"That Jack Burnett needs to talk to us about this meeting he was trying to arrange."

They stepped off toward the elevators, and Colt's phone buzzed in his pocket. He answered it as John waited by the elevator doors.

"What's up, Molly?"

"I was able to get access to some databases," she said. He could hear the excitement in her voice.

"And?" he said.

"There have been several race-related incidents and arrests in Mississippi and Alabama over the last three years, which isn't surprising. But what is interesting is that a few of them call themselves by names that have 'White Nations' in them. White Nations Alliance, White Nations Brotherhood. I'd be willing to bet that the entries in Wallace's notebook are something similar."

"That is interesting," he said. "Keep looking. I'll fill you in on what Dowd just told me and John when I get back."

"Will do."

"And thanks, Molly. Good work." He hung up and stepped into the elevator with John, who looked at him expectantly. "We definitely are going to pay Burnett and Hank a visit."

"There's something else we need to do, Colt," John said.

"What's that?"

The elevator door pinged and John stepped into the fluorescent glow of the first-floor hallway. He turned to look at Colt. "I don't think Sanders is a suspect anymore. Maybe Lucius got killed because of that list of white men."

CHAPTER TWENTY-FIVE

COLT

Colt listened to Becky explain to him her opinion of the current workings of the murder investigation, which, to hear her tell it, consisted of her having to deal with all the unpleasant shit he didn't want to deal with even though he was the one who had caused it all in the first place. First, a damn near riot when the black community showed up in the office to protest and generally raise hell. Then, Colt decides to arrest Reverend Mike Sanders—the most well-known preacher in the county—without so much as a warning to her, and now she was getting phone call after phone call from reporters, notably that impertinent—she actually said "impertinent"—Craig Battles, who, as far as she was concerned, could take his notebook and shove it, and, besides, what in God's name was she supposed to tell these people?

Colt looked across the seat of the Crown Vic for the third time at John, who was having a grand time at his discomfort, not even trying to stifle a laugh.

"Look, Becky," Colt said when she took a breath.

"Don't 'look, Becky' me, Colt," she said, loud enough to make him pull his cell phone away from his ear. "You're not here to see all this."

"I know, and I will make it up to you, I swear," he said, even though he had no idea at all as to how he would do that. And John laughed again. "The word is the same: we are conducting an investigation and we can't comment on anything about that investigation."

Becky let out a ragged sigh. "People are mad, Colt."

"You mean white people."

"Yes, I mean white people. I guess it's their turn now. And some of them, quite frankly, are less than Christian in their comments."

"I have no doubt," Colt said. "I'll deal with that when I get back."

"You better."

"Thanks, Becky," he said, hanging up before she could continue. He tossed the phone to the seat. "Goddam, that woman can rant."

John settled down. "She has a point."

"Point or not, there ain't shit I can do about that right now. Are you ready?"

John's face turned serious. "I am. Question is, are you? You and Hank go back."

"And now you have a point?"

John held up his hands. "I'm just saying. This isn't the average lowlife we're going to question. I know how you get."

Colt opened the car door. "How do I get?"

John looked at him. "Seriously? Just try not to grind the guy down. Not yet, anyway."

"I'll be as charming as a beagle puppy," Colt said as he climbed out of the car.

"Somehow I doubt that," John said.

The same blond woman sat at the same desk on a day that was just as hot as the day of Colt's last visit. She smiled when he and John walked through the door.

"Sheriff Harper, good to see you again," she said.

"Ma'am," he said, stopping at her desk. "I'm sorry, but I didn't get your name last time."

She batted her eyes at him. "It's Holly."

"Is Hank in this afternoon, or does he just have you working on a Saturday?"

"He is." Holly said. "I have every other Saturday off. We work a lot of shifts here, because the farm has to be looked after every day of the week. Do you have an appointment with Hank, Sheriff?"

"Sure don't. I just thought I'd stop by."

Holly rose to her feet at the same time that Hank Claiborne's office door flew open. Hank stood there, hand on the knob, grinning. "Hey, Colt, I thought I heard your voice."

Colt glanced at Holly. "Thanks," he said.

"Anytime, Sheriff," Holly said. She sat and resumed working.

"Thought I might have a word," Colt said to Hank, who looked past him at John. "This is Deputy John Carver."

Hank shrugged. "Sure, y'all come on in."

The three men settled into chairs, Hank behind his desk, John and Colt in chairs opposite.

"So, what can I do for you today?" Hank said.

Colt placed one ankle on his knee. "John and I are still investigating the death of Lucius Wallace, Hank. We're following up on a couple of leads."

"Leads?" Hank said. He leaned back in his chair, smiling at Colt, maybe even enjoying the attention.

"Seems that you and Lucius got into some kind of argument a while back," Colt said. "You care to fill us in on that?"

Hank stopped smiling. Still comfortable, but no longer warm. "Argument? Can't say as I recall any kind of argument."

John leaned forward in his chair. "Had to do with you putting up a Confederate flag here at the farm. That ring any bells?"

Hank cocked his head, gave John a long look. "Oh, that," he said. "Yes, I do recall that. Lucius and I discussed the matter, and I took care of it."

Colt glanced over at John, who wasn't taking his own advice. "Hank," he said, "we heard it was more than a discussion. That the two of you argued about the flag out there on your property as you were putting it up."

Hank shook his head, as if the incident barely was worth mentioning. "It certainly didn't turn out to be anything. I was going to fly that flag about a month ago, on General Forrest's birthday, as a, you know, show of respect."

"Respect?" John said, "For the founder of the Ku Klux Klan?"

Hank sat forward, elbows on his desk. His face darkened; then he thought better of it. "That's actually not true, Deputy," he said, the ingratiating smile back. "And, yes, respect. I have ancestors who fought alongside one of the greatest military commanders in American history. So did you, Colt, if I recall."

John turned his head toward Colt, who ignored him. "That's true, Hank, but it's also beside the point. What was the substance of the argument with Lucius?"

Hank spread his hands. "He said it was offensive to him as a black man, which was something I never intended. Never considered, actually. Which I told him. But he got pretty angry about it. The more I tried to explain, the madder he got. So, I said fine, I'll take it down. And I did."

"And that satisfied Lucius?" Colt said.

"Seemed to," Hank said. "We never talked about it again."

"What about when you put it back up about a week later?" John said.

Hank cut his eyes toward John, then back to Colt. "Like I said, we never talked about it again. I put the flag back up because, after all, this is my damn farm and my business. I can run it the way I like. And we'd settled that issue like grown men."

Colt watched Hank closely. True enough, he'd known the man for decades, save the years he'd been away in the Marine Corps. He'd always been a pretty standard, normal guy. But his answers were too clean, too easy, and he'd caught the looks he'd given John. "You better hope so," he said.

"The hell is that supposed to mean, Colt?" Hank said. No trace of a smile.

"The man did show up dead," Colt said. "Not too long after having an argument with his employer over a racial issue."

"Racial issue?" Hank said, spitting the words like they tasted foul. "I hope you're not accusing me of being a racist. Because that's what it sounds like. And it sounds like you think I had something to do with Lucius getting killed."

"Did you?" Colt said before he could stop himself.

Hank looked like he'd been slapped. "Colt, friend or not, sheriff or not, I ought to throw you out of here for that. I don't think I need to remind you, right here in front of your deputy, that I donated money to both your election campaigns. A lot of money. And I have never done anything that warrants you coming in here with a badge and accusing me of something like that."

Colt let the air hang heavy between them for a few heartbeats. "Fair enough," he said when Hank said nothing else. "Just doing the job you helped get me elected to do."

Hank glared at him, then bobbed his head once. "Apology accepted. Now, do you have anything else?"

"Actually, yes," Colt said. "Thank you for sending the list of employees over to my office. I gave it a look and noticed that Jack Burnett's name wasn't on there."

Hank relaxed. "Jack's pretty new and the new employee list hasn't been put out."

Colt nodded. "Where's he from?"

"He came to me from a farm over in the Delta," Hank said, obviously relieved the conversation had shifted. "He's originally from Montgomery. But he left there, went to the Delta and then here."

"Yeah, I thought he might be from somewhere else," Colt said. "By the way, do you own a gun?"

"Course I do," Hank said. "Ruger nine-millimeter. Like half the men in the county."

"Right. One more question," Colt said. "I was at a community meeting last night. Lot of the black community is really upset over Wallace's death. Not so much the death as much as the way he was killed. Several of them said they heard rumors about a group of men possibly organizing in the county to attack them."

"Really?" Hank said. "That's preposterous. That stuff doesn't happen anymore, and even if it did, I wouldn't know anything about it."

"I didn't think so, but I had to ask. And you know a lot of people in this county. And you have a lot of employees."

Hank grinned. "I'm lucky to have a lot. But I haven't heard anything at all along those lines. Not that I would, of course."

Colt didn't return the grin. "Of course. Thanks for clearing that up, Hank." He stood, and John followed suit. "You hear anything, let me know."

Hank remained seated. "You bet, Colt."

Back in the car, John looked over at Colt. "You're not going to want to hear this, but he's lying."

Colt cranked up the Crown Vic. "I know that. I just don't what know he's lying about."

CHAPTER TWENTY-SIX

HANK

Hank Claiborne watched Harper and his deputy walk out of his office, listened for the opening and closing of the main door, then waited another minute before reaching into the bottom drawer on the left-hand side of his desk and yanking out a half-full bottle of whiskey. He needed a goddam drink. He splashed bourbon into the coffee cup on his desk he used for such things. He took a long pull, felt the hot sting of bourbon slide down his throat, shivered. Took another. Slammed the cup on the desk.

He leaned over to his phone, punched the button for Holly, and told her to have Jack come to the office. He waited until she hung up, then slammed the phone back into the receiver.

He had just refilled the cup when Jack walked in, looking cool even with a sheen of sweat across his cheeks and forehead. Hank motioned Jack into a seat, took another pull of booze, even though he knew he should slow down. He could already feel the buzz wrapping around him like a warm, numbing blanket.

"I just had another visit from the sheriff," Hank said. He wiped his mouth with the back of his hand. "And I don't like his questions."

Jack raised his eyebrows. "I could have guessed that from the smell of liquor. What did he want?"

Hank ignored the booze comment. "He was asking about Wallace. Specifically, about that argument we had over the flag."

"What did you tell him?"

"That it was nothing. That I took the thing down. That we settled the issue."

Jack scratched his beard, his face blank. "I hope your old pal the sheriff believed that. Did he?"

Hank looked at Jack like he was a slow child. Surely he was smarter than that. "Yeah. I mean, I think so. But I don't like him asking questions."

"How did he even know about it?" Jack said.

Hank shrugged. "How in the hell do I know? Plenty of people either saw it or heard about it. It was right there in the open. But that don't matter anyway. He's already sniffing around it."

Jack ran a hand through his hair, like he had somewhere better to be. "Let him sniff. He ain't got nothing. Otherwise, you wouldn't be sitting here. You and him would be having that conversation at his jail."

Hank thought about it. He wasn't convinced it was the booze changing his mood, but Jack had a point. Harper hadn't even made a move to arrest him or bring him in for questioning. "Maybe," he said.

Hank raised his head. "Goddammit, Jack, you really put me in a spot here. Not just me. Us. All of us."

Jack crossed his arms. His eyes narrowed. "I put *you* in a spot? How you figure?"

"You were only supposed to scare the shit out of him," Hank said. "That was the original job. That was the only job."

Jack snorted. "I did scare him, for sure."

"What did happen?"

"I put the scare in him, just like we talked about. He took a swing at me, and I scared him some more."

"Some more," Hank said slowly. "What does that mean?"

"What difference does it make?" Jack shifted in his seat, and for the first time in the conversation, Hank felt a ripple of fear. "Are you questioning me?"

Whatever courage the liquor had given him left Hank's body. He coughed. "No, of course not. Done is done, right?"

Jack's jaw flexed. "Right."

"Right. We have to be as careful as goddam mice now."

Jack didn't move. He just stared at a spot over Hank's head. "I don't need lessons on being careful, Hank," he said. "I can do my job. You need to make sure your pal the sheriff doesn't come around anymore."

Hank nodded. He knew he'd had too many drinks because he wanted another one. Soon as Jack left, he would. "I will," he said.

CHAPTER TWENTY-SEVEN

COLT

Colt walked the corridor to the cells, turned right at the end, and followed the fluorescent glow to the last cell on the right. He worked the key and opened the door. Reverend Mike Sanders, still dressed in his suit pants and white shirt, though both were now nearly destroyed by wrinkles, lay on his back with a forearm over his eyes. Socked feet crossed at the ankles.

"Reverend," Colt said.

Sanders snatched his arm from his face at the sound of Colt's voice. "Sheriff?" he said. His voice was tired, and he looked ten years older than he had just the day before.

"You're free to go," Colt said, sliding his hands in his pockets.

Sanders laughed, a harsh bark, then swung his feet to the floor. "Just like that? I'm free to go? What happened, Sheriff?"

"Just like that," Colt said. "We've gotten more information in our investigation. Enough to show us that you are no longer a suspect."

"I suppose it's too much to expect a man like you to apologize for an unlawful arrest of an innocent man," Sanders said, looking up at Colt.

"It's not too much," Colt said. "But don't push it. At the time, you had motive, means, and opportunity. That made you the most likely suspect. But new information says different."

"New information," Sanders said.

"That's right," Colt said. The man was getting on his nerves, preacher or not. The man-of-God routine was wearing thin. "You want to tell me about this community action group meeting you and Lucius were organizing?"

Sanders stared at him with hard eyes. "You said I'm free to go?"

Colt stared back at him. "You are."

Sanders stood, straightened his shirt. "Then I would like to do that. I have nothing more to say to you."

Colt stepped back and pushed the cell door open. A deputy had arrived unheard—Moore, the new one—and nodded at Colt. "Deputy Moore," Colt said. "Please take Reverend Sanders to Admin for discharge."

"Yes, sir," Moore said. He led Sanders away.

CHAPTER TWENTY-EIGHT

REGGIE

The inside of the Miss-Ala Lounge wasn't very crowded, especially for a Saturday evening. Reggie surveyed the dimly lit room. No players at the pool table in the back of the room. Nobody sitting at the bar. Alan, the bartender, leaned over one corner of the Formica-covered countertop, reading the newspaper spread out before him.

Reggie sipped the longneck beer in front of him. Five of the small picnic tables in the building, which took up most of the concrete floor, were empty. He and two other men occupied the remaining one. Across the scarred wooden picnic table, Rich did the same. Rich was wearing his work shirt—he'd snuck off from the garage he worked at when Reggie had called. Beside him sat Larry Eads, a half-gone mug of draft beer in front of him.

"So, what did you call us out here for, Reggie?" Rich said.

"What, a man can't call up a couple of guys for a beer?" Reggie said, grinning in the gloom.

Larry belched. "Fine with me. Ain't like I was working, anyway."

All three laughed at that. Reggie took another swig of beer and checked his watch. Lamarr was running late. He'd enticed Lamarr with the promise of big cash and an easy score: a bar with a safe full of cash and only one bartender. All he had to do was walk in and take the money. Reggie would keep an eye on things in the place and back him up, and they could split the haul. Lamarr's eyeballs practically turned into dollar signs when Reggie told him how easy it would be to knock over the place. They'd agreed on today for the hit, right about now.

"True," Rich said, "but I'm gone have to get back to work before the boss raises hell about it. I told him I had to take care of some shit at my kid's school."

"Relax," Reggie said. "Drink your damn beer."

Reggie saw the door to the bar swing open—Larry and Rich had their backs to the entrance. Lamarr stepped into the room, sweaty and nervous, and swiveled his head around the room. Reggie ducked his head; Lamarr didn't focus on him and stepped to the bar with jerky steps. The kid was scared out of his mind. He kept his right hand in his pocket as Alan looked up from his newspaper and took in the sight of a skinny black kid in his bar.

Alan sidled down the length of the bar. "You lost, boy?"

Lamarr swallowed and scowled at Alan.

Reggie leaned over the table and whispered to Larry and Rich. "Hey, check this shit out."

Larry and Rich turned their heads, then sat up straight.

"What is *he* doing here?" Rich said.

Larry's hand went to his belly. Reggie saw it and shook his head. "Don't. Neither one of you do anything. I got this one." He eased a nine-millimeter from the back of his jeans and held it with both hands under the table.

At the bar, Lamarr had Alan's full attention.

"I got a gun," Lamarr said. "Give me what you got in the register and the safe."

"The safe?" Alan said, his eyes on the hand in Lamarr's pocket. "I ain't got a safe."

Confusion clouded Lamarr's face for a second, then disappeared back into the scowl. "The register, then. Give it to me."

"Or what?" Alan said, still eyeing Lamarr's pocket.

"Or I shoot every motherfucker in here," Lamarr said.

"Oh really?" Alan said. He reached under the bar, cat quick, and came up with a revolver leveled at Lamarr. "You sure about that?"

Lamarr backed up three steps. "Whoa now, man, you don't want to do that. You hear me? I ain't lying. I know you got money in here and I aim to get it. You don't want to mess with me."

Alan held the gun steady. Lamarr, sweat rolling down his temples, crouched like he was about to steal second, yanked out a small automatic pistol and fired a shot that went wide of Alan. He turned and sprinted for the door.

Reggie jumped to his feet, his own pistol at the ready, just as Alan fired. The bullet caught Lamarr somewhere near his head and he spun a full circle into the door, pushed his way through. A blade of sunlight lanced through the room for a second before the door slammed shut.

The report of the gun in the confined space deafened Reggie, and the smell of cordite cut through the stale air. Alan's eyes were wide, and he looked at the weapon in his hands as if he was surprised to see it.

Larry and Rich leapt from their seats, weapons drawn and pointing at the door.

"What was that?" Larry yelled.

"Holy shit," Rich said, looking at a wide blood trail at the door. "I think you got him, Alan."

Alan plunked the gun on the bar. His now-empty hands shook.

Reggie pulled his cell phone from his jeans and dialed the number for the local TV station. When a woman answered, he said, "Y'all better send somebody out to the Miss-Ala Lounge."

"What? I'm sorry, what did you say?" the woman said.

"A, uh, black guy just got into a whole bunch of trouble with some guys out here. You might want to send a news crew or whatever."

He hung up and stuck his pistol back in his pants. "You all right, Alan?"

CHAPTER TWENTY-NINE

COLT

"Becky, if you're still talking to them, let them know I'm two minutes out," Colt said over the car radio. He pushed the accelerator on the Crown Vic, watched the red speedometer needle jump.

"Will do, Colt," Becky said from her dispatcher's desk, her voice staticky over the air. "John just got there. Ambulance is on the way."

"Roger," Colt said. He tossed the handset to the seat and piloted the hurtling car down Highway 69 South toward the Miss-Ala Lounge. A minute later, the scene loomed in front of him: John's marked car, blue lights rotating like lighthouse beams, sat to the right of the square white cinder-block building, thirty feet from the bar's open front door, which was filled with the figure of a man.

Colt swerved into the gravel parking lot, passenger side toward the front of the building, and killed the engine. Ten feet from the door, John crouched over the supine figure of another man, this one younger than the man standing in the doorway and black. Colt saw a crimson fan of blood around John's feet. Sweat shone on John's ebony face, highlighting his anger and worry. Off to the right sat a TV remote van from Channel 4. A cameraman and a female reporter were going through their equipment checks.

Colt swung his car door open and marched toward the TV truck. The reporter saw him and started walking toward him. "Stop right there," he said to the woman. She stopped.

"You can't be here," Colt said. "This is an active crime scene and we don't have anything contained. You're going to have to get out of here."

The reporter looked back at her cameraman, held up a hand that said *Stay back*, then faced Colt. "You can't make us leave, Sheriff."

"No, but I can arrest your ass for interfering in a crime scene. Just stay back there until I know it's safe." He turned and ran the ten yards to John, his hip screaming in pain. He knelt by John's side and looked over his deputy's sweaty arms and bloodstained hands.

The young man's face—Colt could see he looked to be in his early twenties—lay slack, eyelids fluttering. His neck was bathed in bright red blood around the bandage John pressed against a wound. The kid looked bad.

"What happened?" Colt said.

John jerked his head toward the bar, his eyes still on the man bleeding under his hands. "We got a call. Man with a gun trying to rob the place. We got here pretty fast, but when I was pulling in I saw him on the ground. Then the door flew open and the bartender was there. I told him to stay put and got to work on this guy here. Asshole is just standing there."

Colt peeked over his shoulder. The bartender looked nervous as shit and made an attempt to raise his hands.

"Anybody inside?" Colt said.

John lifted a bloody hand, swiped sweat off his forehead, replaced it on the kid's bandage.

"No idea. My hands been full."

Colt straightened out his left leg to ease the pain in his hip. "He carrying?"

John jerked his head toward his vehicle. "On the hood. A little piece-a-shit .32 auto. Where's that fucking ambulance?"

"On the way," Colt said. He stood and faced the bartender, one hand on his pistol. The bartender clearly didn't know what to do, and he made the stupid decision to put his hands in his pockets. Colt drew on him and leveled the .45 at the man's chest.

"Don't move," Colt yelled. "And keep your hands where I can see them."

The bartender's face flushed, then went white, and he held his trembling hands out to his sides.

"Get down on your knees, hands behind your head," Colt said. The man complied.

Keeping the gun trained on him, Colt moved to the door and got a closer look at the bartender, a thirty-something man, trembling. Jeans, red golf shirt. Worn-out running shoes.

"Hey," Colt said. "Sheriff Harper. Who are you?"

"Alan Wright."

Colt heard the distant wailing of a siren. Ambulance. Glanced at John, who heard it, too.

"Are you armed, Alan?" Colt said as he patted the man down. No weapons.

"No."

"Anybody else in there?"

"About three guys."

"Armed?"

"I got no idea."

Colt drew his handcuffs, slapped them on Alan's wrists behind his back, pulled him to his feet. "Okay, Mr. Wright, I don't have time for a longer conversation at the moment, so I'm sticking you in the back of my car. Don't go anywhere, and don't touch anything."

A nod. Colt half dragged Wright to the Crown Vic, opened the back door, and shoved him in. Slammed the door and turned to the bar just as a car engine roared and another vehicle swooped into the lot in a thick brown cloud of dust.

Molly was out and at his side before the engine had died down, and he stared at her with a mix of bewilderment and admiration.

"Heard Becky on the radio as soon as I got in," she said. "Figured you might need some backup. What's going on?"

"Shooting," he said, pointing toward John, who ignored them. "Bartender is in the back of my car. He said there's three more in the building there."

Molly swiveled her head, surveyed the scene. "Okay, let's go."

"That was my plan, hotshot."

The sound of the sirens grew to a nerve-rattling howl, and Colt watched as a white Lowndes County ambulance swooped into the lot, skidded to a stop ten feet from John and the kid. Two EMTs vaulted out, the passenger-side tech hauling a medical kit the size of a carry-on bag. Both wore blue uniforms and grim expressions. The driver, a sandy-haired woman with freckles and a furrowed brow, scurried to John's side and with a low voice said, "I got him, Deputy," and nudged John away. John clearly wasn't sure about letting go but conceded when the second EMT, a dark-haired man who looked just out of high school, popped open the kit and started yanking out bandages, tubes, and a blood-pressure cuff. The woman nudged John's muscular arm again, and he relented.

Colt and Molly stepped to the door, Colt on the left, Molly on the right, both with weapons drawn. Colt pushed the door with his free hand.

"Hey!" Colt yelled toward the dark interior. "This is Sheriff Harper. I don't know who you are or if you're armed. But one person is already hurt pretty bad. The ambulance crew is about to put him on a gurney and get him to a hospital. If you throw your weapons out right now and walk out with your hands in the air, things won't get worse than they already are. But if you take one more shot or interfere with these EMTs doing their jobs, it's going to get real bad for you."

He glanced over at Molly. All business, like the federal agent she used to be, not the nervous wreck of the night before. He was surprised at the relief he felt. He heard scuffling inside, people moving around. Then: "Sheriff, three of us is carrying. We're putting our pieces on the bar and coming out."

"Do it careful," Colt said.

More shuffling, then three clunks as weapons were deposited. Then three men appeared, single file, hands in the air. All three were variations on a theme: working-class, mean-eyed hard drinkers.

"Against the wall," Colt said. The men lined up shoulder to shoulder, all watching the EMTs with impassive faces. "Molly, search these guys."

He holstered his weapon and quick-stepped to the car, opened the door and stared at Alan Wright's stricken face.

"Okay, Alan, what happened in there?"

Alan drew a ragged breath. "Well, he just walked in and told me to give him the money in the register and the safe. Course, I don't got no safe, and I told him that. He said if I didn't hand over the money in the register, he'd shoot every motherfucker in the place. His words, not mine, Sheriff. He looked like he was about to pull a gun out, and I keep a pistol under the bar. Pulled it out and told him to get the hell out of here. I had the gun on him by that point. He came at me like he was about to come over the bar, then took a shot at me, and I shot him."

"*You* shot him?"

Alan winced at the words, then hung his head. "I didn't really mean to. But, goddam, he was acting like a fool."

"And then what?"

"He staggered out into the parking lot and one of the customers called 911," Alan said, staring at the floorboard. "I's scared shitless, Sheriff."

"I'm sure. You stay here, ahite?"

He walked back to the three men, now leaning against the wall. One, the tallest of the bunch, smirked at Molly, who held her weapon in two hands, pointed at the ground. "Mind if I smoke?" he said.

"Yeah, I do," Molly said.

Colt studied the three. To look at them, they were just three men standing on a street corner, rather than witnesses to a violent crime that had happened within the last half hour. "What's your name?"

A smirk. "Reggie Cash."

"Reggie, what happened in there?" Colt said. Behind him, the female EMT ran in a crouch to the rear of the ambulance. She snatched the rear door open, and he heard her grunt as she heaved out the gurney, followed by the clattering of metal as the gurney wheels extended. Colt turned to face the scene as he heard the ambulance doors slam and the engine crank up.

"That nigger boy there came waltzing in demanding money," Reggie said. "Said he was going to pull a gun."

"Did he? Pull a gun?"

"Hell yeah he did," Reggie said. "Took a shot at the bartender, but he missed. That's when Alan plugged him. I didn't really see it, but I know the bartender was the better shot."

Colt glanced at the other two men, who were listening intently. "You didn't see it? What *were* you looking at?"

Reggie leaned against the wall. "The door, mostly. Figuring out how that little shit was planning on getting away without getting shot."

"Did you pull a weapon?" Molly asked.

He turned his eyes toward her. The movement reminded Colt of a rat. "You want me to pull my piece, sweetheart?" The other two men grinned.

"You want me to take out your kneecap?" Molly said.

Colt found that exchange only slightly funny. "She'll do it," he said to Reggie. "So answer the questions. Did you pull a weapon?"

"No," Reggie said.

"What about you two?" Colt pointed at the other men. Both shook their heads. "Is that the way it went down?" Two nods.

"Did any of you ever see a weapon?"

The man on the end, a short man with a belly under a pale blue uniform shirt with a patch that read RICHARD, said, "I did. But it all happened so fast. The guy told the bartender to give him the money, and then bartender pulls a gun from under the counter. I thought, well, he better get his ass on out of here, but then he pulled out a pistol and fired off a shot. Then he took off for the door, but the bartender shot him on the way out."

"Sumbitch probably deserved it," Reggie said. "About time this started happening."

The other two men jerked their heads toward him. The short one, Richard, scowled and muttered, "Shut up, Reggie."

Colt watched their reaction. "What do you mean?" he said to Reggie.

"He's a damn dopehead, and he come up here threatening folks, disturbing the peace and whatnot. Probably was a criminal anyway."

"Goddammit, Reggie," the short one said.

"All right, that's enough," Colt said. "IDs, all of you."

The men produced driver's licenses from worn wallets: Richard Wayne, the short one; Larry Eads, in the middle; and Reggie Cash, who carried an Alabama license.

"Alabama?" Colt said to him. "Where?"

"Montgomery," Reggie said.

Colt glanced over at Molly, who'd noticed the same thing.

Colt handed the licenses back, then pulled out his cell phone. Stood in front of each, snapped mug shots. "So I don't forget," he said. "Y'all better stay your asses in town for the time being, because I'm going to want to talk to each of you. And don't make me come looking for you. McDonough, let's go."

Colt turned to see John standing in the door of the bar. "Colt, I got three handguns on a table and a revolver on the bar."

"Bag them," he said. "And see if you can find the bullet the perp might have fired."

Reggie Cash took a step toward him. "Hey, wait a minute, those are our guns."

Colt faced Cash. "Get your ass back against that wall. Those weapons are now part of a criminal investigation. And every one of you is going to need to give me an official statement at my office."

Cash opened his mouth as if to say something, then clamped his jaw shut.

As Colt and Molly walked back to the car, Molly squinted at him. "Didn't you tell me Jack Burnett is from Montgomery?"

"I did, and I knew you picked up on that," Colt said. "Meet me back in the office. I have to arrest and book Mr. Wright here."

"That's not a coincidence," she said.

"I don't think so, either, but it's thin," Colt said. "Before you take off, let me ask you something."

"Shoot."

He hooked a thumb over his shoulder. "This place, this bar, you okay with, you know, all the alcohol? Especially those three idiots reeking of booze?"

Molly squinted at him, blue eyes hitting him like lasers. "It's not a problem. This is work. Part of the job. I'm good." She climbed in her car and drove off.

As he approached the Crown Vic, Colt caught his reflection in one of the windows. His own image scowled back at him, black hair sticking out, salt-and-pepper stubble making him look as old as he felt. And the weight he'd lost over the last few months had sharpened his features, making him look tired.

CHAPTER THIRTY

COLT

He walked the corridor after depositing Alan Wright with the booking deputy and confronted a suspicion that had been nagging at him for the last couple of days: maybe there *was* a group of white men up to no good in his county. Two violent racial incidents in the last week. Both connected—even only by the thinnest of margins—to Hank Claiborne's business. Could be a coincidence, despite Molly's doubts. Burnett and Cash both being from Montgomery. Burnett, Dowd, and Wallace all working for Hank. Hank and Wallace having words. He knew better than to trust his gut when it came to investigations, but lumping Hank Claiborne into this mess didn't seem to fit.

He passed Becky's desk. She, as always, sat hunched over her keyboard, headset clamped on her blond head, a yellow sticky note dangling off one finger. Same with Molly, minus the sticky note. She was engrossed in her laptop at the desk she'd claimed since coming aboard, the one next to John's currently empty desk. Molly's fingers flew on her keyboard like a concert pianist's. God only knew what she was digging up.

He entered his office and eased into his chair, sighing relief for his hip. Becky walked in just as he got comfortable.

"What's up?" he said to her, trying not to grimace.

"Channel 4 has been broadcasting from the scene at the Miss-Ala for over an hour," she said. "And protesters are starting to gather downtown at city hall."

"Who's protesting?"

"I don't know, but I think the crowd is mostly black."

Colt shook his head. What next? "Is it violent?"

"No. Not yet, but you know how these things can get."

"Yes, I do," Colt said. "Call the city PD and get word to the chief that if he needs us for backup, I'll support him."

"Will do, Colt," Becky said as she turned and left.

Colt rubbed his head and stared at the window. Thought about the anger he'd seen at the community meeting. And how easily that anger could turn into a protest that would be an outlet for that anger. And confrontation.

He turned to his computer, hit a few keys, and brought up the state crime database. Punched in Reggie Cash's name. He scanned down the report that came onto the screen. Cash was, surprisingly, clean. Only one arrest: disturbing the peace a year ago, at an address he recognized as a bar on the state line.

He sat up in his chair. The man seemed to have a thing for the state line. Cash's record was also flagged by the Mississippi Bureau of Investigation. To view it, he'd have to call the Alabama state office.

He grabbed the phone from his desk and punched in the number shown on the screen. He listened until he heard, "If you are a member of a law enforcement agency, press three." He did so and listened to a few seconds of weird string music before a voice came on the line: "Administration, how may I help you?"

"Sheriff Harper, Lowndes County, Mississippi," he said. "I'm conducting a homicide investigation, and I noticed that one of the files I'm trying to access has a flag on it. Was wondering if you could help me out."

"Sure thing, Sheriff," the female voice replied. "Do you have a case number?"

He read off the number at the top of Cash's file.

"Thanks, just give me a second," the administrator said. He heard keys clacking. "Okay," the woman said, "I can email this to you via encrypted file."

"That'd be great," he said. He dug a pain pill from his pocket and popped it in his mouth. "How long will that take?"

"I just sent it."

Surprised, he brought up his email screen. And there it was. "Thanks very much."

"You're welcome. Anything else I can help you with?"

"No, you've been very helpful," he said and hung up.

He scanned the report, his concern growing with every line. When he'd read the first page, he rose from his desk, went to the door, and called for Molly.

When she was in and seated, he pointed to the computer screen. "What were you saying about the Montgomery thing not being a coincidence?"

Molly tucked an errant strand of hair behind her ear. "There was something about it that triggered my memory," she said. "I've been trying to track it down since I got back to my desk."

"Go on," Colt said.

"I did some digging," she said. "And it came to me. About three years ago, there was a car explosion in Montgomery, a city councilman's car. A black city councilman. And it got classified as a hate crime, which got the feds involved, of course. Especially ATF. I read over some of the reports at the time, but all I remember is that a lot of men—white men—were questioned as being part of some kind of nascent white-supremacy group, but no such group was ever discovered. Eventually, ATF tracked down and arrested the bomber. Don't remember his name, but he was convicted on the hate crimes charge."

Colt turned to his screen. "Then you're going to find this real interesting."

Molly pulled her chair up to his desk and leaned forward.

"I just got this," he said. "Reggie Cash was detained by the Alabama State Bureau of Investigation, questioned by the FBI and ATF in connection with that same car bomb. Part of that search for white-supremacy groups you just mentioned. He was held overnight for questioning but released with no charges."

Molly sat back in her chair, thinking. "And now he's here."

Colt nodded. "Just like Jack Burnett, also from Montgomery. But there's nothing on him."

"Yet," Molly said.

"Right."

"I'll look into that," Molly said.

"Because you know people," Colt said, not bothering to keep the sarcasm out of his voice.

"Hell yeah, I know people," Molly said, grinning.

"Okay, you do that," Colt said. "Meanwhile, I think we should go talk to Reggie Cash."

DAY SIX

CHAPTER THIRTY-ONE

MOLLY

If there was ever a case of a domicile reflecting the personality of its owner, Reggie Cash's trailer would be leading the list. The single-wide had a sullen look to it, perched off the side of the highway in the center of a piece of flat, barren ground. It stood alone, practically daring anyone to approach. Questionable rusted steps led up to a worn aluminum door that was the same faded mustard color of the entire exterior.

Molly stared at the sad shack through the windshield, sipping coffee from a paper cup. Colt sat behind the steering wheel. He pointed at the vehicle parked next to the trailer.

"Looks like he's home," he said. "And I'll bet you that pickup is worth more than that trailer."

Molly shook her head. "I'm not taking that bet."

They walked in step until Colt got to the stairs, which were only wide enough for one person to stand on. Colt banged on the door with a fist while she scanned the area. She heard noises from inside: thumps, cussing, more thumps.

The door swung open to reveal an inebriated Reggie Cash. Wearing the same clothes as before, but more disheveled, if that was even possible. His lips were drawn tight across his face in a kind of slapped-on smile caused by booze, and he planted his feet wide apart to steady himself. It didn't work; he stood there weaving with his drunken grin.

"Well, I be got-dam," Reggie said. "Sheriff Harper." He looked down toward Molly. "And Little Miss Muffet."

Harper put one hand on the door, keeping it from closing. "Reggie, *Deputy McDonough* and I have some questions for you. Mind if we come in?"

Reggie squinted one eye shut; the other tried to focus. "You got a fucking warrant?"

"We don't need a warrant to ask you questions," Harper said. "But we could do this back at my jail, if you prefer."

Reggie reeled backward at the sound of the word "jail," put up his hands in surrender. "Hell naw, ain't no sense in being all assholey about it," he said. He turned, shuffled into the interior of the trailer. "Y'all come on in, ask your goddam questions."

Harper gave Molly a glance over his shoulder and stepped inside the squalor of the Cash residence. She bounded up the steps behind him, then stopped in the doorway. "Whoa," she said, wrinkling her nose.

Reggie knocked some magazines off the couch, and Molly caught a glimpse of naked women on the pages as they rattled to the floor. He collapsed on the couch, arms and legs spread, head bobbing. "Have a seat," he said.

She and Harper surveyed the detritus that filled up the room. A ton of bottles, beer and whiskey, along with the skin mags. Furniture decorated with burn marks and liquid stains. On the kitchen counter sat a lawn mower motor. How a human being could live like this was beyond her.

"We'll stand," Harper said.

"I was talking to that little redhead," Reggie said. He cackled until he doubled over, coughing.

Molly moved beside Harper, put her hand on the pistol on her right hip, hoping Cash would do something stupid. Harper shot her a look that said, *Don't.*

"Reggie, how long you been in Mississippi?" Harper said.

"About a year," Reggie said.

"You should have gotten a Mississippi driver's license," Harper said. "That's what tipped me off."

"To what?" Reggie dug around under his butt, came up with a smashed pack of cigarettes. He pulled out a bent cigarette and held it up for inspection, then stuck it into his permanent smile.

"The fact that you were questioned by the feds a few years ago about a hate crime."

Reggie cough-laughed. "Hate crime? That was bullshit. They didn't know their ass from deep left field."

"What is it that you do over here, anyway?" Harper said. "You got a job?"

"Hell yeah, I gotta job."

"Doing what?"

Reggie pushed himself into a semi-straight position on the couch. "What damn difference does it make?"

Molly stepped toward the couch. "Just answer the question, Reggie."

Reggie heaved himself up and took a tentative step toward her. She didn't move. "I got a job," he said slowly. He took another step toward Molly; again, she didn't move. Hand still on her pistol. "I got something else for you, too."

Molly stared back at him. "We've already covered that ground."

Reggie straightened himself to his full height, as if to tower over Molly. He let out a laugh. "Come on, now, don't be that way." He reached toward her.

Before Reggie's hand could come to rest on Molly's shoulder, she grabbed his wrist and twisted hard enough to damn near break it. Reggie screamed in pain, the high-pitched squeal of sudden agony, and his knees buckled. Molly turned toward him, smashed his left knee with a vicious kick, and took him face-first to the floor. She had the cuffs on him before Colt could take a breath.

Reggie's mouth was tasting carpet, and he was making mewling sounds in between profanities.

"That's assaulting a police officer," Molly said into Reggie's ear, her knee in his back.

"You fucking bitch," Reggie mumbled.

Harper squatted down in front of Reggie. "I told you yesterday she would do it," he said. "You should see her shoot. Molly, I got him. Go check out the bedroom."

She threw him a look over her shoulder. "What?"

"He ain't going anywhere," Harper said. "Go."

She jammed her knee into Cash's back and stood. She faced Harper, who just shook his head: *Not now.* She took a breath. Nodded, then headed down the dim hall.

She stepped over piles of clothes and into the bedroom. Mattress on the floor, with sheets that looked like they'd never seen the inside of a washing machine. More piles of clothes. Two hunting rifles in the corner. Huge Confederate flag tacked to the wall over the mattress. And on the floor next to the bed, a cell phone. She yanked gloves out of her hip pocket, snapped the latex over her wrists, and picked the phone up with two fingers. Harper needed to get an evidence team in here. She spied a plastic zip-close bag on the floor. Picked it up, sniffed it to make sure it didn't have weed residue in it, and put the phone inside. Wasn't an evidence bag but it would have to do. She put the bag in her pocket.

When she walked back into the living room, Harper hoisted Reggie to his feet. Or tried to. Molly grabbed an arm, and together they dragged the drunken, sobbing Reggie Cash to the Crown Vic.

Molly shoved him in the back and slammed the door. She spun around toward Harper, who stared at her with a curious look.

"Don't you say a fucking word," she said.

Harper held up his hands. "Hey, I think that went pretty well."

CHAPTER THIRTY-TWO

COLT

Colt pushed his way into the tiny, fluorescent-weird green-painted interview room carrying a paper cup of coffee in each hand. Reggie Cash sat facing him, one hand cuffed to the steel bar that ran the length of the table.

Molly came in behind him, carrying her own coffee, and pulled a chair from the wall to the table. Reggie glared at her, his rat eyes full of hate. She ignored him.

Colt placed a cup in front of Reggie, then sat in the chair opposite him. Colt sipped the coffee Becky had brewed an hour ago. Apparently, she'd filtered it through a dishrag. He made a face, set the cup down.

"Goddam, Reggie," Colt said. "You look like a wolf ate you and shit you over a cliff."

"Very funny," Reggie said.

"Where were we earlier?" Colt said. "Oh yeah, you were involved in a hate crime in Alabama a few years ago. And you got arrested for disturbing the peace at another bar on the state line. What is it with you, Reggie—can't decide which state to be in?"

Reggie took the coffee with his free hand, blew across the top of the cup, sipped. Winced. "Bad luck, I reckon. I wasn't involved in that other shit. I told you that."

"That's right, you did," Colt said. "What did you mean the other day at the bar when you said, 'About time this started happening'?"

"Huh?" Reggie looked up, confused.

"That's what you said," Colt said. "Deputy McDonough here heard you, too."

Reggie's eyes darted from McDonough back to him. "Nothing. Just that 'bout time some of these criminals running around got what was coming to them."

"Black criminals," Colt said.

Reggie shrugged. "Ain't that who most of them are?"

"What does 'WNC' stand for, Reggie?" Colt said.

"What? I have no idea," Reggie said, a little too fast. "Never heard of it."

"Really?" Colt said. "Over in Alabama, around Montgomery—where you're from—there's a group called the White Nations... What is it, McDonough?"

"Alliance," Molly said over the top of her coffee mug.

"Alliance, that's right," Colt said. "And so now we're having this conversation with you, a fella from Montgomery who was questioned about a hate crime there. And now we're talking about a dead black man, two actually—the kid from the bar died last night—here in my county."

Reggie reached for his coffee again, but this time his hand shook. "I don't know nothing about that. I was just driving up the highway and stopped for a cold drink when that nigger kid busted in yelling he wanted the money from the bartender," he said. "Those two other guys were already there when I got there."

"But you know those guys," Colt said. "They called you by name, told you to shut up. Why?"

"I—Hell. I don't know," Reggie said. "Maybe they didn't want to get in trouble with the law."

"But you do know them?"

Reggie started fidgeting. "Uh, yeah, I know 'em. Hunting buddies. I mean, I know lots of people, you know?"

"If you say so, Reggie," Colt said. "What about Jack Burnett? Or Lucius Wallace?"

"Who?"

Colt glanced over at Molly, who was watching Reggie the way a cat watches a bird.

"Jack Burnett," Colt said. "He's from Montgomery, too. Figured since you know a lot of people you might know him."

"I don't know everybody," Reggie said.

Molly leaned forward. "Just answer the goddam question."

Reggie flung himself back in his chair like he'd been slapped. "No, I don't know him. Or that other guy."

Colt stood, walked to the door of the interview room, leaned against the wall and stared at Reggie. Let him stew. And Reggie was stewing. "I think you're lying, Reggie," he said. "I think you do know Jack Burnett. And the other guy, as you call him, was named Lucius Wallace. Who used to work with Jack Burnett. Who's from Montgomery, same as you. But I'm tired of dealing with your bullshit. I'm charging you with assault on a police officer, resisting arrest, drunk and disorderly, and anything else I can think of on the way back to my desk."

"Because I don't know some guy?" Reggie said. His voice had taken on an annoying whine.

"No, because you're an asshole," Colt said. "And I've got good reason to charge you with the murder of Lucius Wallace."

For a second, Colt thought Reggie might faint at his bluff. His face went white and sweat formed on his forehead. He leaned forward and placed his head on the table. "I didn't shoot him," he whispered.

Colt pushed himself off the wall. "What? You didn't shoot who?"

Reggie rolled his head on the table. Colt walked over, put both hands on the table. "Sit up, Reggie. Who did you not shoot?"

Reggie heaved himself up in his chair, leaving a small pool of spittle on the steel table. "Either of them. That guy in the bar. And that Wallace guy. I don't care that they're dead, but I didn't shoot them."

Colt sat. "Nobody said anything about Lucius Wallace being shot."

Reggie's eyes came unfocused, and he tugged at his cuffed wrist. "What? I thought I heard that."

Colt leaned over the table. "Tell me about Jack Burnett."

Reggie, hungover, scared, and exhausted, sagged in his chair. "Okay, I know him. We knew some of the same people in Montgomery."

Colt looked over at Molly. She took her cue and pulled the bag with Reggie's phone inside from her hip pocket. Tossed it onto the table. "That would explain the calls to and from Jack Burnett, then."

Reggie Cash was defeated, and he knew it. "Yeah, he must have found me through some of the people we know."

Colt shook his head. "That's bullshit, Reggie. Was he involved in the car bombing with you?"

"I told you, I wasn't involved in that," Reggie said, more to the floor than to Colt and Molly. "Got no idea about Burnett, but that wasn't me."

Colt had only one more bluff, and he decided to use it, even though he and Molly hadn't discussed it ahead of time. "Here's the thing, Reggie," he said, keeping his voice steady, almost friendly. "Deputy McDonough here used to be a federal agent. ATF. And when she was working for them, she knew all about the white-supremacy activities in Alabama."

Reggie just stared at the floor. Colt glanced at Molly, and she gave him a look: she got it.

"That's true," Molly said. "Matter of fact, we even knew about the White Nations activity in this state. And that's what got Lucius Wallace killed. He had a list of men he thought were part of something called the WNC in a notebook we found after he got killed. One of those men was, guess who, your buddy Jack Burnett."

Reggie looked up again and stared first at Molly, then at Colt, his eyes black dots of hate.

"Is that what you're doing in my county?" Colt said. "Setting up a group with Burnett?"

"I ain't got nothing more to say to either of you without a lawyer."

Colt stood, and Molly followed. "Good," Colt said. "You're sure as hell going to need one."

He walked into the corridor with Molly trailing behind.

"Hey, wait up," she said.

He stopped. "Sorry."

"Told you it wasn't a coincidence," she said.

"And you were right," Colt said.

"Now what?"

"I'm going to bring Jack Burnett in." He turned and walked toward his office. Molly fell into step beside him.

"When?"

"Right now."

"Want backup?"

"John this time," Colt said. He stepped into his office, dialed Hank Claiborne's number from the desk phone. Holly answered.

"Hey, Holly, Sheriff Harper again," he said. "Is Hank there by any chance?"

"Hello, Sheriff, he is," Holly said. "I'll send you over to him."

"Colt?" Hank said when he came on the line.

"Hank, it's me," he said. "I need to speak to you and Jack Burnett."

"Again?"

"Now."

"Okay, then," Hank said. "Jack's making rounds on the ponds."

"I'll be there in twenty minutes." He hung up before Hank could respond.

John was standing at the door when he walked out. "Molly told me," he said.

"Let's go."

CHAPTER THIRTY-THREE

COLT

The ride out to Hank Claiborne's farm was quick and quiet, mainly because Colt kept the accelerator on the floor as much as possible and because he didn't feel much like talking. He hit the brakes—a little too hard—at the turnoff for the farm. John shot an arm out to brace himself against the dashboard when Colt wheeled the car off the highway.

"I'm getting tired of this shit," Colt said, more to himself than to John.

"I can see that," John said. "You mind telling me which shit that would be?"

The Crown Vic leapt forward down the dirt road toward Claiborne's main building.

"Mostly this bullshit haggling with Hank," Colt said. "But this other shit, too. This fucking narrow-minded racist bullshit that still goes on."

John turned his head to look at Colt. "You and me both," he said. "Would this have anything to do with Hank being a friend of yours?"

Colt shot him a look. "Of course it does, John. I mean, goddam, we grew up together. Saw the same shit—and heard the same attitudes from our parents. You'd think people in this day and age would be a little more, I don't know, open-minded."

"You'd think, right?" John said. "We should have that conversation one day. It's what I hate the most about this place. I can't tell you the number of times I've thought about leaving."

Colt shot him a look. "What made you stay?"

"You, you big dumbass," John said. Then, more quietly: "Rhonda."

Colt thought about that, didn't quite know how to respond. "Thanks, John. I have to tell you this before we go inside, but my reason for bringing you out here is selfish and not at all politically correct." He wheeled the car to a spot near the front door of the building and stopped.

"Because I'm black," John said, as if he'd already figured this out. "That's pretty damn low."

Colt threw the car up in park and killed the engine. Stared straight ahead. "I know it is. But also because there's nobody else I trust in situations like these more than you. That's the smoking-hot gospel truth, and you know it."

John looked out his window. "I know."

"Besides," Colt said, "they see you standing there, they're going to be all kinds of pissed off. It'll make them get sloppy."

"Big nigger befouling their lily-white premises."

"Something like that." Colt opened his door. "Come on, let's get this done."

Hank was waiting by Holly's desk this time. He waved them to his office with a stern look.

The three of them squeezed into the room, where Jack Burnett stood in one corner. Colt watched him closely when he laid eyes on John for the first time. Behind the lumberjack beard and cocky SEAL attitude, Colt thought he saw a flicker in Burnett's eyes. The scene reminded Colt of a spaghetti western, one where somebody was going to do the digging.

He ignored Burnett for the moment. "Hank," he said. "I'm going to get straight to the point. Deputy Carver and I are here to take Mr. Burnett in for questioning in connection with the homicide of Lucius Wallace. I'm doing this here as a courtesy to you as his employer and because you and I have known each other a long time."

Hank was having none of it. He stomped to the door, slammed it, and walked back to face Colt. "Are you out of your mind, Colt?" he said, inches from Colt's face. "This is absolutely ridiculous."

"No, Hank, it's not," Colt said. He turned his attention to Burnett. "Mr. Burnett, we aren't formally arresting you, but we are detaining you for questioning."

"Is that so?" Burnett said. He crossed his arms, a display of muscularity Colt took as vanity.

"It is," Colt said.

"If that's the case, why didn't you just have him come down to the sheriff's office?" Hank said, still fuming.

"Hank," Colt said, "don't tell me how to do my job."

Burnett scoffed and laid his eyes on John. "And if I say no?" he said.

John shrugged. "We can do it with or without handcuffs. Your choice."

Burnett smirked at John. "So that's why you're here."

"Try me," John said.

The two men, each as big as a linebacker, glared at each other. Burnett relented. "Fine. I'll go. But it's a waste of time, because I don't know anything about Lucius Wallace other than the work he did here."

"We'll talk about that," Colt said. He stepped away from the door. "After you."

Burnett wagged his head and took an exaggerated slow step toward the door, John inches away from him. Colt had turned to follow when Hank grabbed his arm. Colt snapped his head around, looked down at his arm, then at Hank. "Move that goddam hand," he said.

Hank pulled his arm away like he'd been snakebit. "Goddammit, Colt, you're out of line here, coming into my place of business and pulling some shit like this. My employees are going to see this."

"That didn't seem to bother you when you got into an argument with Lucius Wallace," Colt said.

"That ain't the same thing and you know it," Hank said. "This is going to have a real serious effect on the people out there that voted for you. And not just them. People all over this county. People are already starting to talk."

"They are, are they? What are *they* saying?"

"That you're protecting the ... them," Hank said. "That you're looking to score points with the blacks in the community after you arrested that preacher."

Colt felt like erasing forty years of friendship by slapping Hank Claiborne to the ground. It'd be easy to do. Hank had never been the fighting type. "Is that what you think, Hank?"

Hank threw his hands out in frustration. "No, but this sure makes me wonder. I mean, maybe Lucius got what was coming to him."

"What in the hell is that supposed to mean? You got something you need to tell me, Hank?" Colt said.

Hank shook his head. "No. No, I don't. But you need to think about how all this looks to the people that elected you."

"You mean white people," Colt said. "This may come as a surprise to you, but I don't really give a shit about what people say about me. Especially at the moment. So, unless you have something else to say, I'm going to get on with doing my job."

He turned and walked out, past Holly, who appeared crestfallen that he didn't stop to speak to her. John had already placed Burnett in the back seat of the Crown Vic and was standing by the car.

The trip back was even quicker and quieter, and that suited Colt just fine. They escorted Burnett into the interview room and took their places.

"Okay, Jack," Colt said once everyone had settled, "let's start at the beginning. Where were you the night Lucius Wallace was killed?"

"I was at a bar that night," Jack said. "Gateway Lounge."

"All night?" Colt said.

"No, not all night," Jack said. "I worked that day, like always, then went home and cleaned up. I was at the Gateway from about nine o'clock until it closed."

"Can anybody verify that?" John said.

Burnett gave John a sly look. "The bartender."

"Do you own a black pickup truck, Jack?" Colt said.

"I do. That against the law?"

"Not that I'm aware of," Colt said. "Do you know a man named Reggie Cash?"

"Yeah, sure we know each other. Ran around with some of the same folks when we lived in Alabama. So what?"

"You were both detained by the FBI and questioned about a car bombing in Montgomery three years ago," Colt said.

Burnett chuckled. "Oh, that. Cash was questioned by the FBI. The ATF questioned me. Same result. We both got released. They had nothing on me."

Colt looked at John and they mentally agreed that "They had nothing on me" was an interesting answer.

"Do you recall the argument between Hank and Lucius over the Confederate flag at the farm?"

Jack idly scratched a tattooed arm. "I heard about it. I was out doing rounds on the ponds at the time. Checking O_2 levels. I didn't see it."

"What was your impression of it?"

Jack shrugged. "Hank put up the flag, and Lucius went ballistic over it and said it was offensive. Hank took it down."

"Tommy Dowd said Hank put it back up a week later," John said.

Jack's eyes narrowed. "Tommy Dowd?"

"Works on the farm with you, Jack," Colt said.

"I know that," Jack said. "How do you know he said that?"

"We asked him," John said.

"Yeah," Jack said, "I think about a week later he put it back up."

"You know why?" Colt said.

"You'd have to ask him," Jack said.

"You said you're in charge of security at the farm," Colt said. "Was Lucius a security threat?"

Jack looked puzzled, then laughed. "A *security threat*? Hell no. Nobody that works there is much of a threat to anything or anybody."

"So, you can't think of a reason anybody would want to do harm to Lucius?" Colt said.

"I didn't know the man," Jack said. "Don't know what he was into. But nobody I knew had it in for him. I certainly didn't."

"Even after he made Hank take down the flag?" John said.

"Deputy, I really don't get hung up over that flag," Jack said. "And it's not my farm. I don't tell Hank how to run it. If him and Lucius had a disagreement, that's their business. I just do my job and do what I'm told."

"One last question; then we're done," Colt said. "Do you own a gun?"

Jack laughed aloud at the question. "Of course I do," he said.

"Pistol?"

Jack nodded. "Glock 19. And, yes, I have a concealed-carry permit. Comes in handy on the job for shooting snakes and such."

Colt tapped the table. "Okay, Jack, that's all we wanted to hear. You're free to go." He stood and nodded to John, who followed him into the hall.

"Not here," Colt said. "My office. Grab Molly."

When John and Molly appeared, Colt didn't bother to offer them seats. He stood behind his desk.

"I don't believe a word he's saying," Colt said. "But we don't have enough to hold him, so we're going to let him go. But I want you two to bird-dog this guy. Do surveillance in shifts. He's an arrogant son of a bitch, and he's going to make a mistake."

"We'll get on it," John said. "Gladly." Molly nodded her agreement and put her hand up.

"Yes, Molly?" Colt said.

"I did some more research. One hit on something called the White Nations Covenant," she said. "Nothing more than that. Listed as a possible 'white-alliance organization.' So, if that's the right name or if this outfit even exists at all, it hasn't showed up yet."

"Dammit," Colt said. "Okay, keep at it when you can, but keeping eyes on Burnett is the priority. Go."

John and Molly left, and he slumped in his chair. Still furious at Hank Claiborne, he didn't like the way this investigation was going.

CHAPTER THIRTY-FOUR

JOHN

John smiled into his cell phone as he listened to Rhonda remind him—again—that they would discuss vacation plans when he got home from work. Through his windshield, rays of orange sunset light streamed through magnolia trees lining a downtown street.

Vacation, he thought, how in the hell did he manage to get here? Five years ago, the thought of living anywhere but Chicago, much less dating a woman like Rhonda, was the stuff of fantasies, worthy only of scorn. Yet, here he sat. As satisfied as a man could be. He could have never guessed that the ugliness of the last three years—in which Rhonda's only child had been murdered, he'd been shot, and Colt had been nearly killed—could have brought them together.

"Rhonda, baby, I swear, as soon as I get home."

"Don't you 'Rhonda, baby' me," Rhonda said. "You just tell Colt you can't work all night. Or do you want me to?"

"No, no, I got it, Rhonda," John said, still smiling. "I'll talk to him tomorrow, I swear. I gotta go, though. Duty calls and all."

"How late will you be?"

He checked traffic and steered his car out of the parking lot, headed toward Jack Burnett's address. "Molly's spelling me at ten, so I'll be done by then."

"Call me?"

"Sure."

He hung up and turned the car into a fast-food place for a large coffee. It took him only ten minutes to cross town to Burnett's place. Another three minutes to find a decent parking spot to see without being seen. Burnett's truck was parked close to the iron stairs that led to his apartment.

His thoughts went back to Rhonda. And Colt—and the conversation he said they should have. John sipped his coffee and wondered if Colt ever took a step back from the death and crime and racism that seemed to thrive in this county and saw it for what it was. He seemed to want to, but what Colt couldn't see—at least, he admitted, to an outsider like himself—was that Colt was part of the fabric of this place, just one thread in a complicated web. And every thread you pulled was connected to all the other threads.

They'd known each other a long time, he and Colt. He just hoped that when all the threads in this case got pulled, they'd still know each other.

DAY SEVEN

CHAPTER THIRTY-FIVE

COLT

Colt had to practically order Molly to ride with him to get coffee. She'd pulled a shift after John the night before, and she looked like she could use ten straight hours of sleep, and maybe a shower, but she'd insisted on working. And truth be told, he needed her on the job anyway. So, he compromised: coffee now or go home. She elected the former.

Colt spent most of the drive to the coffee shop out on Highway 82 listening to Molly yawn. But, he noticed, she didn't complain. Stubborn, he supposed. A characteristic she demonstrated often.

He'd just pulled onto the highway headed back toward his office when the car radio squawked. Becky's crackly voice made Molly wince.

"Colt, what's your twenty?" Becky asked.

He grabbed the handset. "Headed your way, why?"

"We got a report of a body down at Nashville Ferry Landing."

He glanced over at Molly. "Any more details than that?"

"The lady that called said she found a body on the banks of the Tombigbee upriver from Nashville Ferry."

He braked at a stoplight. "All right, then," he said, hitting his turn signal. He turned the car around and swooped over to Highway 69 South, headed to the Tombigbee. "Tell John I need him to contact the bar where Jack Burnett claims to have been, will you?"

"I'll tell him," Becky said and broke the connection.

He cleared the city limits and wound the big car out, speeding but not racing, handling curves he'd known his whole life, blowing past landmarks and memories. Molly stared out the window for a couple of minutes, then turned toward him. "You like it out here, don't you?"

"What do you mean?" he said without looking over. "I like to drive."

"No, that's not what I meant. Out here, you relax, ease into the countryside like this place is your sanctuary. This is home to you."

He shrugged. "I did grow up here. Where do you call home? Memphis?"

She snorted and looked out the window at a wide green field that ended in a wall of white oaks. "Fuck Memphis."

He laughed, glanced at her. "Heard that. That's about how I feel about the place."

"Virginia," she said.

"Huh?"

"Home. I call Virginia home. Waynesboro. But I haven't lived there in years. Not since I graduated college."

"Never heard of Waynesboro."

"Not much to hear of. Little town next to the Shenandoah Valley and the bottom of the Blue Ridge Mountains. Couldn't wait to leave."

He smiled, nodded. "I know that feeling."

She turned her head to face him. "But you came back."

"I did."

"Why?"

"I don't know," Colt said. "All I wanted to do was get away from this place, until I did. Then it was all I ever thought about. But I'm starting to realize that this place is really just deadweight I been dragging around for years."

That seemed to perplex her. Shut her up at least, since he really didn't want to get into his feelings about his past. Or present. They rode in silence, listening to the highway and tires sing their familiar duet. He saw the turn, slowed and wheeled to the right, headed down a narrow blacktop strip, past a decrepit pecan orchard and river shacks that looked like they'd been through one flood too many.

The landing came up suddenly in the glare; even though he knew exactly where it was, had for years, he always felt surprised when he saw the collection of pickup trucks and boat trailers parked at whatever spot the driver could back into. He pulled to the left of the ramp, near the grassy slope leading down to the brown water, killed the engine.

The sign out front said the bait shop on the opposite side of the ramp was open, and through the pines he could see a couple of men hanging around the place. Down at the ramp, on the worn wooden pier, a woman in the dark green uniform of the state Wildlife, Fisheries & Parks Department stood with her hands on her hips, squinting into the state-furnished johnboat, also green. She wore a side arm and a sour expression, and as they crunched through the gravel, she held a hand over her brow to cut the glare. She met them at the end of the pier.

"Ma'am," Colt said. "Sheriff Harper. You the one called about the body?"

"I did," she said in a voice that sounded like bad brakes. "I'm Billie Jack Tunney. Warden."

He tried to suppress a smile but failed. "Billy Jack? Like the movies?"

She spat into the still water. "Naw," she said, "not like them god-awful movies. I spell it with an 'i-e.'"

When he didn't respond, she huffed a breath. "It's on account of my best friend having the same name. People was always getting us confused. So somebody got the idea of keeping us straight by sticking our husband's name on the back of ours. I'm Billie Jack. She's Billie Charles."

"I see," Colt said.

Billie Jack seemed to only just now notice Molly. "Who's she?" she said, tilting her head toward Molly.

Molly stepped up, extended her hand. "Molly McDonough. I'm a deputy."

"Deputy?" Billie Jack said. "How 'bout that? You look like that gal that got shot up with the sheriff here last year."

Colt cleared his throat. "Mrs. Tunney, about that body."

Billie Jack shook her head. "Ain't no Mrs. Tunney, on account of my husband being dead. Got run over by a got-dam tractor."

"Sorry to hear," he said.

"Hell, he was 'bout a halfwit anyway," Billie Jack said. She wiped a leather hand across her forehead. It came away slick with sweat.

"Anyway, Miz Tunney," he said. "You said you found a body."

She jerked her head toward the boat. "I didn't say I was the one what found it. I reported it. I was coming down the river from the Lux when two fellers running trotlines over on this side of the bank started jumping up and down in their boat, hollering, trying to get my attention. Damn near capsized their boat. I pulled up alongside 'em and they pointed the thing out to me. Facedown, hung up in the weeds, right next to the bank. I pulled up close enough to see it was a black male, that's about all."

"You touch anything?" Colt said.

She laughed out a sound that sounded like a dog with a foot caught in a door. "Hell no, I didn't. Soon as I saw what it was, I didn't want to touch the got-dam thing."

"Where is it?"

"Get in and I'll show you," she said. She stepped down into the boat and snatched up a life vest, tossed it into the bottom of the boat, then sat on the bench nearest the Evinrude outboard motor.

Colt looked over at Molly, who simply shrugged back at him. He stepped down into the boat, stood aside as Molly climbed in and stepped to the forward bench. He sat on the middle row, closest to Tunney.

She hit the starter and gunned the engine, shooting the aluminum boat away from the pier and into the main channel of the Tombigbee. She kept the throttle wound out until the boat planed off, the bow lifting from the surface of the river, then made a sweeping turn to the right. She handled the boat like a NASCAR driver—as it if it were an extension of herself. Colt kept his admiration to himself as he watched the thick foliage of the bank fly by in a green smear. After about a quarter of a mile, Tunney cut the engine and the bow of the small boat settled into the water. She steered toward a patch of head-high canebrake that spread out from a clearing at the water's edge. Off to the left, in an eddy choked with weeds and stumps, Colt saw the incongruous shape of a body bobbing in the brown water.

Tunney pulled the boat up short, guided the bow into the muddy bank, cut the engine. Colt gave her a nod and jumped out; Molly followed, so she didn't see him grimace when he landed. Together they made their way through the cane.

"Watch out for snakes," Colt said.

"Fuck snakes," Molly said. "The leaves on this shit are cutting me to ribbons."

He stepped into a clear spot and nearly onto the body. He stopped, and Molly came up on his right. The corpse looked to be that of a black male, twenty to thirty years old. The man was dressed for an event—a night out, a party, something like that. Expensive shoes. Pants, too. The jacket ruined by two black holes in the back that looked like exit wounds. Arms spread out in the water, watch on the left wrist, gold bracelet on the right.

"Goddammit," Colt said.

"Yeah," Molly said, "I was kinda hoping she was wrong, too."

Colt pulled out his phone, punched in Freddie Mac's number, and got him on the third ring. "Freddie Mac, I got a body down here on the Tombigbee."

"I heard," Freddie Mac said. "Becky called me a little while ago, said to expect your call. I'm halfway to Nashville Ferry now."

"Good," Colt said. "When you get there, the game warden will be there with a boat and she'll bring you to me."

Freddie Mac sighed.

"What?" Colt said.

"Nothing," Freddie Mac said. "I just hate boats."

"We all have our crosses to bear," Colt said and hung up. He squinted up at the sun. Not even noon and already hot as fire out here—and guaranteed to be hotter. He whistled—a piercing sound that cut through the still morning air. He heard the Evinrude crank up. A few seconds later, Tunney and her boat swung into view. She idled the motor about ten yards from the bank.

"Ahite, Miz Tunney," he called. "The coroner is on his way to the landing, and I'm going to need you to bring him here. Can you do that?"

Billie Jack gave him a thumbs-up. "I'll be back in a few minutes, then." She cranked up, spun the boat around, and roared off toward the landing.

Colt turned to Molly, who'd pulled her own phone out and was taking photos of the scene. "He wasn't killed here," she said.

"I didn't figure he was," Colt said. "Too hard to get down to the water through that cane, and none of it looked disturbed when we were coming through it."

Molly swiped sweat off her brow with the back of a hand. "No footprints, either. If I had to guess, I'd say he washed up here."

The whine of an outboard motor announced the arrival of Freddie Mac. Tunney steered the boat as close to Colt as she could, grounded it, and watched with some amusement as Freddie Mac hauled his large frame out of the small boat, lugging his kit with one hand while he tried to maintain his balance with the other. He squished into the muddy bank with a labored breath.

"Goddammit," he said, struggling through the slippery ground. "This is why I hate boats."

"Over here," Colt said.

Freddie Mac stood between Colt and Molly and surveyed the scene. "Obviously, he wasn't killed here," Freddie Mac said.

"We didn't think so," Colt said. He turned to Tunney. "These two fellas that found the body. Did you get their names? Are they here?"

She narrowed her eyes at him. "Course I did." She slapped her right breast, or where her right breast presumably would be, had she not been so skinny. "Got 'em right here in my notebook. But they long gone."

He stifled a groan and noticed Molly doing her best to not grin at his discomfort. "Why did they leave?"

She shrugged. "Weren't much sense in keeping them. I got their information, and they weren't much help beyond finding the body."

He wiped his forehead with the back of his hand. "You notice anything else? Today or the last couple of days out here on the river?"

"Naw, it's been dead quiet. I worked both days over the week-end, and it was too hot to fish during the day. Not a whole lot of skiing going on today, it being Monday. Other than a barge or two going up and down the waterway, I ain't seen much of anybody."

Colt decided to end this too-hot, too-long, unproductive conversation. "All right, Miz Tunney. If you would, take me and Deputy McDonough back to the pier."

"Climb on in."

They rode back in silence. Once back on the pier, Colt shook Tunney's hand. "You did the right thing calling it in, Miz Tunney. I'm going to need you to fetch the coroner when he's done. And I'll need the contact info for your two witnesses. And yours, too, of course."

Billie Jack smirked at that. “Sure thing.” She fished a crumpled card out of her pants pocket and handed it to him. “Number’s on there.”

Once Tunney had shot out into the river yet again, he and Molly climbed into the car. He couldn’t hit the AC fast enough.

“Goddam hot out there,” he said.

Molly waited until he dropped the car into gear and spun around to head to the highway before cracking up. Her laughter must have been contagious, because he started laughing, too.

“My God, that was funny watching you,” she said.

“Shut up, McDonough,” he said. But he was smiling. “That’s a tough woman.”

Molly wiped the corners of her eyes. “She looks like a piece of beef jerky with eyes.”

“I’m guessing a pack of Marlboro Reds a day.”

“At least.”

Molly settled down, and when they returned to the highway, her tone was serious. “You know this is connected to Wallace.”

“Crossed my mind.”

“What now?” Molly said.

“Right now, we see what Freddie Mac comes up with. And ballistics. I’m betting the bullet wounds are awfully similar to the ones on Wallace.”

CHAPTER THIRTY-SIX

COLT

Colt pushed through the glass door into the sheriff's office, grateful to be out of the miserable, suffocating heat, but annoyed at his hip—and himself for still having a goddam bad hip in the first place. Molly peeled off and went to her desk, and he tried not to limp past Becky toward his office door.

"John's in there," Becky said without looking up.

Colt turned the knob and swung the door open, wondering what the hell John was doing in his office instead of sitting at his own desk. John sat perched on the windowsill, arms crossed, face like a statue.

"That sure as hell looks like bad news," Colt said. He sat behind the desk, pulled the center drawer open. Shook a pain pill out of the bottle. "Who's got eyes on Burnett?"

"Moore," John said without moving. "Figured he'd jump at the chance for some overtime."

Colt chewed the pill, swallowed. "Well, don't keep me in suspense."

"I talked to the bartender at the joint Burnett said he was at on the night Wallace died," John said. "And Burnett was there."

"Damn," Colt said.

"Wait, that's not all of it. Burnett said he was there until it closed. Bartender says he left *before* they closed. Burnett got there around nine o'clock, just like he said, but the bartender was sure Burnett left before the place closed at one in the morning."

"How sure?"

"When he announced last call, there were two people left in the place, and neither was Jack Burnett."

Colt grinned. "Good," he said. "That blows a hole in Burnett's alibi."

John slid off the sill and stepped over to the desk, sat in his usual chair. "That's not all, Colt."

Colt eyed his friend. So, this was why John was waiting in his office with a serious look on his face. "What else?"

"The bartender is a little fuzzy on the exact time Burnett left, but he was sure it was right after he met up with another guy."

Colt sat up. "Reggie Cash?"

"No," John said. "That was my first guess, too. But it was Hank Claiborne, Colt."

Colt didn't know if it was the Percocet clouding his brain or being out in the heat, but he couldn't quite focus. He shook his head clear. "What did you just say?"

"Jack Burnett was in that bar until Hank Claiborne showed up. They had a drink—Burnett had a beer, Claiborne had Scotch—and they talked for ten, fifteen minutes, then left. Together."

Colt replayed the several conversations he'd had with Hank. "That don't sound right," he said.

"Bartender IDed Claiborne as soon as I showed him a picture on my phone."

Colt stared at John, not believing the words, but then coming to the realization that John was telling him straight. And that brought him right to the same conclusion John had made hours—if not days—before.

"Goddammit," Colt said. "Son of a bitch."

"Yeah."

Colt wanted to throw something, hit something—or someone. Hank Claiborne led the list. The conversation in Hank's office came rushing back to him now in a different tone—all that southern-heritage bullshit. Of course it made sense now. He knew John was reading his face, which was as good as reading his mind. John had been in Hank's office, too, after all.

"You knew, didn't you?" Colt said.

"I suspected."

"Why didn't you tell me?"

John waited a moment before speaking. "Suspicion isn't evidence, for one thing. And this isn't some meth cooker we busted in a trailer. You've known the guy a long time. He's a fixture of sorts in the area."

"I've known *you* a long time."

"That's true, but this is different," John said. "This has so much more in it than two guys who were in the Corps together. Guys from different ... backgrounds."

"Such as?" Colt said, not sure he was liking where the conversation was going.

"You can't turn over a single stone in this county without finding some connection to a racist past," John said. "Even when it's somebody you think you know. Somebody you've been around for years."

"I hope," Colt said, "you're not saying what I think you're saying."

"What?" John said. "That having a black friend and a black deputy proves you're not a racist? And, by the way, how do you think that plays among your constituents? No, I'm not going to say that, and that's not the point."

"What the hell *is* the point?" Colt drummed his fingers on his desk. And thought of overturned stones and the pasts they hid. He had been stepping from stone to stone his whole life. "You're right. Not just people like Claiborne, either. Even me, right? My own father, and his grandfather. Hank was right about that—I have an ancestor who fought alongside Nathan Bedford Forrest and was certainly no friend to the black man. I grew up around it, John, same as anybody around here. White or black. Rebel flags. Bathrooms that were 'Colored' and 'Whites Only.'

The Klan. All that shit. But that don't mean I believe in it, that I buy into it. And to be honest, you should know better than to imply that."

"You, no," John said. "But a lot of folks around here—white folks—still do. Like you said, they grew up around it, too. Makes it harder for somebody like you to spot it."

"The hell is that supposed to mean?" Colt said. The pain pill was definitely in his head.

"Just that it creates a blind spot. Dead space, we used to call it."

Colt stared at his best friend's blank face, his anger rising, then falling just as quickly. John was right. "And we always made sure dead space was covered by indirect fire."

"That's what I'm trying to do here," John said, meeting his eyes. "Cover the dead space."

"I know," Colt said, more to himself than to John.

"So now what?"

Colt slumped in his chair, rubbed his leg. "I can't arrest a man for having a drink in a bar. I'm not going to deny that whatever is going on at the farm, Hank is in it up to his eyeballs. And when the time comes, I *will* arrest his ass, you can count on that. But now is not the time."

"What about Burnett?" John said.

"We stay on him. We know his alibi is bullshit. Sooner or later he's going to make a mistake. I want us on him like barbed wire when he does. When does Moore's shift end?"

John checked his watch. "Twenty hundred."

"Call him and tell him I'll be her relief tonight."

John cocked an eyebrow. "Seriously?"

"Yes, seriously."

"Okay, then."

The desk phone rang, surprising them both. Colt snatched up the receiver. "Harper."

"Hey, Colt, Freddie Mac. Got some prelims on our floater."

Colt gestured at John, grabbed a pen and a legal pad, then punched the speakerphone button. "Go ahead, Freddie Mac. You're on the speaker with me and John."

"Kenneth Wilkinson, age twenty-four," Freddie Mac said. "At least, according to his driver's license. And no reason to think otherwise."

"Time of death?" Colt said.

"Hard to tell, since he was in the water," Freddie Mac said. "But seeing as once a body goes in the water, the skin starts to separate from the digits after about a week—and his hadn't quite gotten that bad—I'd say between two and seven days ago. I think he was dead before he went into the river. I found two slugs in the torso. Too soon to be certain, of course, but I'd say both of those bullets were nine-millimeter. But don't jump to conclusions."

Colt glanced at John—Freddie Mac liked to be an authority. Plus, he knew a hell of a lot about decomposing bodies. "We won't. Anything else?"

"He was decapitated with one forceful blow, I think," Freddie Mac said. "Most likely a machete or some similar kind of big blade. By someone with a hell of a lot of strength."

Colt's mind flashed to Jack Burnett standing toe to toe with John in Hank's office.

"And one more thing," Freddie Mac said. "The kid had skin under his nails."

Colt sat up, his heartbeat quickening. "I like the sound of that."

"Thought you might. I'll be sending that out for analysis today."

"Do whatever you can to expedite it, Freddie Mac," Colt said.

"I'll see what I can do. One last thing."

Colt shook his head. Freddie Mac, always with the drama. "Go."

"Like I said, it's too soon to be sure, but I'll bet you a cold one that the weapon used was the same kind used on Wallace."

"I'm not taking that bet," Colt said. "What makes you say that?"

"The wounds look the same."

"Call me when you're done with the autopsy."

"Will do," Freddie Mac said and hung up.

Colt and John stared at the phone for a moment. "'Bout time we got a break," Colt said.

"Damn right," John said. "Now all we need are DNA samples."

"One thing at a time," Colt said.

CHAPTER THIRTY-SEVEN

COLT

The thunderheads that had been building like giant cotton towers in the western sky all afternoon transformed into a menacing line of low slate-colored clouds heavy with rain by sunset. Colt watched the oncoming storm front approach from his kitchen window as he filled his thermos with coffee. Thunder rumbled, not too far off.

The wind caught the screen door as he left the house, slamming it against the siding with a gunshot bang, and he slid into the driver's seat of his truck as the first fat drops of rain splattered across his dusty windshield. By the time he'd backed out of the driveway and headed toward Jack Burnett's downtown apartment, the sky was black as midnight, the rain a silver maelstrom battering his windows. He idly wondered if the tornado sirens would go off.

The storm suited him. Made for a cooler evening, and if he couldn't see shit through the rain, chances were Burnett wouldn't be able to, either.

He parked on the street, half a block from Burnett's building, killed the engine, and poured himself a cup of coffee in the travel mug he kept in the console. Outside, the storm grew, and Colt watched the trees lining the street bend nearly double as they surrendered leaves, then limbs, to the slashing winds and near-horizontal rain. He thought about turning on some music but decided against it when he realized he could barely hear anything over the din of the storm. So, he sipped coffee and watched Burnett's door for an hour.

Like most summer thunderstorms, this one ended as abruptly as it had started, the sudden violence moving east toward Alabama and leaving a dripping silence in its wake. Rainwater pooled in black and silver circles under flickering streetlights, and traffic returned to the streets as automobiles resumed their journeys.

A few minutes after nine, Colt sat up when he noticed Burnett leaving his apartment, locking the door behind him and making his way down the second-floor walkway to the wrought iron stairs. If he had any sense that he was under surveillance, he didn't show it.

Colt cranked up when Burnett's black pickup pulled out of the lot and turned right, toward Highway 45. He dropped the truck into gear, then fell in behind Burnett at a discreet distance.

Burnett took the bypass off 45, not bothering to use his blinker, and hit the gas, headed east toward the state line; the move gave Colt a moment of concern—he didn't have good enough reason to follow Burnett into Alabama. That concern turned to relief five minutes later, though, when Burnett's truck took the last exit before the state line and headed south.

Colt trailed for another twenty minutes as Burnett took his time driving through the narrow macadam roads and rolling hills in the eastern part of the county, running essentially parallel to the state line, past the enormous new school at New Hope and a brand-new church of vague affiliation until linking up with Highway 69 as night came fully on. Burnett turned south.

Colt followed, at a greater distance now in the quiet, rural area, wondering if this roundabout route was designed to shake a tail.

Burnett drove two miles, then turned left onto a gravel road Colt knew was there even before Burnett hit his blinker, just as he had sensed Burnett's intentions when he'd turned onto the highway. This area was Claiborne property. Colt had been down the road himself plenty of times, though not in the last twenty years or so. Hank's family had used the property for years, mostly for hunting. Somewhere back in those woods was a two-acre pond, one he'd fished as a teenager.

So, what the hell was Burnett doing here?

He slowed to put more space between him and his suspect. When he reached the turnoff, Colt checked the rearview—no traffic behind him—and waited another beat before making the turn himself. No taillights visible up ahead. He swung onto the gravel path, driving slowly down the now-muddy trail that came up in his headlights like a familiar memory. He knew where he was going.

The road was lined on both sides by barbed wire, with red POSTED signs attached to every other worn wooden fence post. Pines three stories high made the trail a black tunnel. Colt followed muddy tire tracks—several, in fact—until they veered through a gap in the wire. Toward the old hunting cabin.

He turned off his headlights and rolled through the tracks, keeping an eye on the dark road ahead while scanning the woods off to the right where he knew the cabin to be, if it was still there. And it had to be—why else would all these vehicles be coming this way?

He rolled over a cattle guard and steered his truck to the side of the road, killed the engine, and eased out into the muggy night air, his boots squishing softly in the mud.

He backtracked to the turnoff, then stepped off in a half-crouch toward the cabin—or where he remembered it to be—off to the side of the muddy path. He stopped once to let his eyes adjust to the absence of light in the woods. Slipped on a downed tree trunk and tumbled headlong in the dark, saving himself by grabbing onto a fortuitously placed but thorny vine. Cursing, he gathered himself and listened. Nothing.

Fifty or so yards later, the shape and substance of the cabin emerged. The squat, tin-roofed shack sat in a tiny clearing amid several sedans and pickups. Colt recognized Burnett's truck nearest the two propane lanterns that hung near the front door. Silhouettes of men, a dozen or so, moved in and out of the house like marionettes under the soft orange glow of the lanterns. Two of the men carried side arms. Colt swung wide to his right to stay away from the light of the lanterns. He moved from tree to tree using the noise of the men to cover his own until he could get close enough to recognize faces.

He'd just decided on his next move when he heard a car engine growl behind him and to his left. The three men standing near the door turned toward the sound. Headlights appeared, lancing through the mist and bugs. Colt ducked, pulled his pistol, and made himself as small as possible, his back against the scaly pine bark.

A car door slammed. Then, a man's voice. An unmistakable voice: "Anybody seen Jack?"

"Son of a bitch," Colt whispered. Hank fucking Claiborne. He dared not look around the tree, bracketed as he was by the twin halogen beams of Hank's headlights. What was Hank up to?

The headlights went out and the area went black, even darker than before Hank arrived. Colt waited.

"He's inside," a man called out. Colt couldn't place the voice, but that didn't matter at the moment.

Boots scuffled, wooden steps creaked, and a door slammed. Then quiet except for the bellowing frogs and screaming cicadas in the woods around him. Colt dared a look around the tree that hid him; no men present. He took a tentative step, tested his hip, then stepped toward the shack, staying clear of the twin orange circles from the lanterns.

The shack had no windows, but the Masonite walls were thin enough that he could hear the murmuring of the dozen men inside. They seemed to be settling down. Then Hank's voice again:

"All right, listen up, all of y'all." Apparently, Hank was leading the meeting. "I know I sent out the word that we have to lay low, and we do, but things haven't gone to plan. So, Jack and I thought we ought to do this meeting tonight."

Colt leaned against the back wall of the cabin. He could hear as clearly as if he were in the room. Plan? What plan? *Jack and I?*

Inside the crowd buzzed.

"Some of y'all already know this, but Reggie Cash got hisself arrested the other day and is in the county jail," Hank said. "I'm working on getting him a lawyer, but right now we don't have any idea what he may have said to the cops."

Another voice cut in. "What are you going to do about the goddam sheriff?"

"Not a damn thing," Hank said. "The hell you expect me to do, Ray? Shoot him?"

"Somebody ought to," said a man—not Ray.

Colt wondered what Ray and the others would think—or do—if they knew he was less than ten feet away.

"We're not here to talk about the fucking sheriff." Colt recognized Jack Burnett's voice. "We're here to adjust what we're doing."

"Adjust?" yelled a man whom Colt took to be Ray, whoever the hell Ray was. "We ain't done shit. You told us we were going to do a Southern Pride march, guns and all, but that ain't happened. And then that nigger got killed. We thought we were the ones gonna be blowing shit up and killing niggers."

"Shut up, Ray," Jack said. "Yeah, well, things change. Shit happens, you know?"

"Ain't our fault," somebody said.

"All of you, be quiet," Hank said, his voice rising. "Like Jack was saying, the original plan was to hold a march, figuring if we did that, the niggers and liberals would show up to counterprotest and we could kick things off. But that ain't going to happen now.

"Truth is," Hank said, "we're only getting started. All this shit with the sheriff is a distraction. Y'all know how the Jew media works around here. They put their liberal slant on everything. But that doesn't matter. We are going to do what we have to do and do what's right. It's just going to take a little more time than I thought. Especially with Reggie getting arrested. So, we have to adjust."

"So now what?" Ray said.

"Patience," Hank said. "Look, before me and Jack contacted y'all, there was nothing going on to stop what's going on around here."

Hank was sounding agitated, Colt thought as he leaned against the back wall to take some pressure off his hip. But what the hell was he going on about?

"But we're doing something now," Hank said. "For one thing, look around the room. There's a dozen of you here tonight. And you all own weapons—and ammo. That's a good thing. I'm buying up more ammo so that we have enough. I've already been working the social media side, recruiting for more people. Pretty soon, it'll be two dozen of us here, maybe more. Jack and Reggie are using their networks in Alabama to bring more people in, too. So, y'all need to be patient. We're going to uphold the Fourteen Words, don't you worry. But we're going to do it when the time is exactly right and works in our favor."

"Then why in the hell did I have to drive all the way out here from Artesia?" Ray said. Ray was clearly pissed off and belligerent.

"You can leave right now, Ray," Hank said in a tone that didn't sound anything like the Hank Claiborne Colt knew, the Hank who was a successful pillar of the community. "Any of you who don't like the way we're running things can walk out the door right now." The comment reminded him of how exposed he was—and that his truck was in plain sight where he'd left it. Not waiting to hear Ray's decision, he took off through the woods, making a wide arc back to the road, trotting as fast as he dared in the darkness.

He climbed into his truck and pulled away, not hitting his lights for a quarter mile and watching the rearview mirror. Back on the highway, his mind unspooled the words Hank had said. He found it just as hard to believe on replay as it was when he heard it live. Hank was talking about some dangerous shit. And what were the "fourteen words" he was talking about?

CHAPTER THIRTY-EIGHT

COLT

The rabbit warren office spaces of the sheriff's department had the feel of a weird sci-fi mausoleum: the silence broken only—barely—by the soft hum of computers with dark screens. Dots of electronic lights glowed red, yellow, blue, at random points in the darkness, looking like tiny creatures' eyes. Colt considered making a pot of coffee as he awaited the arrival of John and Molly—neither of whom was thrilled to be called to work in the dead of night. Times like this, it's good to be the king. Or at least the boss.

He replayed the evening as he slouched in his office chair, now long past his surprise and just plain pissed off at Hank Claiborne. He could feel the rage boiling up inside him like lava. He'd been lied to before, of course. Came with the job. Came with living. But Hank was doing some Olympic-class, full-on lying. He wasn't sure how the stuff he'd heard at the cabin all came together, but he knew redneck racism when he heard it. And that behind that talk was usually a malevolent act. And that's why he was going to take Hank Claiborne right down to the goddam ground.

That last thought rattled around in his head until Molly strode through the door, looking like she'd just woken up, naturally. Jeans, T-shirt, red hair going every which way, pistol on her hip. And all business on her face—either that or she was royally pissed off at the late hour.

John right behind her. Similarly attired but looking like he'd just gotten up from a recliner and walked in, wide awake and ready to go. As always.

"You rang?" Molly said, trying and failing to keep the sarcasm out of her voice.

Colt waved them both to chairs. He'd given each of them the overview when he'd called, so he could get straight to the point.

"I'm taking Claiborne down," he said.

"Hold on," Molly said. "I was thinking about this on the way here. Did you hear anything at all that sounded like a confession?"

Colt glared at her. "No."

"Then you really don't have anything to arrest him on," she said.

John looked at her. "Reasonable suspicion?"

Molly shook her head. "Of what? A bunch of guys having a meeting? That's not illegal, even if it is a racist meeting. Did they even mention Wallace's name? Or Wilkinson's?"

"No," Colt said, shifting in his seat, making more room for the anger rolling around inside.

"Look," Molly said, her tone softening. "I agree with you that you're onto something. You said they mentioned a march of some kind. That's standard tactics for these groups—if this is a real group. They either march, gather, whatever, and hope counterprotesters show up so they can go into attack mode, or they do the counterprotesting themselves. So, let's say that the argument Claiborne had with Wallace prompted that idea. But then Wallace is killed. Why and by who? My bet is Jack Burnett. Same with Wilkinson. Same MO."

"I thought about that, too," Colt said. He looked at John, who nodded his agreement.

"He's the outlier of this whole thing," Molly said. "And he's connected to Reggie Cash and Montgomery, and Reggie Cash is connected to the shit that went down at the bar. And probably more. That all points back to Burnett."

"And Claiborne," Colt said. "Burnett works for Claiborne. And they are the two who were doing all the talking tonight. One other thing. Hank said something about upholding fourteen words or some shit. I didn't get it, but the rest of the room did. You could hear them agreeing with him."

"Is that what he said?" Molly said. "The Fourteen Words?"

"Yep," Colt said. "He told the room that they would be upholding the fourteen words."

"We must secure the existence of our people and a future for white children," Molly said.

John and Colt looked at her.

"What?" Colt said.

"Those are the Fourteen Words," Molly said. "It's a slogan used by the alt-right, white supremacists."

"Are you kidding me?" Colt said.

"You came up with that pretty fast," John said.

Molly shrugged. "Worked a lot of bomb cases. These guys love bombs. You have any idea how many times I read or heard that slogan? But if Claiborne is saying that, then this could be a bigger problem."

"It seemed to be the one thing Hank said that everybody agreed with," Colt said. "And you still don't think that's reason enough to arrest him?"

"Not for murder," Molly said.

Colt stood and started pacing from his desk to the window and back. "Let's back it up," he said. "Here's what I think: Hank Claiborne and Jack Burnett decide they want to start some kind of organization. Burnett recruits Cash. They start getting organized, but then Lucius Wallace gets in the way. He creates a public scene over the flag. And somebody—I'm betting Burnett—kills him over that. Maybe Burnett also found Wallace was onto them. Who knows? But Burnett had the opportunity, if the bartender's story is believable."

"I think it is," John said.

"So do I," Colt said. "But what we don't have yet is real evidence putting Burnett over Wallace's body. But that's what happened, I'm sure of it. Wilkinson, too. John, what's on your mind?"

"That works for Wallace," John said. "But not Wilkinson. What's the motive? Other than the obvious? I'm with Molly. You're onto something here, Colt, and you're onto it hard, but we can't roll up and start arresting people yet. Not just yet."

Colt sat and leaned back in his chair, his gaze going from one deputy to the other. They were right. He was both glad they were right and said so and pissed off that they were. "So, let's come up with a plan to do that before these crackers start doing something we can't manage."

John spoke first. "We have Wilkinson's ID now. I'll track that tomorrow."

"Good," Colt said. "I'm going after Claiborne again. There's more to that drink with Burnett than he's letting on. Molly, stay on Freddie Mac for the DNA results and Wilkinson's autopsy."

"You got it," Molly said. "I think it's worth interviewing Burnett again, too."

"Then do it," Colt said. He looked at his watch. The night was slipping away toward dawn. "Go home, get some sleep. We'll hit it again in the morning, see where we are at noon."

John and Molly rose as one and left without a word, leaving him alone in the office. Just him and his anger.

Rhonda had been right. He'd been stupid not to listen to her; he knew that now. Time, laws, attitudes, had done nothing to erase the line between the two worlds he stood astride. That line was always there, no matter how much the government or society tried to erase it. And everybody knew where that color line was, just as they knew it should never be breached. He'd known it growing up just like all the kids around him—black and white. And yet he'd awkwardly, stupidly crossed that line. With Rhonda—and she of all people knew the risk and consequences of stepping from one world to another. She'd seen with her own eyes, just as he had. And she'd seen his reaction and the violence that a simple friendship brought when it violated the rules.

The goddam rules.

It had been a simple date, nothing more. Or that's what he liked to tell himself. Even then, he knew he was crossing a line that should never even be discussed. That's why he had driven to the movie theater in Starkville, rather than risk being seen in town.

Like that helped, he thought with an odd mixture of shame and satisfaction. To this day, he didn't know how those three boys knew they were there—and what car he drove. He didn't really bother to ask after they swarmed him and Rhonda in the parking lot, spewing vulgarities not dissimilar to the ones he'd heard at Claiborne's cabin a few hours earlier.

He'd managed to get her in the car before the first fist crashed into the side of his head, and Rhonda screamed as she locked the doors. After the first blow, he'd gone on some kind of autopilot and fought back blindly, landing one blow after another until the three attackers lay on the asphalt around him, bleeding and unconscious. His left eye was nearly swollen shut and he was certain he'd broken his left hand, but he was still standing, and Rhonda was unharmed.

They'd driven all the way back to Columbus without speaking a word.

And after an awkward, embarrassing good-bye on the front porch of the Raines' residence, they never spoke of that night again. Because of the line. Because of the rules.

Colt rose, walked out of his office, turning off the lights as he went.

Fuck the rules.

DAY EIGHT

CHAPTER THIRTY-NINE

JOHN

Rhonda was still asleep the next morning when John clicked the front door shut behind him and got back to the job. The conversation in bed still resonated in his head as he stopped for a large coffee and a biscuit at a drive-through on the way to the residence of Kenneth Wilkinson's next of kin.

He finished the biscuit in three bites and had downed half the coffee by the time he pulled to the curb in front of a humble duplex on the south side of town, one of several dozen low-income units spread over a three-block area between the Mississippi University for Women—known as the W—to the east and the skeletal iron and concrete remains of a long-ago-closed marble factory to the west.

The short woman who opened the door peered up at him with unabashed scorn from behind gold wire-rimmed glasses. Skin the color of mahogany set off by a white blouse. Hair just going gray.

"Mrs. Wilkinson?" he said.

"I'm Dot Wilkinson," the woman said. "You find the son of a bitch who killed my nephew?"

He drew a breath, not expecting that response from such a diminutive woman. "May I come in, ma'am?"

Dot Wilkinson stared at him long enough to make him uncomfortable. "I'll take that as a no," she said as she turned on her heels and walked down a hallway into the interior of the house. He waited for her to wave him inside, but she didn't, so he stepped into the house and followed her to a small living room.

She stood facing him, hands on hips. "Go on, sit down," she said. "I'm mad as hell, but I ain't letting you leave here thinking I'm rude."

He nodded, sat on an ancient couch with a faded floral print. Dot sat opposite him in a Queen Anne–style chair that looked older than her. "Miz Wilkinson, "I am very sorry for your loss," he said, and meant it. "No, we haven't found the person who killed Kenneth. That's why I'm here."

Dot looked away, toward what he assumed was the kitchen. "White man killed him."

He wanted to agree with her, tell her he was absolutely sure of it. "What makes you say that, ma'am?"

She turned back to him. "Way he was killed."

He didn't respond. The woman seemed able to read his mind.

"Tell me I'm wrong," Dot said. "Ain't no got-dam way a black man did that to him."

He decided to steer the conversation back to the reason for the visit. He cleared his throat. "I know this is hard, and trust me, we'll find whoever did this. Did Kenneth live with you?"

"He did, ever since his parents got killed in a car wreck when he was eleven."

"You mind if I ask you a few questions about him?"

"That's why you're here."

Grief, he knew, came in different forms, so he let the woman have hers. "Tell me about Kenneth. His friends, job."

Dot leaned back in her chair, hands gripping the armrests, and leveled a gaze at him. "He worked at a clothes store over on Highway 45. Retail, sales, whatever."

"Good worker?"

Dot gripped the chair a little harder, as if she was afraid she might fly away. "Yes, he was. He always showed up on time. No complaints. Always got paid. He worked a lot and he was saving money to go back to school. He wanted to take some classes over at the W," she said.

"Friends?"

"Sure, Kenny had friends," Dot said, her tone softening—a little. "I never paid no mind as to what most of them did for a living. But they weren't got-dam drug dealers, if that's what you're asking."

Her retort embarrassed him, because the thought had crossed his mind. At first. Even though he hated to admit it. "No, ma'am. So, nobody you know of would want to hurt him?"

"No."

"What about a couple of nights ago?" John said. "When did you last see him?"

"Like you said, couple nights ago," Dot said. The façade cracked a bit, and her bottom lip quivered. "He went to that new club, the Marquee. Dancing."

"Did he have a date?"

Dot shook her head. "He most likely met up with a girl he goes with sometimes, though. Tameeka Jones. Pretty thing. She's a schoolteacher at Fairview Elementary."

"One last question, Miz Wilkinson," John said. "Did you expect him home that night?"

Dot's eyes misted behind her glasses. Her hands still clung to the chair. She stared at nothing for a long moment.

"Yes, I did," she said. "Kenny was dependable. And kind. He was a decent boy, never hurt no one."

He stood. "Thank you, ma'am. I'll take my leave now and talk to Tameeka. I appreciate your time."

Whatever emotion had softened the woman evaporated like water on a hot skillet. She pushed herself out of her chair and jabbed a finger at him. "You tell that white sheriff I want some justice," she said.

He couldn't—wouldn't—let that pass. He put his hands on his hips. "Miz Wilkinson, I've known Sheriff Harper since we were both eighteen years old. Served in combat with him. I can assure you he won't rest until we catch whoever did this."

"I heard he went to a meeting the other day and it didn't go well. After he arrested Reverend Mike."

"I was there," John said slowly, reining in his temper. "And I can tell you this: when we find the person, Sheriff Harper won't care what color he is. You take care." He turned and strode out of the house, surprised at how riled he was—at Dot, at Colt, at himself.

Fifteen minutes in the car cooled him off enough to be pleasant to the Fairview Elementary principal, a tall fiftyish man who introduced himself as Mr. Baines and who was all too happy to assist him. Baines paged Tameeka Jones, who walked through the glass door four minutes later. John saw that Dot had been right—she was indeed pretty. Tall and slim, no more than twenty-five. Every little boy's dream teacher.

The principal made introductions, and Tameeka pointed to the teachers' lounge through a side door. John followed her in, and they sat in plastic chairs opposite each other at a round lunch table. Tameeka fidgeted with her hands, pink-painted fingernails clacking. He glanced down at the noise and realized she had no idea about the reason for his visit. She misread the look and jammed her hands in her lap.

"Miss Jones," he began.

"Please," she said, smiling nervously. "The kids call me that. I'm Tameeka."

She really had no idea why he was here. "Tameeka, I'm here about Kenneth Wilkinson. I believe you know him."

Tameeka searched his eyes, her own full of apprehension. "I do, yes."

John shifted in his seat. "He's been killed."

The announcement hit her like a punch to the sternum. She fell back in her chair and gasped, pink nails flying to her mouth. "Killed? How? And when?"

"We aren't completely sure," John said, hoping the vague answer would suffice. "That's why I'm here. Did you see him at the Marquee two nights ago?"

He watched her wrestle her composure back into place, let her take her time. No sense rushing her. When she was ready, she nodded. "He was there. We dance there pretty often. We're not dating or anything like that. Just meet up there to dance and hang out. Sometimes we just happen to be there at the same time. Kenny's a great dancer."

John figured Kenneth Wilkinson had probably considered himself damn lucky with that arrangement. "And you're sure it was two nights ago?"

"I'm sure," Tameeka said. "I had to get home early that night on account of school the next day."

John made a mental note that he could now narrow down Wilkinson' time of death. "So, how well did you know him?"

Tameeka shrugged. "Now that you mention it, not really all that well. I know he worked in retail, lived with his aunt. He wanted to be a teacher, too. That's one of the things we had in common. We met at the club one night a few months ago and started talking, so that's how I know that. But mostly, we were just dancing buddies."

"Did Kenneth use drugs, that you know of?" John said, even though he knew the answer, as well as the question, might incriminate her as well.

"Not that I ever saw."

John considered her response. Neutral. Not fearful, not indignant. Truthful. "Okay, tell me about seeing him the other night."

"I saw him come in around eight or so," she said. "I'd already been there a little while. We danced a little; then he went to the bar to get a drink, and I went to talk to a couple of girlfriends."

"That was the last you saw of him?"

Tameeka shook her head. "No. I saw him about an hour later. I stepped outside to smoke, and I saw him talking to another man. It was at the other end of the parking lot. They had some words, then got into a truck and drove off."

John sat up, heart skipping. "Had words? Did you see this man?"

"Not really," Tameeka said. "His back was to me, mostly. He was big, I know that. He almost blocked Kenneth from sight."

"White guy? Black guy?"

Tameeka cocked her head at him. Curious. "Really couldn't tell you. He was big. Jeans. Dark shirt. Dark hair. *Could* have been white. It was a long way off, and it was dark."

"What about the truck?"

"Dark also. Pickup truck. And that's the limit of my knowledge about automobiles."

"That's okay," he said. "Thank you. This is very, very helpful."

Worry, then alarm, clouded Tameeka's smooth face. "Do you think—did this man kill Kenny?"

John held up a hand. "We don't know everything yet. The investigation is still open, so I can't really comment on it beyond that. But you have helped me out enormously, Miss Jones."

"Tameeka."

"Right," he said, getting to his feet. Tameeka followed him up. "I'll let you get back to work." He fished a card from a breast pocket, handed it to her. "If you think of anything else, anything at all, give me a call."

Tameeka stared at the card and nodded. He walked through the principal's office and out of the building, punching up Colt's number on his cell before he made it to his car.

"Goddammit, that's Burnett," Colt yelled into his ear after John told him about the morning's rounds and the interview with Tameeka Jones.

“I’m thinking the same,” John said. “Question is, how to go at him?”

“Same way I usually do,” Colt said. “Straight at the son of a bitch.”

John shook his head as he steered his car through downtown streets. He remembered Rhonda’s warning. “I think Molly’s following him now.”

“Fine, I’ll give her a call,” Colt said. He hung up before John could answer.

CHAPTER FORTY

MOLLY

Harper was going through some shit with this case, Molly thought as she ate an order of fries at a tiny café clinging to the highway shoulder near the main entrance to Claiborne's farm. From her vantage point, she could clock all incoming and outgoing traffic. Burnett had driven down the dusty road toward the farm an hour ago. She watched a customer swing a six-pack onto the counter at the other end of the place, near the walk-in cooler. She waited for it. That jolt of a craving at the sight of a drink, the total obsession of it. Didn't come. She felt nothing at all. She checked the door. Four steps away, her escape plan. She'd talked with Michelle for a few minutes at the morning meeting. Seemed to be working. For once. Her hands weren't even shaking.

The topic for her early-bird meeting at seven a.m. had been "To thine own self be true," which had prompted no small amount of turmoil in her mind, that very topic haunting her far too often. Trouble was she wasn't exactly sure what self she was. Or wanted to be.

She used to know, had gone through life knowing. She'd mapped her life out since she was nine years old: college for a criminal justice, maybe law, degree. She chose the former. Then federal agent. Check. Done and done.

She stared out the plate-glass window as a flatbed semi slowed, turned, and rattled toward the farm.

But if that version of herself was true, how in the hell did she wind up *here*, eating French fries in a roadside choke-n-puke diner in Mississippi, looking like a crazy redhead staring out a window for an hour? Was this the real her?

She hadn't shared at the meeting—her careening thoughts on the topic were too much—and as soon as the meeting was over, Harper came to mind.

In him she saw a man up to his eyeballs in trying to be true to himself. And he was getting it from all sides, caught in a racial crossfire. This place—not this shitty diner—had scarred Harper somehow, left a mark on him he tried to keep hidden, like when you try to hide a bad tattoo. But the mark remained.

He and Rhonda had history, one that went way beyond the death of her son. She'd first seen it in the hospital a year ago, when Rhonda sat at his bedside. And again at the community meeting. The way they spoke to each other. The exchanged looks. That had to be something difficult to manage in this weird-ass goddam time-warp lost-in-space world.

And his father's shadow. Whatever that man was and did, it clouded Harper's every step. She'd probably never know it all, didn't want to, but she knew what it was like to have a ghost looking over your shoulder.

So, the man was caught in the middle. Where did that put her?

Her cell phone buzzed on the table. Harper's name appeared on the display. She wiped her hands on her jeans and answered.

"You got eyes on Burnett?" he said by way of hello.

"He's at the farm. Been there about an hour. What's up?"

She listened as Harper relayed John's information and his conclusion that Burnett killed the Wilkinson kid. "I want that son of a bitch brought back in," he said in conclusion.

She squinted in the glare of the sunlight pouring into the café. Another hot-ass day.

"I agree he's good for it," she said, tapping a finger on the table.

"But?"

More tapping. Yeah, but what? "Look, Harper," she said, trying to organize her words. "I like Burnett for this, too. But the last interview got us squat. And there are a lot of white guys with pickups in this county. I say we wait. We jump now, he's going to lawyer up, and then we won't be able to touch him. Let's see if the coroner comes back with something more solid."

She heard a long sigh.

"Goddammit," Harper said. "You're right."

She had to smile. "Damn right I am."

"Don't get cocky, McDonough. Stay on his ass."

"You know I will."

Harper hung up. She put the phone down thinking, whoever she really was, right now she was in the middle of a murder case. She went back to work on her fries, watching the window for Burnett's truck.

CHAPTER FORTY-ONE

COLT

Colt slapped the phone onto his desk and pushed away the half-eaten ham sandwich. The conversation with Molly had killed his appetite.

He looked up when he heard tapping on his door. Becky, of course. She stepped in, holding up a copy of the *Dispatch*.

"You want to read it, or just let me tell you the highlights?" she said.

"That sounds like bad news," he said. "Just the highlights, then."

Becky blew a wisp of hair from her eyes and put on a pair of reading glasses. "Looks like Craig Battles has been busy. Three stories, including the front page. Reverend Sanders says he's not suing us."

"What do you know? I guess that's *good* news," Colt said, attempting a smile.

Becky held up a finger. "But," she said. "He isn't sure he would endorse you for another term."

Colt grabbed his sandwich. Might as well finish eating, if nothing else. "Endorse me? The election is three years off. Did he even endorse me the last time?" he said through a mouthful.

"There's a lot of what Craig calls 'lingering resentment,'" Becky said, her face deadpan, "among the black community."

"Lingering?"

"He wrote it, not me." Becky peered at him over her glasses.

"What else?"

"On the other side of the fence, so to speak, the other community—I really hate that word—by which he means white people, are upset that you maybe set a killer free."

Colt ignored Becky's editorializing, even though he, too, hated the word. "Seriously? He *is* a preacher, after all."

"Again, Colt," Becky said, "I didn't write it. Don't kill the messenger."

He crumpled the remains of his lunch into the wax paper it had come in. "It's not that, Becky. It's just that this case seems to piss everybody off no matter what I do. What do *you* think?"

"Me? Really?"

He looked up at her expectantly.

Becky took off her glasses, crossed her arms. "I think you're doing your job. A job that most people have no idea about how complicated it is. Especially one like this. People like that Craig Battles just like to stir things up. All it does is distract you. And you don't need any more distractions."

That caught him by surprise. Distractions?

"What are you talking about, Becky?"

"Nothing," Becky said, suddenly ready to bolt. "Anything else?"

"Nope."

She turned and disappeared back into the main office just as it hit him—she was talking about Molly. "I'll be damned," he said to the empty room.

He tossed the paper into the trash can by his desk and swept the crumbs away with a hand. He grabbed the landline and punched in the number to the Claiborne farm. Receptionist Holly answered right away and transferred him to Hank's line.

"What can I do for you, Colt?" Hank said when he came on. None of the usual congenial, "Hey, man, how's it going?" he usually got from Hank.

"Still working this Wallace case, Hank," Colt said, matching Hank's tone. "Trying to put all the pieces together. Establish timelines, that kind of thing."

"I see," Hank said.

So that's how it's going to go. "It's a lot of information and I'm just trying to make it all fit."

"Not sure I follow. What's this got to do with me?"

Colt pulled a legal pad out of a drawer, started scribbling notes.

"Just trying to account for everyone and rule out obvious people."

"Are you saying I'm not ruled out?"

"Hank, I have to level with you. You did have an argument with Wallace a few days before he was killed. And there were witnesses to that argument."

Hank waited a beat too long to answer, and to Colt the moment felt like when he was fishing and could feel a big bass bumping his line.

"Are you accusing me of killing Lucius, one of my own employees?" Hank said.

"You didn't let me finish," Colt said, hoping he'd set the hook. "Anybody who saw or even heard about that argument could be considered somebody who might have seen an opportunity to do Wallace harm, so we've had to do a lot of checking. Process of elimination is all. Make sure everybody's story checks out."

"Uh-huh," Hank said. He sounded agitated. "And do they?"

"So far," Colt said. "One thing, though. When we talked to Jack, he said he was at a bar the night Wallace was killed. Of course, I had to verify that with the bartender, who vouched for him."

He paused, laid his pen on the desk, giving Hank a chance to react. Nothing.

"So," he continued, "Jack checked out. Bartender said something interesting, though. Said you were with him. Which struck me as funny because you never mentioned that before. Bartender was pretty sure it was you, though. Identified you from a picture."

Another pause; another nonresponse.

"Hank?"

Colt heard what sounded like papers rustling. What was he doing, paying bills?

"Uh, Colt," Hank said finally. His tone was more like the one he'd used at the meeting—authority. "You're going to have to talk to my lawyer."

That surprised him. "Your *lawyer*? Are you kidding me, Hank?"

"I think that would be best, given the nature of this call."

"You got something to tell me, Hank? Now would be a good time. I can't say the next time will be this friendly."

"You heard me, Colt." Hank clicked off the line, leaving him staring at the phone. There were a lot of things he could call Hank Claiborne, but cagey wouldn't have been one of them before this call.

"Have it your way, Hank," he said. He thumbed the button on the phone to get a dial tone, called the courthouse. When the receptionist answered, he identified himself. "I need to speak to Judge Dockery," he said. "I need a search warrant."

CHAPTER FORTY-TWO

HANK

Hank slammed the phone down on his desk. He opened the bottom drawer where he kept the bottle and took a long pull straight from the neck. When he saw his hands shaking, he took another slug, let the burn slide all the way down to his belly, then recapped the bottle.

Fucking Colt Harper. No, no. Fucking Jack Burnett.

He set the bottle on the double-pedestal oak desk that had been his father's and rubbed his eyes. When he stopped, and his eyes had refocused, everything looked the same. Sadly. Photos of Mississippi State football games on the wall to his left, file cabinets on the right. His desktop empty except for one picture of his two preteen kids, taken somewhere in North Carolina where they lived with his ex-wife, Rita.

He pulled his cell phone from his back pocket, dialed Jack's number.

"He's onto us," he said when Jack came on the line after three endless rings.

"Who?"

"Harper, who do you think?" Hank said.

"What happened, Hank?"

"He just called here, asking about me and you being at that bar the night you … the night Lucius died."

"So what?" Jack said, his voice thick with scorn. "That don't mean shit. What did you say?"

"To talk to my lawyer."

The pause on Jack's end was long enough for Hank to down two more huge gulps of whiskey. He couldn't even hear Jack breathing. He wiped his mouth with the back of his hand. "Jack?"

"*You did what?*"

"What did you expect me to do?" Hank said.

"I expect you to not be a dumbass," Jack said. "Jesus Christ, that was stupid."

Hank's head felt light. Either from Jack's yelling in his ear or the booze or both. "Shut up, Jack," he said with more confidence than he felt. "All I told him was to talk to my lawyer. You've got your alibi, right? So do I. Harper doesn't have shit on us."

He could hear Jack moving around, possibly throwing stuff. He drank more bourbon.

"Goddammit," Jack said.

"Look," Hank said. "I'm calling my lawyer right now; then I'm going home to delete shit off my computer. Just sit tight until I call you back."

"Don't tell me what to do," Jack said.

The insolence cut through the whiskey haze and pissed him off. "I'll tell you any goddam thing I please. Remember, you work for me."

He slammed the phone back into its cradle, screwed the cap back on the bottle, and put it away. There'd be more at home.

CHAPTER FORTY-THREE

COLT

Colt laid down the half-inch-thick coroner's report that Becky had printed out ten minutes earlier. He walked to the door of his office just as Molly was slinging a backpack into her chair in the bullpen.

"Molly, in here," he said.

She turned, saw his face, then yanked her laptop from the backpack and headed his way.

He slid the report across the desk. "Take a look at this," he said. Molly grabbed the report, started reading. "John's on Burnett, right?"

"We switched off half an hour ago," Molly said.

Colt got Freddie Mac on the phone, put him on speaker.

"You read it already?" the coroner said.

"The main parts," Colt said. "You're on speaker with me and Molly. Walk us through it."

"Certainly," Freddie Mac said. "I called in a favor to get this moved to the top of the list with the Jackson lab, so you owe me one on that. Anyway, since I was able to do that, I managed to include that tiny sample of blood from the Wallace crime scene, the one we found at the edge of the pit. I didn't think it was enough to extract any usable DNA at first, but I was able to get something. And since I was asking a favor, I figured, why not?"

Colt shot a look at Molly, who was still plowing through the pages.

"Freddie Mac, you're a man among men," Colt said. "I didn't see that in the report."

"Then you didn't read the appendix."

The comment evoked a chuckle from Molly. She held up the report with the pages folded back to the one marked "Appendix."

"I'll get to it," Colt said. "But you're telling me the DNA from both crime scenes is a match?"

"That is correct," Freddie Mac said. "Jack Burnett."

"Finally," Colt said, more to himself than to Freddie Mac or Molly. "How'd you pin him?"

"As you know, having a match is one thing; having an identity is another," Freddie Mac said. "State boys searched the state crime database and came up empty. I cross-indexed the results with the NCIC—the National Crime—"

"Information Center," Colt said, annoyed. "I know what the NCIC is."

"Right," Freddie Mac said. "Both samples hit the same name, Jack Burnett. The rest of the evidence fits. Which isn't to say it matches, of course—that's your job—but the weapon used in both homicides is very likely the same, a nine-millimeter."

"How sure are you?" Molly said, looking at the phone.

"I'd say seventy-five, eighty percent," Freddie Mac said. "The Wilkinson kid had been in the water, which always makes things harder. But both men were killed at point-blank range. Angles of the bullets would lead me to believe your shooter is right-handed. Both victims had entry wounds on the leftmost part of their bodies."

"Anything else?" Colt said.

"Wilkinson fought back, as evidenced by the skin under his nails," Freddie Mac said. "But he had ligature marks on his wrists—his hands were bound. And some blunt-force trauma to his back. That kid was executed, Colt."

Molly looked up from the report and nodded. Colt had already come to that conclusion. "Thanks, Freddie Mac."

"You're welcome," the coroner said and ended the call.

Molly slid the report back across the desk. It spun to a halt at Colt's fingertips. "*Now* we arrest Jack Burnett," she said.

"And Hank Claiborne," Colt said. "Got a warrant working for that." He dialed John's number.

"What's up, boss?" John answered.

"We have Jack Burnett's DNA at both scenes," Colt said.

"Hot damn," John said. "I'm at his place now. Bring him in?"

Colt punched the speaker button. "Molly's on, too, John. No, sit tight. I'll come to you and we'll do it together." He ignored the glare from Molly. "I've got a warrant coming for Claiborne. Molly will execute it at the same time as we take Burnett. You're wearing a vest, right?"

"Of course. Are you?"

"Don't worry about me." He hung up. Molly started to speak, but he shut her down with a raised hand. "It's not because you're a woman. Well, actually, it kind of is."

"You're making my point, Harper," Molly said.

"What I mean is, one, John is the senior deputy. I've known him a long time, and we've done this before. Two, yeah, you're a woman—and Hank Claiborne has never met you. And he damn sure won't be expecting *you*. It's not much of an edge, but it'll help throw him off when you're the one serving his ass, not me."

Molly tapped her foot on the floor. Loudly. Clearly not happy. "Is 'aye, aye, sir' the proper response?"

"Close enough."

"So, when do we get the warrant?"

"As soon as I pry it out of Judge Dockery's hands," Colt said. "Which reminds me." He picked up the phone; Molly took her cue and left.

He drummed his fingers on his desk as he dialed the number to the office of Judge Robert Dockery and waited for his secretary, Mary Ann, to answer. His impatience grew with each passing ring.

Finally, Mary Ann answered: "Judge Dockery's office."

"Hi, Mary Ann, it's Sheriff Harper."

"Hello, Sheriff," Mary Ann said in her always-cordial tone. "What can I do for you?"

"Is the judge available?"

"He's in his chambers at the moment. Anything I can help you with?"

"No, I need to speak to him about a warrant," he said, more sharply than he had intended.

"Hold on, I'll see if he can speak to you about that."

"Thank you, Mary Ann," Colt said. He drummed his fingers some more, as if he could transfer his annoyance at the judge to his desktop. It wasn't like Dockery to take this long on one of his search warrant requests. He had a good working relationship with Dockery, who'd been a judge during the terms of three different sheriffs.

"Sheriff Harper, how're you doing?" Dockery said when he came on the line.

"Judge Dockery, I appreciate you taking the time. I know you're busy."

The judge chuckled. "That's an understatement. Mary Ann said something about a warrant."

Colt stilled his fingers. "Yes, sir," he said. "I'm investigating a homicide, and that search warrant is relevant to the case."

"Yes, I know it's a homicide," Dockery said. "Is the warrant for a suspect?"

Colt leaned back in his chair. "Not exactly, Judge. But the residence belongs to a person who may be a material witness or an accessory. Or both."

"May be."

Colt started the rhythm section on his desk again. "We believe the resident, Hank Claiborne, may be in possession of material information related to the case."

"Hank Claiborne?" Dockery said. "Accessory to a homicide? Are you sure about this one, Colt?"

"As sure as I can be at this point," Colt said in what he hoped was a professional tone. "I have reason to believe that Hank—Mr. Claiborne—may be in collusion with our suspect, who we plan to arrest very soon."

"I see," Dockery said. "I'm guessing you want to execute the search warrant of Claiborne's in conjunction with the arrest."

"Yes, sir."

"I've read over the request, Colt, and I don't necessarily oppose the warrant, but you're asking for a lot, based on what could be argued is dubious probable cause and the fact that Hank Claiborne, I don't have to tell you, is a well-known and respected figure in this community."

Colt balled up his fist. "Your Honor, I'm aware of that. I'm just trying to do my job protecting the people of this county."

"And I'm doing the same," Dockery said. "You do it with a badge and a bullet, and I do it with the rule of law. I'm always sympathetic to your challenges as a law enforcement officer, but, frankly, I'm also a little concerned about your methods."

"My methods, Your Honor?" Colt said. His anger roiled up.

"Considering the last year or so, you tend to attract the same violence you're trying to stop," Dockery said. "And now you want to execute a warrant on a man who has no criminal record and is, in fact—not to use a cliché—one of the leading citizens of the county. Colt, he contributed to my campaign and I'm guessing yours as well. The Claibornes have been a big part of this county for years, you know that. Hank's good people."

Colt squeezed his eyes shut and banged his fist on the desk. He didn't know what to say.

"I'll sign it," Dockery said. "But, I'm telling you, you better be right on this one."

"Yes, sir," Colt said, wishing to be off the phone.

"Anything else?"

"No, sir."

The line went dead. Colt slammed the receiver down, the judge's words burning a hole in his brain like a laser: "Hank's good people."

Money and reputation, all rolled into one unassailable status in the eyes of justice: good people. Didn't hurt that Hank was white. Didn't matter that the victim was black.

And there it was.

Just as John and Rhonda had been trying to make him see. He hadn't been color-blind at all, just blind.

CHAPTER FORTY-FOUR

COLT

He sensed the call from John about a minute before the phone rang. A guy like Burnett wasn't liable to stay in one place for very long, especially when he'd almost certainly been tipped off by now—thanks to Judge Dockery's initial hesitation to sign the goddam warrant to search Claiborne's place. That conversation still burned in his mind.

He'd bolted out the door as soon he'd gotten off the horn with the judge, told Molly to take Deputy Townsend with her to execute the warrant, and blew through a red light and two yellows to join John.

"Hey, Colt, I got a feeling this guy's about to rabbit," John said. "Where are you?"

"Two blocks," he answered.

"Damn it, make it quick. I just saw him casing the parking lot from a window."

"Going as—"

"Gotta go," John said in the voice Colt remembered from a couple of firefights. "Door just opened."

"John, wait," Colt said, but he heard the click ending the call. "Son of a bitch."

He mashed the accelerator and hit the siren. No point being covert about anything now. The Crown Vic leapt underneath him like a rodeo bull, and he swooped down Eighth Street, ignoring stop signs. He swerved into a hard left onto Fifth Avenue and could feel the tires sliding across the pavement. He came up on John's vehicle faster than he expected, and he stood on the brakes, stopping inches from John's car. He threw the car up in park and jumped out with his pistol in hand.

The two-story apartment complex was a long rectangle with the narrow side toward the street. A parking lot half the length of a football field. He scanned the lot. John crouched behind a sedan parked on the far side of the lot. Colt bent double and ran as fast he was able to John's side, praying his hip wouldn't give out now. He pulled up beside John, who had his eyes on Burnett's door. A single track of sweat made its way from his hairline to a point below his right eye.

"Fucker made me, ducked back inside," John said. "What took you so long?"

"Been arguing with a judge," Colt said. "Burnett say anything?"

"No, just ducked back inside."

"Any civilians in the area?"

"None that I've noticed," John said. He twisted around, stole a look over the top of the car. "I don't like this one bit. He's up on the second floor. Clear field of fire across the parking lot. Call for backup?"

"That's a great idea," Colt said, raising up enough to peer over the hood of the vehicle. "Except for the fact we're inside the city limits. We call it in, and it'll turn into a clusterfuck between our guys and the city cops."

John ducked behind the car and stared at him. "So, you're saying we—you and me—are going to do this on our own?"

Colt attempted a grin. Didn't work. "Yep, that's what I'm saying."

"Goddammit, Colt," John said. He took another look up at Burnett's apartment. "No way I can talk you out of it?"

"Nope."

"Well, to hell with it, then. How you want to do this?"

Colt scanned the parking lot, even though he'd already gotten the layout in his head. "We can't go up the stairs here. Too close to his door. Work your way toward the building, then down to the end, take the stairs there. He won't be able to see you because of the angle."

John thought that through, glanced over the car at the stairwell about twenty yards away. He swiveled his head around, computing distances. "Okay, I can do that. What are you going to do?"

"Work my way to the building and then up these stairs so that I'm in position when you get to his door. We go in together."

John took a deep breath. Looked over at him, then nodded. He spun, still in a crouch, facing the building. "Ready?"

"Always," Colt said.

John bolted like a sprinter coming out of the blocks toward the building. Colt trained his pistol on the window next to Burnett's door. John very nearly made it to the shelter of the building when the window exploded in a blast and a cloud of glass splinters that sent John diving to the ground underneath the second-story walkway. Colt ducked and rolled against the side of the car, came up over the trunk with his pistol aimed at the smoking black hole where the window used to be. He fired three shots, ducked, moved back to his original spot. Across his field of vision, he could see John sprinting toward the far stairwell. Then he heard the unmistakable sound of another shell being racked into the chamber of a shotgun. Sawed-off, most likely, judging from the big-ass hole in the window.

Another blast tore the air, causing him to flatten out again and scuttle to a spot behind the car.

Colt stood and aimed his pistol at the hole in the window. "Hey, Burnett!" he yelled at the house. "This is Sheriff Harper, and I'm only going to say this once. Put that goddam shotgun down and come out here with your hands up. You hear me?"

He heard another shell racked into the chamber.

"Why don't you just come on in here and arrest me, Sheriff, you think you're such a badass?" The voice was calm and definitely Burnett's.

Colt took a breath, steadied, let it out, kept the .45 aimed on the window. "Burnett, you make me come in there with a gun in my hand, I ain't gonna arrest you. You understand?"

Silence.

"You hear me?" he yelled. From the corner of his eye, he could see John mounting the stairwell to his right.

Still silence.

This didn't feel right.

John was moving toward the door.

No, this wasn't right. Colt stood up and waved John to a halt.

John looked at him, confused as hell.

"He's going out the back, John," Colt yelled as he took off from the parking lot. "I'm going after him."

"Out the back?" John said, looking down at him like he was crazy. "He's on the second floor."

But Colt was already rounding the building, weapon in front of him, expecting a bullet to tear into him. He scanned the second floor of the back of the building, counted windows, until he saw the open one. He tracked down from the window, scanned the parking lot. Empty except for one blue van on his right and a dumpster at the far end. Woods beyond. On his left, a head-high row of hedges.

And here he stood, he realized, in the wide open, making a target of himself.

He sprinted the ten yards to the van. The doors were locked. He turned from the driver's side toward the dumpster. The window exploded around him, and he felt the hot blast of another load of buckshot passing very near his head. Glass pellets pummeled his face even as his ears registered the sound of the shots. He went down to the pavement on his belly, facing the hedgerow, his eyes scanning the foliage. The shots had come from there, he was sure.

And *there.*

Two worn work boots. He set his sights about three feet above the boots and squeezed the trigger. The big .45 roared and bucked in his hands. He held his aim, heard nothing. No movement behind the hedges. He pushed himself to his feet, his entire being focused on the line of green in front of him. He'd hit Burnett, he had no doubt. His senses kicked into hyperdrive, and even with the report of the .45 ringing in his ears, he now heard the moan of a wounded man.

He squinted in the glare, searching. A wounded man was more dangerous than a wounded animal, and this one was armed. He focused on the sound, took two more steps. He heard a loud grunt, then froze when Jack Burnett pushed his way through the hedge.

The man was a mess.

His face had gone gray, left arm tattered and dangling uselessly as bright red blood coursed freely from the biceps, past exposed bone, to spill on the black asphalt. His right hand grasped a Glock. He took two limping steps, and Colt guessed he must have broken an ankle in his leap from the apartment window.

"Right there, Burnett," Colt said, aiming in. "You take one more step, I'm going to put you down for good."

Burnett's head slumped to his chest; then he looked up at Colt with a face that couldn't believe his predicament.

"Drop that goddam pistol," Colt said. To his left, he heard, then saw John closing on the scene, pistol drawn, sweat pouring off him.

Burnett's eyes followed John for a long moment, then fluttered. He looked back at Colt. The Glock fell to the pavement.

"On your knees," Colt said. Then, to John: "Call an ambulance."

Burnett sank to his knees, then fell, like a sack of grain, onto his back. Colt stepped toward him, pistol still aimed at his head. "John, go."

John pocketed his cell phone, holstered his weapon, and pounced onto Burnett's weak form, frisking him roughly and thoroughly, then flipped him onto his belly and handcuffed him with entirely more force than was necessary. Burnett screamed as his shattered arm twisted behind him. John leaned over, jammed a knee in Burnett's back. "You're getting off easy, asshole. And don't forget that a black cop just cuffed you."

John stood and stepped back. Colt squatted, avoided the growing pool of blood fanning out around Burnett. He could hear a siren—the ambulance—a few blocks away.

"You're in bad shape, Jack," Colt said. "You ask me, you ain't going to live to see the inside of a prison, bleeding like you are."

"Fuck you, Harper," Burnett said, his eyes screwed shut.

"I'm sure you feel that way," Colt said. "But, you know, since you're dying and all, you might as well tell me why. I know you killed Lucius and Kenneth Wilkinson, but I don't know why."

Burnett writhed in his own blood and gasped. "Wallace was a goddam accident," he said. "He'd still be alive, but he wouldn't shut the fuck up."

"What about Wilkinson?"

Burnett wheezed and rolled his forehead on the pavement. "What difference does it make now? Easy target."

Colt glanced up at John, who held his phone toward him. Recording it all. The ambulance was very close.

"So, Jack, what is Hank's play in all this? How did you get him involved in all this white-supremacy shit?"

Burnett rolled an eye toward him. "Me?" he said. "Who the hell do you think started all this? Wanted all this to happen?"

Colt cocked his head, shot John a look. "Hank."

But Burnett had slipped away. Colt heard a siren shriek, then go silent, and he stood. An ambulance rolled to a stop at the curb about twenty feet away. A pair of EMTs jumped out of the vehicle and ran toward them. The driver, a fortyish man with a weary face, was already on a handheld radio with the hospital.

The other, younger and fit, scrambled to Burnett's side and, with a low voice, said, "Holy shit. I need some room." He popped open his medical kit and started yanking out bandages, tubes, and a blood-pressure cuff. He looked over his shoulder. "Can we take the cuffs off him?"

Colt looked at John. "He makes one move, make it his last." He knelt and took the cuffs off Burnett.

"Thanks," the EMT said as he went to work.

Colt and John watched the driver haul out the gurney and roll the contraption back to his partner. He noticed the blood on them both as he went by and grabbed gauze pads from the medical kit and held them out. Colt took one, handed John another, and wiped his hands free of Burnett's blood; John did the same. They watched the grim-faced EMTs work in silence to get Burnett stabilized and onto the gurney.

"Wait," Colt said to them. Both EMTS swiveled their heads and leveled disbelieving stares at him. "He conscious?"

"Barely," the driver said. Then, "We really need to get him to the hospital, Sheriff."

"All right, go," he said. He looked at John. "Thought for sure he was dead."

John shook his head. "I'm going to regret making that call for the rest of my life."

CHAPTER FORTY-FIVE

MOLLY

Townsend didn't talk much. All she knew about the deputy in the passenger seat was that he was supposed to retire in a few weeks. Even though he didn't look old enough for that. Maybe it was the short, almost military haircut, along with the frosty blue eyes.

He'd hardly said a word when she'd come to his desk and briefed him on the Claiborne warrant and Harper's instruction to take him with her. He listened closely, then said, simply, "Sure. Be glad to."

So far, that had been the entirety of their conversation. She glanced over at Townsend now, as the car ascended the tall concrete bridge over the Tombigbee.

"What are you planning to do when you retire?" she said, just to cut through the silence in the car.

"As little as possible," Townsend said, staring out the passenger-side window. "Though my wife might have something to say about that. You been to this residence before?"

The sudden shift in topic threw her off. "Uh, no, I haven't. You?"

"Only driven by it. It's big. This could take a while."

She didn't quite know how to respond to that. "Suggestions?"

Townsend didn't speak for a moment. Then, "You've done these before when you were a fed, so you know we'll separate Claiborne from the house. And anybody else who might be there."

"Right," she said, wondering how Townsend knew she had been a special agent. Then again, small town, small department.

"So, we get Claiborne out of the house. I'll isolate him while you execute the warrant, do the search."

Molly glanced over at Townsend. He was serious. She'd expected him to say that he'd handle everything, no need to worry her pretty little head over anything. A flash of embarrassment jolted her.

As if reading her mind, Townsend chuckled. "I got no problem with you being in charge."

She grinned back at him. "Fair enough."

"But I do wish we had more bodies for this," he said.

"Me, too." She hit her turn signal and wheeled onto the shaded road that led to Claiborne's house. The massive two-story brick house—Townsend had been right—came into view as the road curved gently to the left, away from the broad river glittering in the sun on the right. Hank Claiborne lived very well for a catfish farmer. She slowed, parked the car near the entrance to the residence. A set of three crosstie steps flanked by low, ornate brick walls surrounded by beds of marigolds led to a lush green carpet of golf-course-quality Bermuda grass bisected by a sidewalk leading to the house itself. The place looked like something out of a real estate brochure.

"Ready?" Molly said.

"Yep," Townsend said, swinging his door open.

She and Townsend climbed out of the cruiser and mounted the steps to the sidewalk. She felt a familiar nervousness, a sort of muscle reflex all cops get when approaching the unknown. But its familiarity, in a world that was lately unfamiliar, gave her an odd comfort.

She banged on the door as Townsend scanned the area in front of the house. No answer. She hammered the door again with her fist. "Mr. Claiborne, sheriff's office," she called. The only answer came from her words echoing across the lawn. She looked over at Townsend, who shrugged. He stepped over to a ten-foot bay window and peered in, his hand cupped around his eyes.

"Dark," Townsend said. "Nobody's here. You sure he was supposed to be home?"

"I assumed so," Molly said. Goddam assumptions. She knew better. "Hold on." She yanked her phone out and tapped in Harper's number.

"Yeah, Molly?" Harper said after the first ring.

"Claiborne's not here," she said.

"What do you mean he's not there?" Harper said. She could tell he was pissed off or in the middle of something—most likely Jack Burnett.

"Just what I said," she said. "Not home. Nobody answering the door."

"Goddammit," Harper said. "Townsend's with you, right?"

"Yep."

"Kick the fucking door in if you have to. You got a warrant." He clicked off.

Well, screw him. She'd already thought of that. She slid her phone in her pocket and beckoned Townsend. He stepped over, his face a question.

"You might want to step back," she said, pulling her pistol.

Townsend blank-stared her but drew his weapon as well. She leaned back and kicked the door near the handle as hard as she could. The door gave way in a shriek of splintering wood and swung open, its hinges protesting in one long squeal. She leveled her pistol at the dark interior of the residence.

"Come on," she said.

CHAPTER FORTY-SIX
COLT

"What's up with Molly?" John said as he and Colt walked back to their vehicles.

"Claiborne's not home," Colt said. He swiped sweat from his brow and punched up Becky's number on his cell phone. "Hey, Becky," he said when she came on, "patch me through to Hank Claiborne's farm."

"Sure," Becky said. "Hold on."

John started to say something but Colt held up a hand. The phone rang twice; then he heard Holly's now-familiar voice: "Claiborne Farm. This is Holly."

"Hey, Holly, Sheriff Harper. Is Hank in?"

"Oh hey, Sheriff," Holly said in a too-courteous voice. "'Fraid not. Hank left about an hour ago."

He beckoned at John, who was about to climb into his car. John shut the door and walked toward him.

"He say where he was going?" Colt said.

"No, sir, he didn't," Holly said. "He usually does, but not today."

"Thanks, Holly," he said and hung up. John watched him, his eyes a question.

"He's not in the office, either," Colt said.

"You think Burnett tipped him off?"

"I'd bet my badge on it."

"So, where's he headed?" John said.

Colt didn't even have to think about the question. "His cabin."

"Where you saw him the other night?" John said.

Colt opened his car door. "Get in and we'll find out."

Colt cranked up the car and spun out of the parking lot, headed south. He weaved through the city streets until he reached the highway, then lowered his foot on the pedal until the car was nearly sailing down the asphalt. John stayed quiet. He hit the lights and siren when he saw vehicles ahead, and he didn't wait for them to move to the shoulder. He swooped past the too-slow ones in the other lane, yanking the wheel left and right to avoid oncoming traffic.

He made the turnoff in five minutes and slowed as the car rattled down the worn gravel path.

"There," John said, pointing at a BMW and a green Ford in front of it. "Who else you figure is here?"

Colt skidded to a stop behind the BMW. "Beats the hell out of me. Grab the shotgun."

"You looking for a firefight?" John said as he reached over the back seat and grabbed the short-barreled twelve-gauge loaded with buckshot.

"Looking? No," Colt said. "But if I had to guess, I'd say there's liable to be one."

John racked the slide to put a round in the chamber. "Better safe, I guess."

They climbed out, and Colt led the way down the dirt path toward the cabin. He found the going much easier and faster in the daylight, and they could make out the shape of the building through the trees after a few minutes. Just as Colt spied two men, both armed, standing outside the door, one of them turned, raised his weapon to his shoulder, and fired at them. The staccato burst of automatic fire tore through the dense air and they both dove for cover behind pine trees.

"I'd say they are definitely armed," Colt said to John, who lay prone ten feet away.

"What now?" John said, staring ahead at the two men. "That backup we couldn't call earlier?"

Colt squinted at the cabin, still thirty yards away. Give or take. "Backup's at Hank's place, remember? It's me and you, partner."

"I was afraid you were going to say that," John said. "So, what's the plan?"

Colt watched the cabin. Both men were staring in their direction, weapons at the ready. No other movement around the cabin. Impossible to tell if those men knew they faced another pair of men or just one. "You take the left, and I'll take right. Get them looking in opposite directions," he said.

"That's what I would have done," John said. "See you at that door?"

"Yep," Colt said as he worked himself into a kneeling position. John pulled up into a crouch. "All right let's go."

"Get some," John said as he moved off to the left.

Colt worked his way from tree to tree, bent at the waist even though his hip ached. He kept an eye on the two men, neither of whom seemed to be aware of his and John's movement. He closed the gap quickly and knelt behind an oak tree wide enough to block him from sight. From this position he could tell both men held military-style rifles, which had clearly been modified for automatic fire. He gathered his feet under him to move again.

One of the men sprang up and pointed his weapon in John's direction. Before Colt could take a step, the shooter cut loose with a shrieking burst of fire that ripped through tree branches and leaves. A half second later, Colt heard the cannon boom of John's shotgun and saw the shooter fly backward as a geyser of blood erupted from his chest. He crumpled at the feet of his fellow shooter, who had turned toward the firing and away from Colt.

Colt sprinted into the open and stopped twenty feet from the remaining guard. Drew a bead on the back of his head just as John stepped into the clearing, shotgun on his shoulder.

"Drop that weapon right there," Colt said. The man froze.

"Hands," John yelled. The man raised both hands. His rifle dangled from a combat sling around his neck. Colt came up behind him and pressed the .45 into the base of his skull. "Get on your goddam knees."

"Hey, man, I'll do whatever you say," the man said. He was young, maybe thirty at the most, skinny, and shaking in a near seizure. "I ain't dying over this shit."

"Good call," Colt said as the man lowered himself the ground. "John, watch that door." Colt reached over his shoulder and undid the sling, snatched the weapon away, and flung it aside. He patted the man down, then cuffed him quickly. John stood like a big cat about to pounce, aimed in on the door. The dead man lay between them, lifeless eyes skyward, chest a mangled mess from John's shotgun.

Colt stood and faced the door. "Hank, it's Colt. You in there?"

Silence. He and John exchanged a look.

"Goddammit, Hank, answer me," he said. He heard feet scuffling on the wooden floor inside the cabin. "What the hell are you doing?"

"What do you expect me to do?" Hank said.

"Burnett's already confessed," Colt said. "Told me and Deputy Carver that he killed Lucius Wallace on your orders." It was a lie, but this wasn't a deposition. No lawyers, either.

"Bullshit," Hank said, but his voice quavered.

"You'd be surprised how honest—and talkative—a dying man can get," Colt said. "I shot him less than an hour ago. He was making a run for it, leaving you hanging."

Colt moved toward the door. Two small, quiet steps. He could hear Hank panting like a dog.

"He wasn't supposed to *kill* him," Hank said.

Hank's words shocked him. He knew he shouldn't be surprised, but he was.

"What the hell is wrong with you, Hank?" he said.

"He wasn't supposed to kill him," Hank said. His voice trailed off in a sob. "He was supposed to scare him."

"*Scare* him?"

"Yeah."

"I don't believe that for a second," Colt said.

"I don't care what you believe," Hank said, his words slurring. "That son of a bitch Wallace got what he deserved. That's right. Jack was only supposed to scare him. He was uppity and didn't know his place and he disrespected the flag and my people. And yours, too, not that you give a shit anymore, seeing as you've forgotten where you come from."

Colt looked at John, who just shook his head.

"So, that's why you and Jack were forming some sort of redneck vigilante group," Colt said. "To get some kind of twisted revenge."

"Goddam right," Hank said. "Me and Jack and Reggie. Wallace was exactly the reason we need somebody—a group of men, white men—to enforce some discipline and traditions around here. To preserve the race and save it from extinction by the goddam mongrels."

Hank's words were slurring more. Colt could feel John's anger, and his own, rising.

"You drunk, Hank?"

"What difference does it make if I am?" Hank yelled. Clearly drunk.

"I'm asking the questions here, Hank. Don't forget that. I'm coming in there now."

"Don't come in here, Colt," Hank said in a shaky voice. "Don't make me shoot you."

He stepped to the side of the door, back against the wall. "That ain't the way this ends, Hank," he said. "You know that. You know me. And I'm not alone." He turned to look at John. Nodded.

John took the cue. "This shotgun will take that door right off the hinges," he said.

"You hear that, Hank?" Colt said. "You got nowhere else to go, no more cards to play. You might as well come out right now."

"Right, so you can shoot me," Hank said.

"Not unless I have to," Colt said. "But if I have to, I *will* put you down. So, you better put that weapon down." He looked at John, jerked his head—*Come here.*

John came close and Colt whispered, "Use your pistol and get behind me. If he takes a shot at me, put his ass on the floor."

"You sure?" John said. "He sounds a little crazy at the moment."

"He's a lot crazy," Colt said. "And, yes, I'm sure." He turned back to the door as John laid the shotgun on the pine needles and drew his nine-millimeter. "Hank, I'm coming in. Don't do something stupid."

He stepped in front of the door, put his hand on the weathered brass knob. Locked. He stopped and took a step back. He felt John behind him, and he raised his good leg and kicked the door with all his strength. The door flew open and slammed against the wall with a bang. He leveled his pistol and moved in a crouch.

Hank stood at the far end of the room, pistol in his right hand. His face was a mixture of anger and despair. Colt eyed the man he'd known since junior high, one who'd always had it made, even if he never realized it or appreciated it. And his own anger returned. "Put it down, Hank," he said over the top of the .45. "I'm not going to tell you again."

Hank shook his head slowly. Tears stained his face but didn't wash away the rage in his eyes. "We were going to set things right in this county," he said. He began to raise the pistol in his hand.

Colt didn't think, didn't feel, didn't blink. He squeezed, and the .45 roared and jumped in his hands.

The bullet hit Hank in the forehead and launched him backward into the wall, into his own gore. The pistol fell from his dead hand as he stood flattened against the wall for a half second, then slid down into a sitting position, leaving a wide smear of blood on the wall.

Colt smelled the cordite and blood, kept the pistol on Hank's body and stepped across the room. "Goddammit," he said, finger still on his trigger. The suddenness of Hank's death left him stunned for a heartbeat. Then: "John."

"Right here, Colt," John said over his left shoulder. He hadn't even heard him move into the cabin.

Colt holstered his pistol and stared at Hanks' shattered head in a wide arc of bright-red blood. "Son of a bitch."

"Yeah," John said. "He still got off easy."

Colt dragged a hand across his face. "That's a hell of way to get off easy, John."

They stood in the silence of the cabin for another moment, the coppery smell of blood permeating the humid air. Colt's cell buzzed in his pocket; he yanked it out of his pants and looked at the display. Put the phone to his ear.

"What is it, Molly?"

"We're in," she said. "You find Claiborne?"

"We found him." He looked at John, who was on his phone calling for the coroner and backup, and pointed toward the open door. "Meet me back at the office when you're done."

John finished his call as Colt walked past him. "There's one more person to talk to."

CHAPTER FORTY-SEVEN

COLT

John didn't say much on the drive back to the office. Then again, neither did Colt. Once inside the sheriff's office John went straight to his desk, and Colt to his office.

He tapped a Percocet out of the bottle in his desk and flopped in his chair. Closed his eyes, saw Hank Claiborne's dead face falling away. He opened his eyes and pushed himself out of his chair, limped to the window. A drink would be good right about now. More than one.

He heard a tapping at his door, turned to see Molly step through.

"Townsend said he'd do the paperwork on all the shit we took out of Claiborne's house," she said in a low voice. "I can't wait to see what's on his computer."

"Good work." He leaned against the windowsill.

Molly crossed her arms. "Becky told me you shot Claiborne."

"I did."

She stared at him long enough to make him look back out the window. Out in the graveyard, a crew of four men worked at mowing and trimming the grass.

"You okay, Harper?" she said.

He pulled his eyes from the activity below. "Yeah, I'm fine. Come on, let's go talk to Reggie Cash."

She looked startled but said, "Sure."

He walked past her, and she fell in step, then followed him to Becky's desk. He reached over and grabbed the key ring, then moved down the corridor to Cash's cell.

Cash must have heard them coming because he was at the bars, neck craned to his left to see who was coming. Colt stopped inches from Cash's face.

"Face the wall, hands behind your back," he said.

Cash complied and Colt cuffed him. He stepped back into the corridor. "This way."

Cash shuffled out of the cell, and Colt took him by an elbow, then led him into the interview room, Molly close behind.

Once Cash was seated and cuffed to the table, Colt pulled up a chair. Molly stood against the door watching in silence.

Cash was scared, he could tell. As it should be.

"Reggie, you're in deep shit," Colt said.

"What do you mean?" Cash, still scared but now alert, glanced at Molly, then back at him.

"One thing I haven't been able to figure out," Colt said, "is how you just happened to be at that bar when Lamarr Purvis tried to rob the place."

Cash's eyes flickered back and forth between Molly and Colt. "Told you. Just bad luck, I guess."

"See, I don't believe in luck, mostly," Colt said. "You're going to have to do better than that. Because that kid died."

Cash shrugged. "So?"

"So, here's what I find interesting," Colt said. "Jack Burnett killed two black men in my county, and he and Hank Claiborne were looking to do a lot more than that. And a third man, also black, gets killed in a bar full of white men. And you, a man with a history of race violence and a buddy of Jack Burnett—who has a similar history—was just there by, what, coincidence?"

Cash's cuffed hand started twitching on the table. "Don't know what you mean."

"Reggie, few hours ago, I shot Jack Burnett," Colt said. "He might not make it through the night. Lost a lot of blood. And I killed Hank Claiborne after that. Hank was drunk and stubborn, but he mentioned your name."

Cash's trembling hand had started to affect his whole body.

"You set Lamarr up, didn't you, Reggie?" Colt said.

Cash shook his head.

"Deputy McDonough," Colt said over his shoulder, "what's the federal guidelines for hate crimes?"

Molly pushed herself off the door and walked to the table. She slid her hands in her pockets and stared down at Cash, who looked back at her with a mixture of hatred and fear.

"Since this one involves murder," she said, taking Colt's cue, "life or the death penalty."

Colt nodded at Cash. "Guess which one the DA will go for. So, like I said, you're in deep shit."

Cash leaned forward, head bowed. "Okay," he said. "I hear you."

EPILOGUE

Colt cut the engine, took a breath, and looked through the passenger-side window at Rhonda's house. She was waiting for him, as he knew she would be, on the porch.

He climbed out of the Crown Vic and took his time reaching the steps. The Percocet was starting to wear off. He groaned as he mounted the steps and spied the tall glasses of iced tea on a small white wicker table between two similarly constructed chairs. One chair was his. Rhonda occupied the other one. She smiled but did not rise. He lowered himself into his chair, the wicker shrieking with his weight, shifted his pistol so it didn't dig into his side.

Rhonda's eyes found his, as they always did. "Thought you might like something cold to drink."

He raised his glass. "Sure thing. Thank you."

"You're welcome." She sipped from her own glass, looked across the small front yard. "You see the paper today?"

He chuckled. "I saw it. Craig Battles did a real good job on that one, don't you think?"

She turned to look at him. "I thought you didn't like him."

"I think he and I have come to an understanding."

"Really? Do tell."

He set his glass down on the table, stretched his legs out in front of him. "Ah, hell. Ain't much to tell. We just agreed to put to rest a whole bunch of shit that happened a long time ago."

Rhonda's eyebrows raised, and Colt became acutely aware of her stare. "You did this? Colt, you hardly let go of anything."

"I know," he said. "I know. I can't explain it myself. I guess when it comes to Winston, I'm still trying to outrun a shadow."

"Oh," Rhonda said. "So it had to do with your father."

"It does. Or did."

"You know, Colt, you aren't him. And you're not responsible for his actions."

He looked over at her. "I thought you were going to say 'sins.'"

"I almost did. You're not accountable for his sins, either."

"I'm starting to understand that."

"Good," Rhonda said, a faint smile creeping back to her lips. "Enough of that. How are you doing at work?"

He cocked his head at her. "Fine. Why?"

She took a breath, let it out. "Colt, you killed another man. And nearly killed another."

He closed his eyes and grumbled, mostly to himself. "Burnett had it coming, Rhonda. I guess, in the end, Hank did, too."

"I don't doubt you, Colt, you know that. But from what John tells me, it was a little more than that."

He looked down at a june bug skittering across the wooden boards of the porch. "He said that?"

"He did." Rhonda sipped her tea.

Colt sighed. Thought back to the moment he'd shot Jack Burnett, the satisfaction he thought he'd find eluding him as his rage refused to yield the stage. Turning to see John run to him, eyes fierce and hard as flint staring at him. And then the surprise and something else—was it pity?—when he shot Claiborne. It had been as if they'd suddenly become blind to each other. Especially after he'd killed Claiborne. Damn few conversations since. John all business, nothing more, nothing less.

She reached across the table and laid a manicured hand on his tree-bark arm. "Colt," she said in a trembling voice, "you know I love you. Always have. I just worry about your heart. Your soul."

He put a hand on hers. "What's left of it."

Rhonda squeezed her eyes shut. "Don't," she said. "What happens now?"

He drank from his glass. "Craig Battles will be busy for a while, I would reckon. He'll have plenty to write about. I never would have thought Burnett would have lived, but live he did, and his trial will start as soon as he's discharged from the hospital. Two counts of first-degree murder, and my understanding is the DA is going for the death penalty. Same for Reggie Cash."

Rhonda looked over at him. "I know this has got to be hard for you. You knew Hank Claiborne a long time."

"I should have seen it a long time ago, though," Colt said. "His office looked like some kind of shrine to the Confederate Army. And his computer had enough white-supremacy stuff on it to make the Klan look like amateurs. I mean, I'm not blind to the fact that even in today's supposedly enlightened times, there's still a lot of racism out there, but when you look it in the eyes, you see a different kind of—"

"Evil," Rhonda said.

He looked over at her. "Yes. Evil."

Rhonda held up a hand. "Not your fault. You never really know what's going on inside a person. Sometimes 'til it's too late."

Colt looked at her, wondering if she meant those words to hit so close to home. He could tell by her eyes she did. He patted her hand. "*I'll* be okay, Rhonda. But there's something different about John since this happened."

Rhonda dabbed at her eyes with her fingers. "He's worried, too."

"About me?"

"About himself."

Colt sat up. "What?"

Rhonda folded her hands into her lap. "He'll be fine, too, I think. He just needs to get away for a while. I know it's starting to get to him. This place. The never-ending lack of peace."

Rhonda's words surprised him. "John said this?"

Rhonda stared into the distance. "We talk about it all the time."

"He never said anything to me."

Rhonda smiled. "You're his boss, Colt. And his best friend. He'd rather die than let you down. And I know y'all have been friends since you were kids in boot camp, but y'all aren't the same person, you know? He's not you."

That stung him, made him feel somehow that he'd been the one to let John down. "I'll talk to him," he said.

She shook her head. "No, don't. We're going away for a little while. I've been after him for weeks now to take some vacation, just the two of us. To get away from work and just spend time together."

He smiled—he couldn't help it. "You love him, don't you?"

She looked cross for half a second, then smiled. "I do. And he loves me, too."

"I have no doubt. Well, I think it's a good idea. Take as long as you need. This county will be here when y'all get back." He drained his glass and realized he had nothing left to say. He stood to go. "Thanks for the tea. And the rest."

Rhonda stood and threw her arms around his neck. "Watch your soul, Colt," she said. "And tell Molly I said hello."

He held her for another moment, relaxing in the quiet space of their friendship. He stepped back to see a single tear track glistening on her cheek. "Talk to you soon," he said, then descended the steps to his car.

Colt pulled into the parking lot of the sheriff's office to find Molly flinging a backpack into the back seat of her car. When she saw him roll up, she pushed her hair out of her eyes and straightened up.

"Hey," he said when he got out of the vehicle. "Leaving?"

Molly nodded, looked around like she was surveying the terrain. "I got stuff back in Memphis I got to get back to."

He slid his hands in his pockets. "What about the job here?"

She slammed the car door shut. "What about it? I appreciate you bringing me on for this. I needed it. To keep myself occupied. You're going to get that asshole Burnett locked up, hopefully for a long time. And Cash."

He shrugged. "You did a lot of the work, too, you know."

"Then my job here is done," Molly said.

Colt watched her eyes. "And now you're going to quit?"

She crossed her arms, leaned against the car. "What are you saying? I thought this was temporary."

Colt walked over, leaned against the car beside her. "Molly, I'm about to be down one deputy when Townsend goes. And I just found out John and Rhonda are taking some time off together. I need a good cop. One I can trust and count on."

Molly looked down at the pavement. "And you think that's me?"

"I know it is."

Molly pushed a rock across the asphalt with the toe of her boot. "Even if I'm barely sober and going to AA meetings every day?"

Colt turned to look at her but didn't speak. He waited until she raised her face and turned toward him. "Absolutely," he said. "Do whatever you need to do. But do it here."

Molly stared off into the distance at a line of pecan trees, fiddled with her keys. "Holy shit, you're serious," she said.

"Damn right I am."

She sighed and slid her hands into her pockets. "I have stuff in Memphis."

"Fuck Memphis," he said. "Go get your stuff. Job's yours if you want it."

She turned and looked him, squinting in the sun. "I'll let you know." She opened the car door.

He pushed himself off the car. "Ahite, then."

"What are you going to do, Harper?" she said as she slid behind the wheel. Cranked the car, looked up at him.

He smiled. "Me? I'm going to get out of this heat for the rest of the day."

She smiled, dropped the car into gear, and rolled out of the driveway. He stood and watched her disappear out of the parking lot and down the street that led to the highway, then turned and climbed the steps to his office.

ACKNOWLEDGMENTS

As always, I'm indebted to several people who helped me along the way. BJ Ramos, a trusted friend and honest broker, took the time to review the chapters and offer thoughtful suggestions on the characters. Jason Kraus read the initial draft of the manuscript, and his insights were invaluable. Joe Studdard helped me understand some of the inner workings of the law, for which I'm grateful. I'm also grateful to the following for their camaraderie and suggestions: Kim Baer, Tom Pitts, Shawn Reilly Simmons, and Joe Clifford. Eileen Chetti is a fantastic editor who handled the manuscript with care. And, again, my thanks to the team at Brash Books: Lee Goldberg and Joel Goldman. Finally, my undying thanks to Brenda for her support, patience, and encouragement. Casablanca!

ABOUT THE AUTHOR

A native of rural east Mississippi, Phillip Thompson served in combat as a Marine, covered capital murder cases as a journalist, and wrote speeches for top military leaders in the Pentagon. He has worked as a reporter and editor at newspapers in Mississippi and Virginia.

Publishers Weekly described his first novel, *Enemy Within*, "...as timely as the morning headlines [and] asks some probing questions about national apathy, the abdication of responsibility for one's own country and the resulting decay of US civil rights." Thompson's other novels include *Outside the Law, Deep Blood*, and *A Simple Murder.* His short fiction has appeared in *O-Dark-Thirty; The Dead Mule School of Southern Literature; Out of the Gutter Online; Thrills, Kills, and Chaos; Near to the Knuckle; Yellow Mama;* and *The Shamus Sampler II.* He attended the Bread Loaf Writers Conference as a fiction writer in 2003.

He lives in Virginia. Find him on Twitter at @olemissgrad38 and online at his blog, "Grace & Violence," at *http://kudzucorner wordpress.com*

Made in United States
Troutdale, OR
08/30/2024